Bleeding Hearts

K. iller

Playlist

Scan to listen Bleeding Heart's Playlist or click here:

Song list-

Meet You At The Graveyard - Cleffy

Please Please Please Let Me Get What I Want - Deftones

Bad Moon Rising - Mourning Ritual, Peter Dreimanis

Ballad In The Blood Spill - Jiinzo

Straitjackets & Roses - Diggy Graves

Gory Model - Jiinzo

Working On Me - Russ, 6LACK

broken - lovelytheband

Blood Sport - Sleep Token

Carousel - Melanie Martinez

Zzz - Diggy Graves

Say Yes To Heaven (slowed&reverb) - Vallvete, eyeroze, Melodyz Town

MONSTERS - Shinedown

Don't Freak Out - Huddy, iann dior, Tyson Ritter, Travis Barker

Session 9 - sKitz Kraven

The Red Means I Love You - Madds Buckley

In The Shadows You'll Hear My Voice - KIRRA47

Lonely Day - System Of A Down

I Think I'm OKAY - Machine Gun Kelly, YUNGBLUD, Travis Barker

The Things I Do For Love - bludnymph

Issues - Julia Michaels

I Want Your Feelings - Jake Webber

Mental Handcuffs - Jake Webber

Flatline - Jared Benjamin

Antidote - Breaker

EXISTENTIAL DREAD - Dutch Melrose

To The Edge - Jiinzo

Who Do I Call Now? (Hellbent) - Sofia Camara

DiE4u - Bring Me The Horizon

Love And Violence - Pixxy Lua

If u think i'm pretty - Artemas

MATCH MADE IN HELL - Dutch Melrose, benny mayne

Love Plug - donavns

Only Love Can Hurt Like This (slowed down version) - Paloma Faith, sped up + slowed

My Vigilante - Jiinzo

Heathens - Twenty One Pilots

break me! - Maggi Lindemann, Siiickbrain

First edition July 2024

Paperback Book Cover by Kim Giller and Vanessa Mena

Ebook Cover by SKDesigns

Cover Model Rem!x

Editing and Formatting by Vanessa Mena, Dark Queens Author Services

Ebook ISBN: 979-8-9897308-5-8

Paperback ISBN: 979-8-9897308-6-5

Editor's Note

As someone who struggles with various mental health disorders, it is very rewarding to participate in books that represent not a romanticized version or a pink-lens version of mental illnesses, but handles it with love and compassion while still showing the realities of living with these struggles. Please remember these characters are in a psychiatric ward, where many of them, including Karver, are long-term residents and therefore have some heightened symptomatology. Thank you to those who provided insight as to what it's like to live with BPD. Thank you, readers, for supporting K; it means the world to me.

If you also struggle with mental illnesses, I see you and I leave you with these quotes from a movie close to this project ...

V.

"Rejoice! The broken are the evolved."

~The Beast, portrayed by James McAvoy in the M. Night Shyamalan film *Split*, 2016

"We are what we believe we are. Let's show them how powerful the broken can be."

~Dennis, portrayed by James McAvoy in the M. Night Shyamalan film *Split*, 2016

"Et cetera."

~Hedwig, portrayed by James McAvoy in the M. Night Shyamalan film *Split*, 2016

Trigger Warnings

Your mental health is important. This is NOT a happy, cute love story. It is a dark book with a lot of anguish and gore. Please be honest to yourselves and mind the triggers.

Trigger Warnings

Body Horror

Stalking

Self-Harm

Mention of Suicidal Ideations

Graphic Sexual Situations

Necrophilia

Bloody Heart Sex Toy

Murder

Stabbing

Mention of Psychiatric Symptoms

Knife Play

Blood Play

Masks

Gore

Intense Emotional Volatility

Use of Drugs and Alcohol

Suicide

Hanging

Strangulation

Drug Overdose

Forced Drug Use

Isopropanol Poisoning

Head Injury

Blunt Force Trauma

Smothering

Desecration of Remains

Bodily Fluids

Exhibitionism

Voyeurism

Dedication

Not everything is sunshine and rainbows. Just remember you deserve to be loved for exactly who you are, broken pieces and all. Find someone that will stand with you in the darkest of times. The person that will take your hand and dance with you while your demons surround you.

To My Darling Karver,

If you're reading this, then I sadly have left you on your own. I'm so sorry I couldn't hold on longer. I promise you, I really did try to stay with you as long as I possibly could. I know things are scary right now, and you're probably having a hard time holding on to one feeling at a time. That's okay. There are many stages of grief, and I know when the anger hits, you're going to feel like I abandoned you like your parents did. I need you to know that this isn't the same thing, but it's okay if you feel that way in moments of anger.

With me gone, it's going to be very difficult for you to get a proper education. I need you to learn as much as you can, Karver. The world is scary enough, but living in a world without knowledge is even worse. Read as many books as you can. They even have lots of information and history on those computer things at the library. It won't do you any good right now since you're too young, so I put it in my will that Uncle Harkin will be your conservator. I've had a lot of conversations with him about this and he's willing to do this for you because, as he says, he owed your Pops one. He's not really in a place to live with you and take care of you, which he's very sorry about. So am I.

This is the only way I could make sure you were taken care of. I put the house, my car, and Pop's truck in your name. I left an inheritance behind for you.

Its hidden behind the biggest picture of me and your Pops.

You won't be able to use any of this until you're eighteen, but it's all yours. It breaks my heart that I have to tell you this, but I'm no longer around to protect you and it's important. Do you remember the stories I told you about the history of masks and how they were used to ward off evil? Over the years, I've learned that everyone wears a mask. Some for protection, and some to hide their true intentions. My fear is that you will come across evil in this life and you must do all that you can to ward them off, even if that means wearing a mask of your own.

It may not be the best option, but I need you to do everything you can to not be put into foster care, Karver. I've heard horrific stories about those places. I think... I think it might be best if you make people believe that my death took a horrible toll on your mental health. This way, it's more likely you'll be put into a facility, which will keep you away from those awful people who would hurt and touch you while getting money from the state.

In a facility you'll be safer, have a roof over your head and food in your belly. Always protect your mind, body, heart and soul, my darling boy. I don't want you to live this life all alone, but you must be careful. I want the best for you, and you'll have to fight through life to get it.

Don't let just anyone in. Do not give yourself or your heart freely. When you find the one, you'll know. They'll make you feel alive, light up a room and take your breath away just by looking at them. They're the person you would live, die and kill for.

There will be trials and tribulations, as there is in any relationship. But if you two can make it through those, you can make it through anything together. You'll find yourself as obsessed with them as your Pops and I were with each other. When you find that... that is when you know they are the one who deserves your heart. They will be the one who deserves every piece of you, every beat of your heart.

Though I won't be there to see you grow up, I believe in you, Karver. You are stronger than you know, and you will find your way.

Stay smart, strong and vigil, my darling Karver.

Nana Cordelia
143

1

Karver

13 years earlier

When hearts fail, do you think they shatter like glass? Or maybe they explode, leaving us with bleeding hearts that never truly heal?

I sniffle, regretting it instantly and pressing my nose against my hoodie as the pungent smell invades my senses. When characters in my favorite slasher flicks talked about the stench of death, I never really thought anything of it. I don't think this is what they meant, though. It's like taking Nana's powdery and flowery perfume, then mixing sour gummies with it. They're nice on their own but the musty combination is awful.

I peek out of my hood and see Nana's still asleep, the oxygen mask on her face fogging up with every shallow breath she takes. My eyes drift down to the silver chain around her neck with the homemade pendant I made. It's a dull silver rectangle, with one line etched at the top, followed by four in the middle and three at the bottom. 143.

The hospital room slowly disappears as I'm immersed in a memory.

I walk into the kitchen for a soda, when I stop at the sight of Nana sitting at the dining table. She's holding a picture frame in her hand, smiling wide as a single tear falls down her wrinkled cheek.

"Nana?"

She slowly lifts her head and dabs her tear away with an embroidered handkerchief. "Oh, Karver. Come here, come here, I want to show you this." I shuffle her way and look over her shoulder. It's a wooden frame with '143' painted on the bottom in red. Inside of it, there's a picture of Nana and Pops. The picture is a sepia print where she stands next to him in a puffy dress, while he's dressed in what Nana called his Navy SDB. Nana looked so happy while Pops looked almost mad except for this sparkling look in his eyes. I never knew him, Nana said a heart attack took him away from her. I point at the '143' on the bottom and ask, "Nana, what are the numbers for? Every picture of you and Pops has them."

Her shaking hand traces the numbers with her finger. "Take a seat, baby. We'd be here an awfully long time if I told you the full story, so we'll just stick to the short and sweet version."

I pull out the chair next to her and plop down. The chair creaks as I tilt it on two legs. Nana picks up her cane and swings it towards the chair. The whoosh of air makes my hair dance and I yelp, dropping the chair down just as it bounces off the back legs. She lifts the cane and points it towards my face. "You know the rule. Four to the floor, Karver."

"Yes, ma'am."

She smiles at me, which deepens the wrinkles next to her mouth and eyes. She pushes a plate of cookies my way and then places the picture down in front of her. "Back in Massachusetts, Pops was in the Navy and a lot of them would tell stories about the Lover's Light. The lighthouse would flash the light once, then four times, and then three."

I take a bite of my cookie and play the numbers over and over in my head trying to find the connection. Cookie crumbs fly from my mouth as I ask, "What does it mean?"

Nana pulls the plate away and scowls. "Karver Damon Murphy. Where are your manners today?"

I quickly finish my bite and wipe my mouth with the back of my hand. "Sorry, Nana."

She leans forward and pats my cheek twice. "143 means I love you. The numbers correspond with the amount of letters in each word. Once your Pops heard the story, he was as obsessed with the history as he was with me. He came home and started painting it on all of our picture frames and signed off every note to me with it."

An icy grip pulls me from the memory. I look down and see Nana's hand on top of mine. "You… were… very… lost… in… thought… Karver," she wheezes. Panting into the mask, she works to gain the oxygen back that she lost talking to me. I put my other hand over hers to warm it up.

"I was just remembering the story you told me about 143." With her other hand, she slowly reaches towards her neck and briefly touches the pendant. Moving past it, she starts to pull her mask down. I leap up and gently put my hand over hers to stop her. "No, Nana, you can't take that off. It's helping you breathe."

She places the mask to her face and sucks in a rattling breath. Dropping it to her chin again, she says, "Listen... Karver... please." I move my hovering hand and place it on the bed railing. "I need... you to listen... to Nana. Take... the necklace."

My eyes widen at her words and I shake my head. "I made that for you, Nana. It's yours."

"I can't... take it with me... my dear boy. I want... you to have it." I swipe away the tears falling on my cheeks and reach behind her to unclasp the necklace. My shaking fingers fumble with the clasp a few times until I catch hold of it and pull it from her. I put it on and tuck it inside my shirt, wiping my runny nose on my sleeve.

"No more tears, Karver. One... one more thing." She slowly points at the table next to her bed. "Drawer. Letter... for you." I slide the drawer open to see an envelope with my name on it in Nana's handwriting. I pull it out and start to open it. "No."

I stop and look up at her, confused, "Wha-?"

"Not... here. I need... I need you to go, Karver. I don't... I don't want you to see this."

"No. No, Nana, I'm not leaving you. You're going to get better. Everything will be okay. Your heart will heal and we'll go home together." She breathes in from the mask again. "I don't want this to... to be our last m-memory. And if... you're here they'll... they'll t-take you. Don't ever... ever let them... take you. Go home. Read... letter. Follow everything I say. 1... 4... 3." She barely rasps out the three and coughs hard, her labored breaths rattling in her chest. I rush towards her and push the mask against her mouth. "Breathe, Nana, just breathe."

The machines she's connected to start beeping like crazy, I can't understand anything it shows other than the flashing red light. I quickly look back at her, my heart racing. Her hand resting on the bed has one finger pointed towards the door. Her eyes look almost like she's pleading with me to listen. The door bursts open with nurses and doctors and I back against the wall, watching them. I watch the green bouncing heart rate line get smaller and smaller until it goes flat with a loud beep. I can't hear anything the nurse in front of me is saying. Nana's words bounce around in my head. I whisper, "143," and run around the nurse and out of the room.

My eyes shoot open, my heart racing through every ragged breath. I pull my drenched shirt off and wipe the sweat pouring down my face. I thought I was done having that dream. *What are you trying to tell me, Nana?* I look around the room and shake my head. She told me I would need to pretend I was something I'm not in order to seek safe shelter here. There are a lot of things in my life I fake, but this wasn't one of them.

She didn't realize my past with my parents, and then her leaving me would mold me into who I am now. A man diagnosed with BPD. Then again, maybe some part of her did know. After all, this is where she told me to go.

As far as we knew, there was no name for what I dealt with. It was easier to blame my drug-addicted parents for my issues. They neglected and abandoned me, always choosing drugs over me. Even though Nana saved me from that life, loved and cared for me, the damage was done. If my own parents couldn't stick around and love me the way they're supposed to, then nobody ever would. I have so much love to give, but they didn't want it. So along with all of my love comes all of the anger, all of the sadness, just… all of it. Every emotion is all-consuming. It's all too much for people, hell, I'm too much for my own damn self. To top it all off, Nana left me, too. I know that it's irrational, the therapists all remind me that dying wasn't her choice. They've explained it until they were blue in the face, but I don't give a fuck. Leaving is leaving and there is no in between, no explanation or understanding. All I see is she left, just like my parents did.

The bunk above me creaks, pulling me from my spiraling thoughts. I roll my eyes and huff. "What the fuck did I tell you about that bunk, Decker?"

The bed shakes and squeaks as he hops down to the floor cackling. He makes a show of spinning around to face me with a shit-eating grin on his face. He tosses his head like it's a shampoo commercial for hair he doesn't even have and says, "To not to."

I wad up my sweat-soaked shirt and throw it at his face. He cradles it against him and loudly inhales with a sigh. "Aww, for me? You know how much I love the smell of man juices."

I keep my face neutral and relax my body the best that I can. I refuse to give him any indication that his shit is annoying or he'll just use it to push me over the edge for the hell of it. With a calm and even tone, I say, "Give me my shirt back, you skinny fuck."

He slowly rubs my shirt down his face and tosses it at me with a wink. I catch my shirt before it pelts my face and stand up, tossing it into my yellow pop-up mesh hamper. I open my drawer to get some clothes, when a knock on the door stops me. The door slowly opens, the rubber-padded tread squeaking across the linoleum.

"Knock, knock. Med time." The mousey little voice that grates on my nerves tells me exactly which nurse it is. Christ, I almost feel sorry for the poor bastard who has to listen to that while fucking her. Almost. His own damn fault if he isn't using that opportunity to gag her.

Pulling myself from my thoughts, I grab a stack of my clothes and slam the drawer shut. I turn towards the door as she pops her head in with a bright, fake smile that only rivals the Joker with her red lipstick. "Gooooood morn-ingggg," she chirps in a sickly sweet voice.

Don't react, Karver, just return the favor. In a deadpan voice, I say, "I'm here voluntarily. Guess that means no meds for me." I return her fake smile and give a nonchalant shrug.

Her smile wavers for a moment as she takes a steadying breath, "Mr. Murphy, you and I both know that's not true. When you check yourself in voluntarily, the paperwork you fill out specifically states that you will adhere to your treatment plan during your stay. Any refusal of said plan means you agree to check yourself back out. Don't you think you already get away with enough around here?" She pointedly stares at the chain around my neck, which we're not really allowed to wear. I drop my clothes on top of the dresser and walk over to her, grabbing the paper cup of pills.

I tilt my head back as I toss the pills in my mouth and mumble, "Whatever you say, mouse."

Decker giggles as she gasps. "Excuse me?!"

I dry swallow my meds and look at her. "Whatever you say, *miss*." I grab a cup of water from the tray and swallow the pills down. Decker walks around me and takes his meds next, followed by our other roommate, Axel. He quietly thanks her and quickly shuffles back over to his bed to sit, his bulky build causing the bed to groan in protest. Without another word, the nurse quickly leaves the room. As the door shuts, I dry heave until I puke the pills and water into my cup.

I grab my clothes and throw them over the cup to discard in the bathroom. I look over at Axel, nervously pull on his overgrown scruff. "Ax, if you want to take a shower today, then it's time to go now, okay?" He quickly nods and scrambles over to his drawers. I can feel Decker's stare and slowly turn my head to look at him and lift a brow in question.

"You're not even going to invite me to shower with you guys?" he pouts.

"Nobody is stopping you from taking a shower, Decker. Take a shower, don't take a shower. Go hang out with Thumper, don't go hang out with Thumper. I really don't give a fuck what you do, just go do it."

I ignore his fake hurt and push past him to the door. "Let's go, Axel. You get first dibs on the shower while I watch the door for you."

He quickly catches up to me and murmurs, "Thank you, Karver."

Walking into the hall, Decker shouts in a childlike voice, "Wait fo me, I have wittle wegs!"

Even with us all wearing the same slip-on shoes, it's easy to decipher who is who behind me. The annoying squeaky footsteps let me know Decker is to the back left of me, and Axel's heavy-footed shuffle tells me he's to the right. Walking into the rec room, I immediately spot old man Thumper in his signature look, a blue cap with NAVY stitched in white letters on the front and his matching blue crew neck. Taking quick strides, we reach the table tucked in the corner of the room by the window. His cloudy green eyes land on me as I pull out the chair facing the entrance doors.

Taking a seat, I place one of my blank masks down on the table in front of me. Decker and Axel follow suit and pull out their chairs on either side of me. He shifts to push himself further into the corner of the adjoining walls and blinks a few times. The wrinkles around his eyes deepen when he smiles at me. He pulls his cap off and tips his head at us. I take note of his salt and pepper hair and see that it's slightly longer than he likes.

I cover my mouth with my palm to hide my smile, knowing he'll make a remark about it and how his superiors would give him shit about it if he was still in the Navy. I jump to it first and nod towards him. "Hey, what's up with your hair, shipmate?"

He throws his head back and laughs. "Nice try, kid, but my skivvies have more time on this earth than you. Decent attempt at sounding like a superior, though. So, what's the scuttle, boys?"

To the left of me, Decker whines. "Aww, come on Thumper, you missed the best part of that term. You're supposed to say *butt*, scuttle *butt*." Like a child, he snickers each time he says butt.

Thumper chuckles as he runs his fingers through his hair, scraping at his scalp. "Ah, you kids keep me young. Anyway, Karver, my boy... before I forget, I got you something."

He puts the cap back on, and I tilt my head in question as he pushes an old, crinkled magazine across the table towards me. I pick it up and shake it. "Best present ever. Uh, what's it for?"

He leans forward and taps my blank mask. "I know you like to do different designs on these. Figured you could find some pictures in there to tear up and glue them on during arts and crafts time."

I stare at the magazine and down to my mask, mulling it over in my mind. "Hmm. Never thought of that. Good idea. Thanks, Thumper." I drop the magazine on the table and flip through it while Decker and Axel listen intently to Thumper's war stories. I quickly realize that I might not find many pictures in the gardening magazine so I work on tearing out random article titles that are in bold letters, until the obnoxious door buzzer rings. I glare at the doors as if that will quiet the noise.

The doors slowly open and the first person I see is Dr. Dead - our forensic psychiatrist - with a sad woman on his arm. I swear this man is obsessed with all things involving death. If he's not cutting up the deceased, he spends a lot of time up here with the living dead. Following closely behind is a woman with her head down and wavy brown hair hiding her face. I wonder who they are?

I watch as they make their way to the check-in desk. Dr. Dead speaks animatedly to the security guard, his expressions in contrast with the solemn one on the woman's face.

The younger woman lifts her head and stares at the exchange happening and then slowly turns to scan the room. Her face comes into view and it feels like the air is sucked from my lungs. My heart pounds in my chest as if it's been jump started. I try harder than I ever have to mask how this feels. A metaphorical mask isn't enough and I quickly pick mine up from the table. Just as her eyes fall on me, I lift the mask to my face and tilt my head. Our eyes connect, the mask obscuring how intently I'm staring at her. Right now, nobody else is here and nothing else matters other than the voice in my head screaming '*mine*'. Something catches her attention, and she blinks a few times, shaking off the moment before turning away. I toss my mask on the table and glare at the intrusion that pulled her away from me. I faintly hear Thumper's reverent tone as he says, "I used to look at my bunny that way."

Unable to look away, I blindly tap at the table behind me. "Axel. Go listen to them. Find out what you can for me." The squeak of his chair sliding across the linoleum almost pulls my attention. *Almost.* As he walks past me, I start making plans in my head. This voluntary stay has just been shortened.

People with borderline personality disorder may experience intense mood swings and feel uncertainty about how they see themselves. Their feelings for others can change quickly, and swing from extreme closeness to extreme dislike. These changing feelings can lead to unstable relationships and emotional pain.

2

Sloane

I barely have a chance to appreciate the man's handsome face before he covers it with a blank mask. For a split second, I wondered why I was so mesmerized by him, until it dawned on me that just looking at him gave me the feeling I've been yearning for my whole life.

It takes me a moment to realize Corbin is trying to get my attention. I turn towards the counter and try to subtly pull away from his touch. Ignoring the word exchange he's having with the security guy, I stare at my mother. Everything about this is wrong.

The woman beside me is not the Denise Moriarty that I've grown up with. The woman I know screams and manipulates. That woman has never been as broken as she's portraying now. If you told me we would be looking into committing her to the psych floor of St. John's Damascus, I'd call you a fucking liar.

Shuffling footsteps behind me catch my attention. A man whose demeanor does not match his stature is pacing back and forth behind us, chewing on his fingernails. On every turn, he peers over at us through his shaggy black hair. After a couple of turns, I smile up at him as he looks over. With a sharp intake of air, he quickly averts his eyes, and starts muttering against his fingertips.

"Hey, Sloane?" Corbin questions.

I turn towards him with furrowed brows. "What?"

He taps a pen against the paperwork. "I need you to sign this visitation form and emergency contact form. Please don't sign as Sloane or Sloane Flanagan, you need to write out Sloane Teagan Flanagan. Okay?" I swear he thinks my lack of emotions and feelings means I'm devoid of intelligence. I step closer to the counter and skim the paperwork. Printing and signing my name, along with the date, I put the pen down and push the forms forward.

Before I step back, the security guard nods at Corbin and says, "I know what you and your dad–,"

I cut him off and correct him. "Stepdad."

With a quirked smile, he continues, "What you both are doing for your mom is a very difficult decision, but everyone knows it comes from a place of love."

Ignoring his statement, I ask, "Since when do security guards handle the paperwork? Or do paperwork here for that matter? Aren't we supposed to go to some private office or something?"

He chuckles at my question, "Probably not the usual at other facilities, but around here we work with what we have. We're pretty short-staffed, so they showed me the ropes. Even gave me fun little dummy stickers to guide me through the process."

Corbin grabs his attention and I turn to look at my mother. Maybe if I look hard enough, I can reach into her brain and figure out what the fucking game they are playing is. She turns her head and a flicker of the real Denise flashes behind her eyes. It shows up in a flash and is gone just as quickly. Refusing to cause a scene and bother everyone here, I file away my confrontation for later.

After Corbin is *finally* done running his mouth, we head for the doors to leave. I chance one more glance over at Mr. Dark and Delicious. I find his eyes are already on me and a zip sparks through me. My steps falter and he winks. The brief feeling of being electrified has turned molten and I glare back at him for catching me. By the time we reach the parking lot, the feeling has faded. I find it difficult to continue walking away when all I want is more of that feeling. I fear I'd morph into a succubus, siphoning every bit of his essence just to keep that buzz going.

I open the car door and plop in behind my mother, the leather squeaking beneath me. As I shut the door, Corbin grits, "*Sloane.* You may not feel shit, but the Benz does! You don't throw yourself on pristine leather seats, and you certainly don't slam the door shut!"

Ignoring his attempt at verbal assault, I pull my ear buds from my pocket and pop them in. I scroll through my playlist, hit play and max out the volume. I swear he thinks bringing up my emotional constipation all the time will magically reverse it. Aren't doctors supposed to be smart? Then again, he plays with dead people. Maybe their education isn't as extensive. I close my eyes and lean my head against the window, letting the music wash over me. I think of the constant reminders I'm given about my feelings, or lack thereof. What they fail to realize is I was crafted to be this way. It was like my mother wanted herself a rare plant, but didn't bother to follow the instructions of proper care. Instead of being given the right amount of love, sunlight, and water, I was drowned and stamped out when I didn't bloom properly. I was thrust into darkness and left there to try to survive on my own. I had one last leaf that could've been salvaged if she just tried hard enough, but decided it was too much work. That last leaf that's barely hanging on is what's left of me. So it's not that I don't truly have any feelings or emotions; I just learned that they needed to be watered down to almost nothing.

I lurch forward and open my eyes, my head sliding against the window as Corbin parks the car. I quickly pull my hand back as I feel something cold and wet touch it. I look down and see a wet wipe laying on my hand, then look up and see him eye the wipe and then the window. I swipe away the non-existent smudge, pocket my ear buds and get out of the car.

I trail behind them along the cobbled path to the front door. I shut the door behind me with a click, and lean against it as I watch Corbin help my mother with her jacket and hang it up. Their interaction seems normal, but it's not. They're acting as if we didn't just leave the hospital where they plan to admit my mother. It was the equivalent of setting her up with some extended stay hotel reservation. They slide their shoes off in sync and place them in the shoe organizer. He attempts to push strands of her stiff and brittle hair back, the hairspray she doused it in keeping it immovable. He kisses her forehead and murmurs, "I'm going to get lunch started for my girls."

She smiles up at him, but as he passes, she glares in my direction. She turns to follow him, but I quickly catch up, grabbing her elbow. "What are you guys up to?" I demand. She yanks her arm free and spins to face me, her finger jabbing towards my face. "There's nothing to discuss, Sloane. Some things you'll just never understand."

I pace back and forth as I start rambling about the day. "How am I going to understand if you don't tell me what's going on? Anybody would be confused right now. We go to this hospital where you're going to be checked into and act like a completely different person. Then we leave and the two of you are acting like it's just a regular Wednesday morning."

My pacing stops when she lunges forward and gets in my face, shouting, "LEAVE IT ALONE, SLOANE! STOP ASKING QUESTIONS! IT'S NOT LIKE YOU GIVE A FUCK ABOUT ANYONE OR ANYTHING! QUIT PRETENDING YOU GIVE A SHIT!"

I open my mouth to respond when Corbin sighs, "Girls, can we please not fight? Let's all give each other some space and take a breather. Honey, why don't you go put on one of your favorite shows while I finish lunch? Sloane, is there some art you want to work on while listening to music?"

I watch as my mother scoffs and stomps towards the living room. Corbin steps between the two of us and pats my shoulder, whispering, "I'm sorry she's acting like that. You know how she gets when she feels cornered. She's having a really hard time these days. I know it seems sudden to you and you have questions, but this has been a long time coming. Maybe after I get home from work tomorrow morning, we can sit down and discuss this as a family."

I nod. "Okay, that's all I wanted. Just a discussion. I'll be in my room."

He pats my shoulder again and steps away. I head towards the stairs, planning to retreat to my room, but stop when I hear Corbin growl, "Really, Denise?!"

I tip-toe back to the mouth of the kitchen and listen behind the wall. My mother sniffs, and puts on her fake innocent tone. "What? I didn't do anything."

"The fuck you didn't!" Corbin booms.

"Don't you talk to me like that!"

"Oh, right, of course! The only one who can be a raging, vile bitch in this house is *you*. Could you, for once in your miserable existence, try not to bring everyone down with you? What's it going to take for you to figure out that *you* are the problem? You treat everyone like shit, and then play the victim wondering why, oh why, nobody wants anything to do with you. *Newsflash, wife*, the reason is you," the vileness in his tone makes a shiver run down my spine.

When I hear the tap of his shoes on the hardwood floors, I turn and run up the winding staircase, passing the second floor to reach the top where my loft room is. I pull my ear buds from my pocket and toss them on my dresser, switching them out for my noise-canceling headphones. I push my window open and sit on the window seat, pulling my knees to my chest and light up a cigarette. "What the fuck is going on?"

Karver

I couldn't help but be an ass and wink at her as she left. God forbid I allow some vulnerability and smile at her, maybe even introduce myself. My thoughts continue to swirl. Be vulnerable. No, don't be vulnerable. Tell the truth. Don't tell the truth. Take off the mask. No, don't take off the mask. I'm pulled from my thoughts when Axel's shy voice registers.

"Hey, Karver?" I look up and see Axel standing there, wringing his hands. "It's time for arts and crafts. I-I can tell you what I know while we're there. Is that okay?"

My knee starts bouncing and I look over at Thumper. "You coming with, old man?"

He looks out the window longingly. "No, you go on ahead. I'm waiting on my bunny."

I grab the magazine and my mask and stand. "Good luck with that." I can hear the clock ticking above his head and stare at it. There's not enough time. "Let's walk and talk, Axel. No time for arts and crafts. Just tell me everything I need to know. I still have to pack up and head out. Why were they here? What was her name? Everything. Leave nothing out."

Reaching our room, I head over to my clothes hamper and pull everything out. I toss it on my bottom bunk and walk over to the dresser. I yank all the drawers open, ignoring their loud squeaks of protest with the swift movement. I pull out stacks of clothes from each drawer and toss them over to my bunk.

"Bag, bag, bag. I need my bag. I'll have to get that." I spin towards Axel, causing him to jump. "Alright, make it snappy, Axel. Lots to do, not enough time."

I pull my knife out of my jeans pocket and repeatedly flick the blade in and out. Axel nervously stares at it and blinks with every click.

Decker steps between us and smiles big. "Next time you sneak shit in, can you bring me one, too?"

I look him dead in the eye and say, "No." He pouts and then climbs up to his top bunk. I realize I won't get anything out of Axel with the knife out, so I pocket it. "Better?"

He lets out a long breath and nods. "Much. Thank you."

With nothing else to do and unable to sit still, I fold my clothes while Axel tells me about Dr. Dead's plan to check his wife in. I've seen a lot of shit being in and out of this place, and that's definitely a first. I'll have to try to get more information on what the hell that's all about. I pause my folding when Axel says, "Her name is Sloane Teagan Flanagan."

Well, well, well... I found myself my very own lucky charm.

Sloane

I drop the charcoal stick on my desk when the cramp in my hand worsens. I look down at my sketchbook and the realization of what I drew hits me square in the chest. A buzz pulsates through my whole body as I stare at the intricate details of the man from the hospital. He's holding a mask just below his eyes. I see the same intensity in his eye that I saw when he winked at me as I was leaving. Looking closer, I see that I added in my blurred silhouette in the reflection in his eye. The mask is almost completely blank except for a crack I left, as if I could somehow put a crack in his carefully crafted facade. I run my charcoal-stained finger along his cheekbone, leaving one last remaining mark on him. I stand up and head over to my small bathroom to wash my hands.

The food on my dresser catches my attention and I realize I've been up here for a while. Not only is there a plate of lunch, but Corbin left a plate of dinner as well. I grab the black-stained soap bottle I use specifically for cleaning off charcoal, and turn on the faucet with my elbow. I rub my hands together until the soap starts to lather, getting lost in the swirls of black water and soap suds slowly fading down the drain. I look up and gasp when it's not just my reflection in the mirror. "What the fuck, Mom?"

She rolls her eyes and points to her ears and then to me. I dry my hands , slide my headphones off my ears and drop them to my neck. The music is so loud you can still hear every word playing.

"You would have heard me calling for you if you didn't have those things blaring in your ears."

"Did you need something, or is this round two of your one-sided fight?"

She narrows her eyes at me and sighs. "How can someone as emotionally dysfunctional as you still be so dramatic? This is important, Sloane. We need to talk."

I push my arms out. "You think we could have this conversation in my room rather than in my *one* person capacity bathroom?"

Without a word, she turns on her heel and walks into my room. I follow behind her and drop down on the chair by my desk, spinning it so I can face her. I open my mouth to ask her what she wants to talk about, but she cuts me off with her hand in the air. She sits on the edge of my bed across from me and looks around my room. A small smile crosses her face while she stares at some of my artwork on the walls. Bringing her gaze back to me, she says the last thing I'd ever expect. "I know you won't believe me when I say this, Sloane, but I really do love you. You're my baby, I've always loved you. I know that's hard to understand when we either don't speak at all or we're butting heads, but it's true. I just," she pauses and wipes away a tear, "I just needed you to know that. I'm… I really am sorry that I wasn't a better mother to you. Maybe if I was, things could have been different for both of us."

Alarm bells are ringing in my head with this conversation and the memories of this morning. "What's going on, Mom? Other than yelling at me in the kitchen, you haven't been yourself at all today. And the shit at the hospital? Did something happen?"

She sniffles and runs her finger underneath her nose while shaking her head. "No? I mean, no, no of course not. Like I said, there are some things you just wouldn't and couldn't understand."

She stops and stares at me, a few more tears falling as she stands. "Goodnight, Sloane."

"Night."

I watch as she leaves my room, and the events of the day play in my head like jagged puzzle pieces that I'm struggling to piece together. I spin the chair around to face my desk and reach for my sketchpad. I can't shake the feeling that my mind is playing tricks on me; I swear I see a flash of light outside my window and feel like a fish in an aquarium, being watched.

More people have BPD than schizophrenia and bipolar disorder combined.

3

Karver

After Axel filled me in on everything he overheard, I ran to the front desk to request my bag and sign myself out. The security guard and the resident therapist escorted me to my room to pack my bag. The therapist asked the usual twenty-one questions and reminded me that my constant check-outs weren't conducive to getting better. It's the same spiel they've been feeding me since I was in the children's side of the facility, when I refused to communicate during therapy. What the hell do they know? There is no getting better permanently, it's always just a temporary thing. Even if I'd somehow manage to work on myself and subdue the worst of my issues, there would still always be this dark hole inside of me. I'd still have demons to fight for the rest of my life. You don't just get over years of neglect and abandonment issues.

On my way out, I wave to Thumper and he gives me a sad smile. Since I checked myself in, I had Pops' old Chevy truck waiting for me in the parking lot. It took a few tries, but I finally got the old bitch to run and head to Nana's house. Harkin, my pop's old Navy buddy, was assigned to be my conservator after Nana's death and took care of things for me. Even now that I'm an adult, he still chooses to take care of utilities and puts the equivalent of an allowance in a savings account for me. He kept in touch with me over the years, very brief letters to see if he needed to fuck anyone up. When my head isn't a fucking mess, I understand why he didn't come take care of me. He was dealing with his own demons. He didn't need some fucked up kid with demons as well. But when my brain fights me, I can't fucking stand him. I hate him for not choosing to be there for me when I needed him most.

I fire up my laptop and look Sloane up. Unable to find an address for her, I decide to look up Dr. Dead. Bingo. There you are, my sweet clover. I run to my room and grab one of my black hoodies from the closet and throw it on. I shuffle through my collection of masks and grab my blue and red light-up mask. I grab a pack of smokes, a lighter and head out the door. I jump in the truck and fire her up, black smoke pouring out of the muffler behind me. I turn the lever to lower the window and it squeals the whole way down.

The only new thing in this truck is the stereo and right about now proves why I'm glad for the upgrade. I connect my phone to it and hit shuffle on my playlist. I look in the rearview mirror and run my palm over my overly grown scruff. I'm tempted to shave when I get home, but I'd much rather know if my little clover is into it or not. I make my way to the rich side of town. Damascus is still so small it takes under ten minutes to get anywhere you need to go.

Not wanting to be caught, I find one of the hidden private roads that lead to the marsh and back the truck up there. I get out, drop my smoke to the gravel and stamp it out, the rocks crunching below my boot. I look up at the sky and notice that the sun will be setting soon. The mix of pinks, purples and yellows have always been the only breath-taking view in this town… until her.

Not bothering to check the road first, I cross to the other side and walk along the short stonewall that surrounds their property. I take a right around the corner and walk until I reach the big leaf maple tree just on the other side of the wall. Thank you, satellite view. I slide the mask on before pulling myself up on top of the wall. The tree is close enough that I'm able to reach out and grab one branch while placing my foot on another. I hop a little on the branch to test if it will hold my weight. When it doesn't budge, I push up and climb until I find the perfect branch to sit on; the bark scraping against my boots and clothes as I try to get in a comfortable position. Settling against the base of the tree, I have a perfect view of Sloane in her room.

Fuck, she's beautiful. Drops of sweat form an itch at my temple and I reach under the mask to scratch it. My finger-nail gets caught on the switch for the mask and I acciden-tally click it on. I grit my teeth. "Fuck." As quick as the light is on, I turn it back off. I quickly look up and catch Sloane looking in my direction. There's too many leaves, she can't see me. She can't see me. It's fine. It's good. A laugh bubbles up and I clamp my hand over my mouth to stifle it. With every shake of laughter, my hoodie gets caught on the bark of the tree. With my other hand, I punch my fist over my mouth. Shut up, shut up, shut up. My laughter dies down and I slowly exhale after removing my hand. A slight breeze ruffles my hair and the scent of incoming rain hits me. I look through the gaps in the tree to see dark clouds rolling in. The once beautiful colors slowly fade out to grays and blacks as the sky opens up to a downpour. The leaves do fuck all to keep the raindrops from pummeling me and soaking my clothes. I pull my mask off and slip it into my hoodie pocket with one hand, and with the other slick my hair back from my forehead. Thunder rumbles above me and I hear a screeching noise. I watch as Sloane pushes her window open, closes her eyes and breathes in the air. She takes a seat, leaning against the window frame, and lights up a cigarette.

I'm mesmerized every time Sloane sucks on the end of her cigarette and purses her lips to blow the smoke out. Fuck, I want those lips on me. All over me. Wrapped around my cock. A streak of lightning paints the sky a purplish blue. She drops her cigarette out the window and shuts it. My eyes drop to the window on the floor below my clover. I watch as her mother, Denise, I think her name is, sits on the edge of her bed and sobs into her hands. She pulls her hands down and even from here, I can see her body shaking as she looks around the room. I look back up at Sloane to see if she can hear any of this, and realize that's not possible with her headphones on and the sounds of the storm.

I drop my eyes to the floor below and see the woman bloody and lifeless. I see the glint of a bloody kitchen knife on the fluffy comforter. Without thought, I'm already crawling across the thick tree branch that just about touches the window. Before I even have a chance to hit the window and shout, I can see she's still alive, but just barely. I watch the small movements of her chest rising and falling with every ragged breath. Blood paints her lips and I suck in air when our eyes connect. "Shit." This is only the second time I've witnessed death, and that's enough to tell you, not everyone has the same look in their eyes when it happens. What was once panic and desperation is now transformed into something resembling euphoria and a serene calm. Fuck, fuck, fuck. What am I supposed to do? Sloane. She needs me. She needs me right now. I have to be here for her. I drop my head and look at the blood-soaked sheets surrounding her mother. No. No. I have to leave. I can't be caught here. Fuck. Stay. Go. Stay. Go. I grip my hair and pull until it stings. *Meet in the middle, Karver.* Get the fuck off this property, but stay close by. Yes. Yes, I can do that. I watch as Dr. Dead runs into the room shouting and grabbing hold of his wife and I scurry back to the middle of the tree. I'm so sorry, sweets.

I climb down and skip the wall, jumping straight down to the ground. I slip on fine gravel and barely catch myself. I can already hear the sirens getting closer and run to my truck. Fucking small towns. Just as I jump in, I watch as an ambulance and cop car fly by with lights and sirens. I light up a smoke and bounce my knee, the urge to run back and comfort Sloane almost unbearable. The feeling is so visceral, it's as if ants are crawling under my skin. Fuck. I may not be able to go over there, but I'm sure as fuck not leaving now. I have to make sure she'll be okay. She may not know it, but she needs me.

People with BPD commit suicide at 400 times the rate of the general population.

4

Thursday - One day later

Sloane here. I really don't know what good this is going to do, but Corbin handed me a journal and told me to just write whatever I felt like. I think one of his therapist friends at the hospital suggested it. The outcome is unclear, but my hope is maybe it will unlock the block I have on my emotions once and for all. For the most part, it's always been my choice to water down my feelings. Remain in the background. Not cause unnecessary waves. Although, if you asked my mother, she'd tell you I was still a problem. Well... I guess you can't ask her anymore. Not after last night.

Last night's events took my already numb emotions and completely obliterated them. My mother died. Correction. She killed herself. Slit her arms and died, cradled in Corbin's. I didn't even know anything was wrong at first. My art and music consumed me completely. The flashing lights bouncing around my room were the first sign something was wrong. I pulled my headphones off and just over the sounds of the storm could hear my stepfather screaming and crying. I rubbed my hands down my pants and walked down the staircase to their floor. On the way down, I saw police walking up the stairs and some congregated by the door. I pushed past an officer who stood in the doorway of their room.

Corbin was sitting on the edge of the bed with my mother cradled in his trembling arms. He kept screaming 'why, why, why?' over and over. Blood was all over both of them and their bedsheets. None of it felt real, it's as if I was watching a movie. You would think that would be the moment I'd feel something, anything. But it never happened.

Uhh, interlude? Do I write that when I take a writing break? Whatever. Corbin just walked in and handed me an urn pendant with my mother's ashes in it. He seems to be holding all of his emotions inside. Don't get me wrong, his eyes are red and tear-filled, but he's somehow still going. I search for grief, but my mind is blank. Nothing. All that I feel and all that I am, amounts to absolutely nothing. Does that make me broken or a monster? Perhaps, I'm both. I just stood there, pendant in hand, still no glimmer of feeling. Not even after I placed the chain around my neck. What's wrong with me? I know we never got along, but she was my mother. Why isn't this the key to crack open the floodgates and feel everything? There's been no tears, no screaming out to the abyss and asking the universe why.

Wednesday - One week later

Sloane, here... again. It's been a week since my mother killed herself. Her wake is happening right now, but I needed to get away from everyone. I was standing there in one of her black dresses, listening to all these people share their bullshit stories about a pretend version of her that never existed. I closed my eyes and listened to all their words, trying to picture their perception of her. I grasped the urn pendant tightly, and still... nothing. Everywhere around me there were laughs and sobs, while her only daughter sat there like a fucking statue. It was just a matter of time before I was asked why I was so quiet and withdrawn, or even worse, to speak. Fuck that. I ran upstairs, ripped that itchy-ass dress off and put on a hoodie and sweats instead.

I figured I should write something down, but really all I can think about is my artwork. It feels weird to be so numb, yet have a new obsession... but when your newest obsession is the only thing that's making you feel alive... you just gotta run with it, right? I keep all my drawings of him in my sketchpad. The last thing I need is Corbin finding endless drawings strewn across my room and walls of the man from the hospital. I don't see that going over very well. I hope nobody ever reads this. I've been thinking of him so much... sometimes I have these little moments where I feel like I'm being watched... and even though it's impossible, I always hope it's him.

Wednesday - Two weeks later

Surprise, it's me... Sloane... again, again. Can I just say, thank fuck my mother chose to kill herself when I was of legal drinking age. I'm on an emotional journey... no, no... an emotion-seeking journey? Fuck, whatever. I didn't have to steal Corbin's alcohol like a rebellious teenager, so I was able to go buy a bunch of random shit at the liquor store. I've spent the last week trying out different things. I didn't want to mix anything so I could decipher what gave me some sort of emotional response. Look at me being all scientific with my experiments. It's science, bitch! Or whatever the hell Jesse Pinkman says in Breaking Bad. Unfortunately, the only successful part of this first experiment was figuring out the quickest route to the porcelain throne to aggressively expel my liquid demons. Oh, and I smoke like a fucking chimney while drunk. On to the next experiment. I'm in my last semester at the university for my art major, so I've been keeping an ear out for parties although I only have one class left to take so I'm rarely on campus. What better way to work through shit than to dip your toe into the drug pool?

Thursday - Two weeks, one day later

I've hit a new level of fucked up on this journey.
I was just drawing and for some reason, the
glint of the blade in my charcoal sharpener caught
my eye. I don't know how long I sat there
staring at it. Calling to me. I picked it up and
twirled it in my fingers; the sun hitting the blade
over and over. Flashes of my mother's fileted
arms played in my head and I thought... this... this
could be it. This could be the one thing to break
the dam and make me feel. Make me truly mourn
the death of my mother. If anything will make
me feel something, slicing my wrists like mommy
dearest would definitely do it. Corbin was gone
again, he practically lives at the hospital now,
either working his shift or spending time with his
friends on the psych floor. He says they're hanging
out, but I think maybe he's actually seeking
therapy to deal with the loss of his wife.
I pulled the sharpener apart and grabbed the
blade inside. My fingers slipped and I hissed at
the sting in my finger and watched as blood
droplets fell from my fingertips. Does this count
as some sort of feeling? It's not an emotional
one, but this is one step closer, right? I rolled up
my left sleeve and pushed the edge of the blade
into my arm. There was a pinch and blood pooled
around the blade. I laid the edge of the blade
against my arm and slowly dragged it up. There
wasn't enough pressure at first, so it left a trail
of scratches with pinpricks of blood.

I pressed harder and watched as my skin separated, trickles of blood now running down my arms. I inhaled a deep breath and savored the feeling. There was a sting of burning pain... and control. Relief. If nothing else, this... this I could take control of. This may not be a full blown epiphany, but it's something.

Wednesday - Three weeks later

Cuz I got high, cuz I got high, cuz I got highhhhhhh... yeah this was a bust, in more than one way. The experiment was a bust, and damn, my jeans are about to bust from the amount of munchies I've consumed. I think weed would be fantastic for those who have a hard time eating. Those that need to make all of their overwhelming feelings, emotions and anxieties just shut the hell up. For pain, nausea, I mean the list is endless. But for me... right now... this is not what I'm looking for. I've consumed the whole kitchen, mixing foods that normally would be fucking foul, but goddamn, it was delicious right now. Other than that... I just need to melt into my bed. Sloane over and out, bitches.

Saturday

So last night was... Something. I turned in my final art project and overheard talk about a "killer rager", whatever the fuck that means. I quickly pulled out my phone and took notes of where they said this thing would be happening and how there's always so many party favors available. I got home as quick as I could and started doing research. God, how fucking lame am I that I was doing searches on drugs and what kind of things happen when you take them? I'm amazed the headline of the article wasn't 'Boring, Good Girls Trying to Be Bad'. Anyways, my search helped me decide that I'd be tackling an acid trip. It was just too hard to ignore the kinds of reactions that people have when taking it. This had to be the golden ticket, right?

Shortly after arriving, I was a woman on a mission and immediately was on the prowl for the dealer of party favors. I got what I needed without any issues other than his creepy stare, and ran to one of the open bathrooms. Did I attempt to look up video tutorials on what I needed to do? Yes... yes, I did. When that was unsuccessful, I did an online search of what I needed to do. I skimmed the forum of what it needed to look like, taste like, smell like. I guess that was my first clue I was supposed to stick the strip in my mouth. I opened the small baggy and was smacked with the scent of mint. My eyes watered and my nostrils burned.

I dropped the strip on my tongue and tasted the overpowering mint flavor. I started to feel weird in the amount of time it took me to walk from the bathroom to an open seat. Noises sounded like I was underwater, my vision kept going in and out of focus.

The only thing that sticks out is a hallucination that started with a fight breaking out. Or maybe it was a dance. I'm really not sure. And then there was a man hovering over me with a blue and red light up mask. There were x's for eyes and a stitched mouth. I think it felt like there was a bunch of him hovering over me at once. I didn't realize you could have, what I now know, is called olfactory hallucinations as well. But you can. Along with seeing this brightly colored masked man, he smelled fucking delicious. My heart was racing, and I felt all tingly... free... almost blissful. Part of me really wants to feel that again... but I don't really like the gaps in my memory, or how I ended up in my bed in different clothes. I don't think anything bad happened to me... I checked to make sure. My thighs weren't soaked with blood, no horrific pain or soreness in my pussy or ass, and no bruising I can see on any part of my body. This feels like a partial success, but I'm not sure if it's really worth the potential risk of being so vulnerable. I'll have to revisit this. Maybe it's something I can just do here at home, alone.

5

Karver

I've been watching my girl spiral for the last few weeks. As much as it pains me, I've been keeping my distance. For the most part. I have to keep her safe. Only when she sleeps do I run home to shower and eat, then I'm back here again. I either stay in my truck or I settle myself in the tree across from her room. The best thing about hiding in the shadows are the things you learn about a person. You can cut through all the lies and secrecy by just simply observing.

Her favorite color is blue, but she only wears black with small pops of color.

She prefers comfort over style, but she could wear a fucking potato sack and I'd find her just as beautiful.

She prefers having her hair in her face with her hood drawn up to hide, but she seems more comfortable with it up in a messy bun.

She doesn't have any friends, but she's polite to everyone around her, unless she's given a reason not to be.

When she watches shows, they tend to be the same ones over and over... Supernatural, Criminal Minds, Bones, Teen Wolf, and anime.

She would probably tell people that she doesn't have a favorite flower, but based on the ones she stares at a little bit longer, or tosses into her art, then I'd tell you she loves roses and lilies.

She listens to all different genres of music. I've learned that she loves to get lost in her art and music. If Dr. Dead is home, she's sure to be polite and keep her headphones on, but when he leaves she blasts the music so loud it shakes her windows. She's an amazing artist and even goes to school for it. My favorite thing about her artwork as of late... it's all me. I'm starting to think my sweet clover is as obsessed with me as I am with her. Every piece I've seen her draw is me with my mask, just barely revealing my face. The ones I love the most are when she adds herself to it. Various poses of us holding each other, smiling, laughing, me holding her as tears fall from her eyes.

I haven't seen her cry once since her mother died, but if her artwork tells me anything, it's that she's fucking intoxicating when she cries. The strength it takes to keep from marching in there and making her mine was truly tested the first night I caught her slicing her arms. I sat there watching as my cock grew hard and I imagined myself licking drops of her blood up. I saw myself rubbing her blood all over my cock, bending her over her art desk and fucking her until we both came. What better way to color her art than using a mix of her blood and our cum?

I know she senses me sometimes. She'll pause what she's doing and look around. I blend in well enough that she hasn't seen me everywhere I follow her. That is, until last week, which I don't think really counts, though. I overheard the fucker that gave her what she thought was an acid strip. Apparently it was a *Listerine* strip with fucking drops of Rohypnol on it. Fucker deserved far more than the quick beatdown I gave him for trying to take advantage of my clover. I don't think she realized I was really there when I swooped in to save her ass.

She was too far gone, and there were far too many fuckers eyeing my girl. Thank fuck Dr. Dead was working that night, so I was able to take her home without getting caught. I put her pajamas on and did the best I could not to stare too long at her sinful body. I kept my mask on so it was only a minimal peep show. I tucked her in and brushed strands of her hair from her face. She smelled fucking delicious. Best way I could describe it is like a fruit salad sprinkled with cinnamon. Before I stepped away, she ran her hand down my mask and whispered, 'I wish you were real'.

Movement catches my eye and I look up to see her throwing clothes around. Ah yes, another party tonight. I'm not sure how much longer I can remain in the background. She needs me. As much as it pains me to not have her any closer, it's also what's best. I can watch over her from afar. I can keep her. She's mine, and there's no risk of her seeing my darkest parts. There's no risk of her leaving me, because eventually she would.

A few minutes after the taxi picks her up, I drive to Nana's to drop off the truck. I pop open the glove box to grab my knife and remember that I still can't find the fucking thing. Dammit.

As fate would have it, the party is at a house at the other end of Nana's road. It's about a mile walk, but if I kick my ass into gear, it shouldn't take long to get there. I unzip my hoodie and roll up my sleeves. A bead of sweat falls down my temple and I slap it away. I can already hear the party and see the lights of it through the trees before I hit the curve in the road. Nana's house is the only other one around here, so there won't be any calls to the police for noise complaints. Then again, they can probably hear the party with the department only being a stone's throw away.

I walk up the steps and slip into the house, turning every which way to keep from the various bodies surrounding me getting too close. How the fuck is anybody comfortable being slammed together like sardines in a tin can? By the state of most of the people here, my girl is fashionably late. I look around the house for her, needing to minimize the distance between us.

I head towards the back of the house to check outside. I wait for a few people to walk through and once I step outside, my excitement to see her burns to ash in an instant, and my heart stops.

Fuck this.

Fuck this party.

Fuck these people.

Fuck that motherfucker who's going to die for touching what's mine… no, not what's mine. She's not mine, she's nothing.

My body vibrates with rage and my stomach coils in disgust as I watch *Sloane* flirt with this douche-canoe frat boy. She's laughing with him. Touching his arm. I'm gonna break that fucking arm. Right before I smash his fucking skull in. And *her*. I'm going to make that traitorous bitch hate me as much as I fucking hate her. I stomp over and push myself between them. Sloane gasps and her eyes go wide. Bitch boy taps my shoulder and shouts, "Hey, what the fuck, man!?"

I glare at him over my shoulder, "Shut the fuck up. I'll deal with you in a minute." I look back at her and sneer, "Why the fuck are you doing this? Did it all mean nothing? Do I mean nothing? You know what, don't fucking say a word, I already know the answer to that."

She flinched as if struck before settling her wide-eyed stare on me. I look down at her urn pendant and immediately get the urge to rip it off. I know I have to do it. She did this. This is her fault. She deserves this. I reach up and yank the chain from her neck, tossing it into the punch bowl on the table beside us. Tears fill her eyes as she grasps at her neck. She starts looking around, grits her teeth and then tries to shove me. "What the fuck is your problem?! Why would you fucking do that?!"

I lean in further, our lips a breath away. I can't believe I ever wanted these lips on mine. "YOU KNOW WHY!"

I spin around to dismiss her and focus on the punk-ass frat boy. He takes a step back as I jab my finger in his face.

"You touched the wrong one, motherfucker!" I rear back and throw my fist into his jaw. He stumbles, crashing into the table which crumbles beneath him and make the drinks splash everywhere. I don't give him a chance to get up and climb over him. I grasp the collar of his polo shirt with one hand and hit him in the face over and over with the other. I will end this piece of shit. I can't believe she's making me do this.

Why did she do this to us? Ashes. Ashes. Ashes. Oh, she's gonna fucking hate me for destroying her mother's ashes. Good. I'm going to make her hurt as much as she hurt me. I'll give her a reason to disappear from my life. The blood plastering his face makes my fist slip every which way. I barely hear the shouts around us as I continue beating his face to a pulp. Tired of my hands sliding off his face, I grip his shirt with both hands and yank him up as I slam my head to his, the crack of his nose deafening. I shake my head as my vision blurs from the hit.

Sloane

It's him. He's here. He's here, and he's mad at me. For what? I don't know, no matter what he says. He's acting like a jealous boyfriend and I don't even know the fucking guy. Nothing makes sense right now. Him screaming at me doesn't. Ripping my necklace off and throwing it in the punch bowl doesn't. My reaction definitely doesn't make any sense. First I'm screaming at him for what he did, and now I'm just transfixed. I'm finally feeling something, and it's not even the feeling I was searching for. Tears fall down my face, but it's not for my mother, or for her ashes, which he discarded like trash.

Why don't I care about that? I should be heartbroken he did that. I should be furious he's acting like this. But no instead, I'm rocked with feeling everything. Despite his actions and spewed venom in my direction, I'm happy to see him. I'm relishing in his apparent jealousy. Something's wrong with me. I squeeze my thighs together to ease the pulsing ache. Jesus Christ, am I seriously turned on watching him beat the fuck out of some random guy? With every hit, every blood spray, I feel a zip through my whole body. This is a work of art. He. He is a work of art. I'm pulled from my heated haze and jump when two police officers tackle him. Before I can stop myself, I'm shouting, "Don't hurt him!"

One officer holds him down as he kicks and squirms while the other cuffs him. They yank him off the ground and turn him around. I barely notice the EMT's helping the bruised and bloody guy as one of the officers sighs, "Are you fucking kidding me, Karver? You wonder why everyone keeps telling your frequent flier ass to just stay at the hospital and work on getting better."

Through his blood-stained face, he gives them a sinister smile. "And miss out on these heart-to-hearts? No way. Take me away to my tower, boys." He looks past them at me and his smile sours, "Nothing left here for me, anyway."

His hateful words strike a chord and the tears start to fall again. How the fuck does he have this effect on me? I don't even fucking know him. The officers turn around to see who he's looking at and for some reason, recognition crosses both of their faces. "Uh, is that you, Sloane Flanagan? Corbin Moriarty's daughter?"

"Stepdaughter. Or, I was. I'm not really sure how that works now that my mother is dead."

The other officer steps forward. "We're really sorry for your loss. Corbin's been really concerned about you. You're not in any trouble, but we're gonna need to take you to him."

"What? Why? I'm an adult, and I'm not doing anything wrong."

He puts his hand up as if I'm some rabid animal he needs to placate. "You're right. You are an adult and you've done nothing wrong, but you seem to be a part of whatever caused this fight to happen. So we just want to get you home safe."

While one of them shoves Karver, I guess his name is, into the back of their car, the other guides me in on the other side. I settle into the seat and he tilts his head, "We're going to give Corbin a call and give him a heads up to meet you at home. Just a sec."

The doors close on each side, making me jump. We may be on opposite sides of the seat, but his body heat and scent envelops me. It's enticing for a moment and then becomes too much. Every quickened breath between us, the sound of the music, static of the CB radio, the lights, it's all too much. My head spins and my heart races, saliva pools in my mouth as if I'm going to throw up. I suck in air like it will be my last breath and scratch at my chest over and over. Tears fall down my face and the squeak of the leather seat rings in my ears. He hovers over me and for a moment, I think he's going to kiss me. His voice deepens and it sounds like he's swallowed gravel when he says,

"That's right. Cry for me, *sweetheart*." He spits the endearment out as if it tastes vile. Flicking his tongue out, he roughly licks the fallen tears and groans. "Even your betrayal tastes sweet."

The doors open in the front and Karver throws himself back, the car shaking with the movement. I barely hear what they say while I'm lost in what just happened. I spend the ride to my house squeezing my hands to keep from touching the spit trails he left on my cheeks. The squeak of the brakes bring my attention ahead and I see Corbin standing in the driveway. My door opens and even if I tried, I couldn't have stopped myself from looking at Karver. He wordlessly looks away from me, the pain is overwhelming and confusing. I slowly step out of the car and Corbin rushes over. "Are you okay? He didn't hurt you, did he?"

"No." I shake my head, realizing he asked two questions. "I'm okay. No, he didn't hurt me. I think… in his own way, he was protecting me. I– I don't know. I just wanna go to bed. Sorry for the inconvenience, Corbin. I'll be okay, you can go back to work." I run up to my room and stand at the window, watching as the police say goodbye and back out of the driveway. I place my hand on the window, the ache inside me growing as I realize I'll never see him again. One last tear falls as I whisper, "Goodbye, Karver."

Splitting: Also called black and white thinking or all-or-nothing thinking is a pattern of unstable and intense interpersonal relationships characterized by alter-

nating between extremes of "idealization and devaluation".

6

Karver

My mind is a fucking hurricane as I look up the bunk above mine. The war within me and these annoying ass scrubs have had me on edge all weekend. Note to self, always bring a packed bag everywhere when out in society. I left at least one outfit in my drawer before leaving the last time. Fuck. I miss my clothes. I miss *her*. I've played that night in my head a million times. Why does every single thing in my life have to be all or nothing? Why can't my emotions just be… normal?

I know I shouldn't have screamed at her. I know I shouldn't have thrown her mother's ashes in the punch bowl. I still stand by beating the fuck out of that pussy in a polo. I was just so mad. So hurt. I needed her to hurt like me. I also knew I had to make sure I was hurting at the end of all this as well. And I am. I'm stuck in here involuntarily and have no clue when I'll get to see her again. Even if I do, she hates me now, that much I do know. I could see it written all over her face. I broke her. I took away the one thing she had left of her mother. She kept grabbing for it in the cop car. In the moment, I was glad. I was glad she was hurting like I was. I needed her to feel my pain. Why the fuck do I do this shit?

I'm laying here, knowing I fucked up. I purposely fucked up. But at the same time, she's at fault here, too. Right? It couldn't have been a fluke that she was making her art all about me. About us. She felt it, too. So she should have known better than to get close to someone else. *Obsession. Hatred. Good. Bad. Mend her. Break her. Fight for her. Fight with her.* I growl in frustration and punch the bunk above me until my knuckles split. Decker's fit of laughter rumbles through the door before it even opens. I clench my jaw and glare in his direction as he barrels through. Bending down with one hand on his knee, he tries to point behind him with the other. Through his giggles, he chokes, "Tell. Him. Axel. Tell. Him."

Axel shuffles in with his shoulders hunched and head down. I sit up and rub my bloody knuckles against the front of my scrub shirt. "What's up, Axel?"

He slightly lifts his head and looks at me. "Um. Well. You."

Decker shouts, causing Axel to startle. "Dude! Fine, I'll tell you. Your girl is here, man. And it's not to check her mama in." Well, no shit. Her mother is dead. "Like. She's *here*. For herself. This is toooooo good."

"Are you sure she's not just here with Dr. Dead? Dude practically lives at this hospital nowadays."

Axel quietly says, "It's true, Karver. They're getting her checked in, now. She… well, she… don't get mad at me

52

when I say this, I don't know any other way... but she doesn't..."

I stand up, completely unprepared for whatever he needs to say, "She doesn't what, Axel?"

"She doesn't look so good, man. I don't mean it in a, eww, way. I just mean... what's that saying? The lights are on, but nobody's home?"

Tread carefully, Karver. Fuck. That. I pull one of my masks out of my drawer and slide it over my face. "Decker, go flirt with the new orderly. Make sure Sloane gets roomed with us. *Both* of you will keep tabs on her. If she needs help, help her. Guide her. You tell her *nothing* about me tasking you with this." I walk out of our room and halt, looking over my shoulder. "And, Decker... *don't fucking touch her.* She's mine," I mutter as I walk away.

Sloane

The aftermath of Friday night makes me wonder if having feelings is all it's cracked up to be.

I barely make it through my shower, then drop to my bed and crash... hard. When I finally roll my ass out of bed and trudge down the steps, I find Corbin in the kitchen with a cup of coffee. When he hears me, he looks up over his cup and frowns, pointing to a chair. "Have a seat, Sloane."

I pour myself a cup of coffee, adding an insane amount of creamer and take a seat. "What's up, Corbin?"

Setting his cup down, he says the last thing I expect. "I've let this go on long enough. I understand your mother is gone, but this hasn't exactly been easy for me, either. The things you've been doing," he heaves a sigh, "it's just not right. It's not safe. I think... I think it would be best if I took you to St. John's."

My eyes bulge out of my head. "What? Why?"

He leans over the counter, "You're out of control. You can't keep going like this. Parties. Alcohol. Drugs. For fuck's sake, you're cutting your-self! I will not standby and let you kill yourself. I was too late with your mother, I won't make that mistake with you. So you can either come with me like a responsible adult, or I'll drag you there like a fucking child."

I get up from the chair and pour my coffee down the sink, unable to stomach another sip. Isn't the hospital for people with real problems? Ones who can't escape the torment their brains put them through? My brain isn't the one doing this. I'm doing this. Doesn't that make a difference? Karver. I'll see him again. Do I want to see him again? Will he want to see me again? I breathe in through my nose, slowly releasing it and turn towards Corbin. "Okay."

His tense shoulders fall and he nods. "Thank you. You're making the right choice. I'll give you one more day to rest here at home, and then take you first thing on Monday."

A nudge pulls me from the memory and I look up to see Corbin staring at me. "Sorry, what?"

"We need to sign the paperwork, Sloane. Please, focus."

"Where's my mom's paperwork? I mean why waste trees and fill out new shit? Just cross her name out and me as an emergency contact and we're good to go right?"

He gives a strained smile to the security guard that was here last time and turns to me. "Sloane. I thought we were going to be responsible adults about this? You know that's not something that can be done with medical files. Plus, you have questionnaires to fill out."

I give him a mock salute and look down at the piles of paperwork. I'd say I crossed my t's and dotted my i's, but there's only one t in my name. Finishing that, I move on to the questionnaires and my eyes unfocus at the extensive list of questions before me.

The pen hovers over the paper as I think of what I should write. As I see it? Uh, trying not to be a piece of shit daughter who can't mourn her suicidal mother. I jump when Corbin's voice is directly in my ear, "Just put what you've been doing since your mother died. Why you're doing it."

I mumble under my breath, "Well, *now* it'll sound worse than it really is."

St. John's Damascus Hospital

12 Knell Road, Damascus, Oregon
458-555-0124

Psychiatric Ward Intake Form

Name _Sloane Teagan Flanagan_

Birthday _June 21, 2000_

Primary Physician: _n/a_

In your own words, describe the current problems as you see them?

I've always had an issue with feelings and emotions, mainly by my own choice. Since my mother killed herself, they've completely shut off without my doing. I thought it made me a bad person to not feel some sort of way about her killing herself, so I started a journey... experiments to see if I could somehow flip the switch and turn them on. I drank different kinds of alcohol, tried out different drugs, and cut myself. ~~I only feel when~~

How long has this been going on?
About a month.

Feeling numb? ✓
Intrusive memories? ✓
Flashbacks? ✓
Sense of lack of control? ✓
Difficulty meeting role expectations? ✓
Self-mutilation/Cutting? ✓
Self-Harm ✓

After each question, I find myself taking longer and longer to answer. I can feel Corbin hovering impatiently right before he reaches over and grabs the clipboard. "I'll finish the rest of this." He shuffles through the pages and pulls one out, sliding it over to me. "You can fill this one out, it's about birth control."

I grimace. "Birth control? What about it?"

The security guard chuckles and I look at him, lifting a brow. He waves his arm around the room. "Co-ed facility. *Everyone* has needs, no matter the location. So we need to know if you're already on birth control or if we need to provide it. Nobody wants an oopsie-baby in the psych ward."

I'm not even gonna touch that. I'm not stupid enough to believe oopsie-babies happen just from patients *consensually* fucking. I've heard about people being taken advantage of in places like this. I sign the form confirming that I'm already on birth control and they have permission to access my hospital records to prove it. I put the pen down and shove the paperwork towards the guard. I lean against the counter to look around the room. My eyes fall on an old man who smiles and waves, greeting me like I'm a long lost grandchild of his. I return his smile and wave until my view is blocked by a woman in scrubs. My eyes are drawn to her fiery red finger waves plastered to her head, her matching lips standing out against her fair skin. She smiles wide and without meaning to, I get lost staring at the lipstick stains on her teeth. Her mouth is moving, but the words aren't registering until she lets out a squeaky, "Yoohoo!"

I blink back into focus. "Sorry, what?" I do my best to keep my face neutral when my ears take notice of her squeaky, syrup-like tone. "Hiiiii. I'm one of the RN's here."

She points to her hair as she says, "You can call me Nurse Red, *everyone* does. Security will go through your bag and then take your clothes to be washed," she leans in and whispers, "while we go do your strip search."

Looking past me, she wiggles her fingers. In a tone that's far too flirtatious for a recent widower, she says, "Hi, Dr. Moriarty."

I look over my shoulder at him to see how he reacts. "Hello, Nurse Regan," he murmurs, refusing to look at her.

"Are we all set here, Corbin? Apparently I have to go help the nurses get their rocks off and get felt up."

He grimaces at my words right as the nurse behind me gasps. "Don't be crass, Sloane. I'll visit soon. Please let them help you."

Without another word, he waves at the guard and stands by the doors waiting to be buzzed out. Effectively dismissed, I turn to the nurse, "Alright, Red, let's get this molest-fest out of the way."

Her eyes bulge and she stammers, "I-I… we…" Taking a deep breath, she rubs her hands down the front of her scrubs, "We don't do that. Please, follow me."

With her back towards me, I smirk as I follow behind. We turn right down a hallway and I freeze in my tracks, my shoes squeaking against the floor. There's a masked man walking down the hall. Karver. Before I can say anything, or even decide if I *want* to say anything to him, he scoffs and then stomps away. I roll my eyes and mumble, "Good talk."

Red turns towards me squinting, "What was that?"

I shake my head, "Nothing."

BPD is the 3rd leading cause of death for young adult women between 15-24.

7

Karver

I walk around the corner and lean against the wall. I tilt my head to watch her walk away and whisper, "Sorry, sweets." I pull the mask off and bite my cheek to keep from smirking, when I see Decker flirting with the new orderly.

Thumper sees me and waves me over to the table. I walk over and take a seat across from him. "Your sweetheart is back, Karver, my boy."

I trail my finger around the design on my mask, "Yeah, I saw that."

"She seems like a sweet girl. A little lost, but aren't we all?"

A hollow laugh escapes me. "You got that right, Thumper."

"I think she can save you. Like my bunny saved me."

Unable to keep the comment to myself, I throw my arms out and snap, "Does this look like she saved you? Look around. Look where we're at. Nobody can save us."

A heavy thud on the table makes me look over at him with his fist against the table and an angry expression. "I may be an old man, but I'll still kick your ass, you little shit. You watch your tone with me and show some respect. You're not mad at me. You're not mad at anyone but your own damn self, so why don't you pull your head out of your ass and fix it."

The chair squeals as I push away from the table, placing my palms on the table. "You don't know a fucking thing about me," I growl.

Before he can respond, I slide my mask on again and walk over to the door that leads to the courtyard. I wait for the buzz and push it open. I lift my head to the sky and soak in the sunshine and light breeze that ruffles my hair. I find an open bench and sit down, spreading my legs wide, my rubber slides scraping against the concrete. I pull out a smoke, shoving it through the mouth hole of my mask and light it. I take a deep inhale as I listen to one of the patients whine to a guard. "I just don't understand how this is completely open. I mean, we can go anywhere, and anyone can come here. So what exactly is the point of the locked doors with a buzzer inside?"

The guard heaves a heavy sigh, "Are we going to talk in circles about this every single day? Did you forget there's a buzzer on the door that leads here as well? Not only that, but look at me. What am I? What are the other guys dressed like me? Friggin' security guards. We keep an eye on all of you, so it doesn't really matter that this area is technically open. Okay?"

"Yeah, okay."

"Awesome. I look forward to having this conversation with you again tomorrow."

I look over to the door when I hear it buzz and see Decker strutting out with a big shit-eating grin. He curls his fingers in and brings them to his mouth, huffing on them and then rubbing them across his chest. "Done and done, my friend. Your lady luck is now our new roomie. This is gonna be awesome." His eyes gloss over and he licks his lips. "So much fun."

I clench my jaw so tight it clicks, and breathe in deeply. I stand up and angrily throw my cigarette away, yanking my mask to the top of my head. I prowl towards him ready to strike. I stop when our slides bump against each other and his smile grows.

"Are we gonna make out right now?"

"I wasn't fucking around when I told you not to fucking touch her, Decker. You haven't even begun to see the things I'm capable of. Don't fucking test me."

He giggles like a schoolgirl. "Kinky."

"HEY!" The guard behind me shouts. I hear his footfalls scraping the pavement as he approaches. He stands to the side of both of us and huffs with his hands on his hips. "We got a problem here, fellas?"

Ignoring his question, I cross my arms and narrow my eyes at Decker. He puts his hands up and takes a few steps back. "No problem, here. Toodles." Blowing a kiss in our direction, he spins around and skips to the door to head inside.

I start to walk away when the guard's words stop me. "Karver. You get away with a lot of shit around here. Could you at least *try* to not make waves?"

I look at him and salute. "Sure thing, 2.5."

A mask of confusion crosses his face and he scratches his head. I see the moment it clicks when his eyes grow, and my lip twitches trying to hold back the smirk. "Half of five! 5-0! I am not half a cop, fucker."

I walk backwards and shrug. "But you're not a full one, either."

Sloane

I focus on the buzz from the lights above and the random scratching of her pen on paper. I refuse to look at the nurse while she gropes, rubs and probes my naked body with her glove-covered hands. Once she shut the door to this room, the immediate change in her demeanor and voice was eerie. The fake smile dropped and her voice dripped with venom. The back of my neck prickles and waves of goosebumps pepper my skin. I thought it was just the chill in the air causing my nipples to pebble and my teeth to chatter, but realization dawns on me. It's not just the cold, I'm uncomfortable. Here I am again, questioning if emotions are really worth it.

She runs her fingers through every bit of my hair, starting at the scalp and working her way down. She taps my chin with her forefinger. "Mouth open." I open my mouth, and count the dots in the ceiling. "Wider. Tongue out."

I try to say dirty, but with my mouth wide open, it just sounds like the nonsensical noises you make while brushing your teeth and talking.

"Tongue to the right."

"To the left."

"Up."

"Down."

I hear her scribbling on the paper again and the clang of the clipboard on the table when she puts it down. "Turn around and touch your toes."

Jesus Christ, as if this whole thing wasn't fucked up enough. I do as she says, but jolt when I feel her spreading my ass cheeks apart. "Whoa!"

Her grip tightens, sure to leave finger-shaped bruises in its wake. "Hold still!" She spits.

"I'm not asking for hearts and flowers here lady, but maybe ask me to dinner first. Hell, I would've settled for a fucking warning."

Ignoring my retort, she barks, "Cough!" I let out a small cough. "Again. Harder."

"Hey, isn't that my line here?"

"Stand up." I do as she says and then turn. There's a light knock on the door before it slowly opens. I instinctively attempt to cover my body the best I can and watch as Red messes with her hair, as if it could ever be out of place with it plastered to her head.

Her lips curve into a smile just as a quiet voice says, "Hi. Sorry." A young woman with thick, curly brown hair and olive-toned skin peeks through the door. "Hi, Sloane. I'm one of the orderlies. My name is Leeba." She giggles as she says, "We're both newbies here. We can stick together. To find your room, you'll take a right and your room is the last one at the end of the hall on the left. If you take a right, you'll find the showers."

I nod. "Okay, thank you." She smiles at the both of us and ducks back, closing the door behind her. Fabric smacks me in the face, I grab at it and pull it down to see that it's white scrubs.

I lift them up. "I thought we were allowed to wear our own clothes here? Minus the belts, strings and shoelaces, of course."

"Security has your bag, remember?" She scans my body and looks at me with disgust. "I doubt you want to waltz around naked in front of everyone."

I don't need to look down to see what she's looking at. It's the one thing that ever did stir some sort of reaction from me while growing up. I learned to cope with what haunted me in the mirror by refusing to look at it. My boobs grew too fast, lining them with flesh-colored stretch marks. Over the years, bad eating habits and sitting in front of my sketchpad more than moving around, left me with extra weight on my stomach and thighs. I got so good at ignoring it, that the only reminder of my sizable difference compared to girls like Red here, was the thinly frayed fabric of the inner thighs of all of my pants.

I steel my spine at her words and immediately make a spiteful decision. I tuck the clothes under my arm and grab my now laceless Converse, shoving them on my feet. I walk to the door and when my hand is on the doorknob, she hisses, "What the fuck are you doing?"

I attempt to yank the door open, the hydraulics keeping it from flying against the wall. "Don't ever doubt me." I lift my head and walk into the hall. Nobody cares. I don't care.

Fuck that bitch. I look forward and recognize the man pacing at the end of the hall. Red's screeching behind me catches his attention and he looks in our direction. His eyes go wide and he quickly throws his head up to the ceiling.

He puts his hands up like blinders and shouts, "KARVER! HURRY! KARVERRRRRR!"

I slice the air across my throat , hoping he magically looks at me again. Stop it. What the fuck? Why is he calling for him? I reach the end of the hall just as the guy pacing turns in my direction. He gasps and quickly spins away from me. I stop in my tracks and all bravery vanishes when I hear, "WHAT THE FUCK?!"

My heart starts to race and it feels as if my bones will burst through my skin with how much I'm shaking. With the guys here, Red's fake-ass persona comes back and the sickly-sweet tone is back. "Sloane, honey. Please don't do this. Let's get you in your room and get your clothes on, okay?"

I gasp when I feel the heat of his body at my back. "We got it from here."

"B-but."

"*Go.*"

"Fine," she replies with a pouty tone.

I swear the bitch even stomped her foot. I feel his body press further against me and I jump. My whole body feels like it's on fire. Why does he have this effect on me? His breath fans my hair, and the pressure of his mouth against my ear somehow feels fucking sinful. I clench my thighs in the hope to stave off this newfound ache… and the very real possibility I further embarrass myself by dripping on the fucking floor like a bitch in heat. What the fuck is happening to me? On a growl he seethes, "Get in the fucking room, *sweetheart.*"

There's a whimper, and I realize it came from me. Yup, definitely a dog now. I feel Karver's icy fingertips on my back, urging me forward. As I cross the threshold, I hear a man's hysterical laughter as he hoots, "Hot damn, now it's a fucking party."

People with BPD say it feels like: An emotional burden to me and everyone else in my life.

8

Karver

I've always heard the expression 'my blood is boiling'. Right now, I'm actually wondering if it's possible for your blood to turn to lava? This was the last thing I expected to find when I walked around the corner to see what the fuck Axel was shouting about. I push Sloane further into the room, shielding her the best I can, especially now that she's caught Decker's attention. I shout over my shoulder, "Fuck off, Decker."

His only response is his annoying laughter. I hear Axel whisper-shouting, "No, Decker. Don't go in there. Just leave them alone. Come on, go do your Jell–O switcheroo in the rec room."

There's loud clapping as Decker shouts, "Yes! Fantastic idea! Let's go, Axel!"

I grab hold of her by the shoulders and she gasps as I spin her around. I wrap my hand around her throat and she instinctively grabs my wrist. Her shaky hold pushes and pulls like she can't decide if she wants me to hold on or let go. I push her back against the door as I shut it with the other hand. The door shuts and her hiss matches the one from the door. My eyes dip down to her heaving chest and I can't help but take in the view of her big tits and hardened nipples. I bite my lip in an attempt to suppress my groan. The moment is shattered by her whispered plea, "Please stop staring at me."

I stare deep into her eyes and watch as they dilate. "Funny. You sure weren't shy when you were walking the hall in all your glory."

I squeeze her neck on the final word and she lets out a gurgled, gasping moan. I push my knee between her clenched thighs until I feel her wet heat pressed against my thigh. Her muffled moans continue, and I look down when I feel my pant leg go slick. I loosen my hold on her neck to a barely there touch and she squeezes my wrist. I lean in and run my nose along her jawline, noticing the goosebumps following the trail I leave. "I think you *love* when I look at you, sweet clover."

She pants, "I... I was just trying to make a point."

I drop my head to look at my thigh and then slowly look up. "My thigh suggests you've made quite a point."

She shakes her head the best she can. "No, I," she growls in frustration, "that's not what I meant. That bitch was trying to make me feel like shit about myself, so I was making a point to her."

I step back and rip my mask off. I don't miss the look of disappointment on her face. "What bitch? Who's making you feel like shit about yourself?"

She nervously crosses her arms every which way over her body as if to hide herself. I blindly throw my mask to my bed. "Don't do that."

She throws her hands out and slaps them back around her body, "Do what? And I said she *tried* to make me feel like shit. Not that she was successful."

"Really, sweets? Cuz it looks to me like you weren't making a point for her. You were doing it for yourself in order to feel better about the fucked up shit she said to you. Not to mention the fact that you're trying to hide from me now, as if you've realized your fake bravado got you in quite the *sticky* situation."

She scoffs at my words, "You don't know a fucking thing about me, *Slasher.*" Did she...? She just gave me a nickname. Fuck, I thought my cock was hard before. I knew it. She's mine.

I stalk towards her and press my body to hers. I place my index finger below her chin and press my thumb against it to tip her head up. Her eyes widen when she feels my cock stabbing her stomach. "Oh, I know more about you than you could ever imagine. Now. Tell me who the bitch is that's fucking with you? You've been here all of two seconds and already finding trouble. I didn't realize clovers had thorns. I fucking love it."

The fire in her eyes is fucking breathtaking. "What the fuck do you care about anyone fucking with me? You *don't* know me. And last I checked, you were the one who fucking screamed at me and trashed my mother's ashes at that party."

I look away, the shame of what I did welling up inside me and I mutter, "That was different."

"Unbelievable. Get the fuck off of me. I'd like to get dressed now."

I'm frozen, unable to let go. I don't want to let go. I need to keep her here. I feel the anger building from my shame and at the same time, I know I need to get the fuck away from her. Why do I always do this? *Keep her. Let her go. Tell her everything. Tell her nothing.*

The haze of my ping-pong thoughts is broken by Sloane's shout, "SLASHER!"

I whip my head in her direction. "Now you pay attention. I've been saying your name over and over trying to ask you a question."

Barely able to get the words out I breathe, "What?"

"So it's okay for *you* to treat me like shit, just nobody else?"

My jaw clicks when I clench it. Don't yell. Don't yell. It's a perfectly acceptable question. No. No it's not. She's fucking questioning you. She's not understanding. Why is she not understanding? She starts pushing at me again. "*Stop.*"

She pushes once more. "ANSWER MY QUESTION OR LET ME THE FUCK GO!"

"NO! OKAY!? NO!"

I release her and step away, pacing back and forth while

pulling my hair. "You wouldn't understand. Nobody does. Fuck, I don't even understand it."

I stop when I feel her pulling on my wrists. "Stop that. You're hurting yourself." I slowly release the hold on my hair when I see the concern in her eyes. She pulls away and covers herself again. I already miss her touch. I need it tattooed onto my skin. I need it wrapped around every fiber of my being.

She grabs her scrubs from the floor and kicks her shoes off. Yanking the scrubs and socks on, she shoves her feet into her shoes. The look on her face shows that she doesn't like the way the non-slip socks feel in her shoes. She starts to pull her hair out of her scrub top and I march over and stop her, murmuring in her ear, "Let me."

I slide one hand around the front of her and pull her back to my front. She melts against me and in that moment, I feel like I could conquer the fucking world. With my other hand, I caress the side of her neck and she shivers. I gather her hair in my fist and pull her head back. She moans and allows her head to fall against my shoulder. Her chest heaves with every breath. "How are you doing this? I don't... I don't understand."

She squeezes her eyes shut. "I'm not doing anything, Clover. Not yet."

"Remember how you said nobody understands you? Not even yourself? It's like that for me, too. I can't feel. I do whatever I can to just feel and have emotions and I can't... until you. I don't even know you and any time I'm near you, I'm flooded with... everything. I don't know what to do with it, I don't understand it. I love it. I hate it." Fuck, she's just as lost as me. Can we save each other? Or will we bleed each other dry?

Before I have a chance to answer her, there's a frantic knock on the door followed by Axel's muffled voice. "H-hey, Karver. It's group time. They-they said if I can't get you guys out of here, they're going to think something is wrong and it'll be real-really bad. Please, Karver. I don't know what they mean by that, but I don't like it. Please come out."

I push my nose against her temple and breathe her in. "Let's go. He'll freak out even more if we don't go out there." I murmur into her hair.

People with BPD say it feels like: Being constantly worried, fearful, and suspicious.

9

Sloane

The intensity of being alone with Karver in the room was intoxicating. I felt... everything. I didn't realize the magnitude of having feelings until now. I keep waiting to crash like I did the night of the party. That's not the only new discovery I've made in the short amount of time I've been here. Apparently, my shadow has tripled in size. I'm not sure having three men standing behind me makes me appear weak. Maybe it makes me powerful, as if I am a magnet who can pull them in any direction I go. From behind me, the pacing man I now know as Axel whispers, "They said group time will be in the courtyard. Don't wanna waste the sunshine."

My steps falter when I realize I'm unsure of where to go. "I don't-"

My heart races as I feel Karver at my back again. "There's a door that leads outside in the rec room where you checked in at. That's where you'll go, sweets."

"How," I shake my head, nervous to voice my question in front of his friends. "Okay."

We turn the corner to enter the rec room and I see that it's almost empty, except for an older woman in a wheelchair by the window and Nurse Ratchet bent over, whispering to her. Chuckles behind me, better known as Decker, says in a high-pitched voice, "Hiya, Nurse Red."

She bends over further and slowly swings her hips side to side. Does this really turn men on? This scene is… God, I'm embarrassed for her. I reach the door and snort. Her head whips in my direction, and her lame attempt at a seductive smile falters. She abruptly stands ramrod straight and starts messing with non-existent stray hairs and wrinkles in her scrubs. As the door buzzes to let us out, I smirk. "Subtle." Her mouth drops as I open the door and walk away before she can respond.

The warmth of the sun wraps around me. Luckily, there's a light breeze to stave off the brunt of the heat. Decker snickers, "Dude, she wants my dick so bad."

I spin to face the three hulking shadows that now plague me. "Hate to break it to you, Deck, but that bitch wants any cock she can wrap her holes around."

He closes his mouth and his cheeks balloon out. Before his face has a chance to turn tomato red, he bursts out laughing. "Holy shit. I can't believe you just said that. You're a dirty girl." He elbows Karver in the side, "Dude, she is a dirty girl."

Karver side-eyes Decker and walks away. I turn to follow and see that there are picnic tables to the left hand side arranged in a square, leaving enough space for people to get to the seats towards the inside of the square. From the looks of it, everyone is already sitting and waiting. There's one table left pushed up against the building, where the old man I saw earlier is sitting.

From behind me, Decker shouts, "Aww, Thump, Thump, Thumper left a table for us. Thanks, gramps."

Instead of being annoyed by his antics, the old man's green eyes twinkle with his big smile. He pats the table beside him, "I'm so happy to finally meet you, darling girl." I leave some space between us and straddle the bench so I can still see the other groups of people. The guys all take a seat on the other side, Karver in the middle, Decker on the left and Axel on the right. Karver leans against the building, and within seconds, the other two follow suit. I turn my attention back to the old man to introduce myself. "I'm Sloane, by the way. What's your name?"

The wrinkles in his face deepen with his smile, "Ahh, pretty name for a pretty girl. I go by Thumper. I'm so pleased to meet you." I start to squint and bring my hand up to shield my eyes as the sun shifts. "Here, let me."

I put my hand down and look at Thumper as he drops his Navy hat on my head. I can hear murmurs of, "what the fuck?" and "no way" to the left of me. I fix the hair stuck in the front of the hat and slide them to the sides.

Decker chuckles, "That's crazy. You never let anybody go near that hat, let alone wear it."

Thumper looks over at them and shrugs. "My bunny wore it all the time."

Through gritted teeth, Karver says, "She's not your bunny, old man. Back off."

Thumper shakes his head, Karver's anger not even fazing him. "She's old enough to be my granddaughter. Don't make it weird, kid."

A familiar chuckle catches my attention and I look in the direction it came from. The same time I'm thinking it, Karver mutters, "What the fuck is Dr. Dead doing here?"

I'm preparing to stand up and ask him just that, when the man I'm guessing is the therapist speaks up. "Alright, everyone, who wants to kick this meeting off? What about you, Sloane? You want to just dive in?"

"Oh, no, no, no. I'm good, thank you. I've never done this before, anyway. I think I'll just… observe."

I meet Corbin's disapproving stare from across the way and he sighs. "Sloane. You promised you'd try."

"And I intend to. But like I said. I've never. done. this. before. I don't know how it works or what to say, so I would like to observe before I join in. And what the fuck are you even doing here, anyway? Last I checked, this is *group* therapy. For *patients*. Did I miss you checking yourself in as well?"

He looks around and rubs the nape of his neck. "I… I've been coming here for a few sessions ever since your mother died."

"Jesus, small towns run shit weird. Well, good for you getting the help you need, but this isn't a family therapy

78

session. So it would probably be best if the things we discuss were done separately."

The therapist looks back and forth between the two of us. "I mean, I think it can still be discussed here. Everybody already shares in front of each other, anyway."

Corbin stands and puts his hand up with a tight-lipped frown, "No, no. You're right, Sloane. I apologize. I just got used to coming here and having a place to talk about how much I miss your mother. I will go find myself someone to talk to so I don't interrupt your time here. I'm sorry."

He whispers, "Sorry, everyone," and heads to the door to be buzzed back into the building.

After a moment of stunned silence, the therapist gets the session started. I watch and listen as everyone talks about various things, their thoughts and feelings for the day, last week, month, year or a traumatic experience. Some talk about their favorite meal here. A few remain utterly silent. There's anger, fear, sadness, confusion. How do they deal with these whirling emotions day in and day out? I guess that's just it, though. They're not. Nobody really seems to be coping with it at all. At least not in the way that people say we should.

Axel murmurs a few quiet words, stating he wishes he could be more outgoing, wishing he wasn't afraid of so many things, real or perceived. Who knew that people's emotions get to be so much? That they even battle things that don't truly exist? To them, it's very, very real. It's Karver's turn and I can't help but watch every move he makes. He holds his hand to his chin and his thumb over his mouth. With every word spilled from his mouth, he smiles. He continues to smile, even when he says things that would usually break a person. He talks about experiencing the most horrific past, but from murmured remarks, they all agree on one thing. Nobody knows what's the truth and what's the lie.

At one point, I even hear, "Oh, here we go again. His story changes every time." I zero in on the thumb near his bottom lip, and it dawns on me. Nobody has noticed that he has a tell. I haven't known him long enough to know if he has others, but I'm certain I just caught one. Has nobody else ever noticed? For some of his stories, there's a barely-there twitch of his thumb against his lip, as if he's trying to push the lie back into his mouth.

Karver

For years I've been told that you have to follow the treatment plan in order for healing to take place. According to them, having elementary-style storytime for all our problems is supposed to be the key to that. I've hated group therapy since the first one they ever had me join as a kid. Nana told me to wear a mask, to lie if I have to. It became a game, a source of entertainment in such a mundane activity, to come up with the most outlandish stories just to see the looks on people's faces. Plus, when you share the sordid details of your past in between all the lies, nobody will ever know the true horrors of your life. What can I say? Old habits die hard. So when it's my turn, I keep it up. "I didn't talk until I was 10. My parents taught me that it was best if I just shut my mouth. If I didn't, they would whoop me all over my body with a belt. If I shed a single tear or let out even a whimper, I'd have to go to bed hungry that night." Lie. "My parents loved drugs more than they loved me. Food was non-existent in the house. When they'd have friends over to shoot up, they'd lock me outside so they didn't have to deal with me. It never mattered how little I was or what kind of weather we were having." Truth. "My parents would get really fucked up and their laughter and dancing would quickly morph into shouts and violence." Truth. "One night, they got so high that my dad passed out with a lit cigarette in hand. Since I was outside, I didn't realize anything was wrong until I saw the flames eating away at the curtains. I ran up to the windows and knocked as if that would make a difference. It didn't. We lived in a bad neighborhood, so it took a lot longer for police and fire to show up. I can still hear their screams." Lie.

I take a deep breath and pull out a smoke. I wiggle it between my lips and the flick of my lighter makes a few people jump. I blow out the smoke and laugh. "Ironic, right?" My eyes fall on Sloane, who looks like she's in a trance staring at my mouth. I pull the cigarette from my lips and slowly mouth, 'hi, sweets'. Her eyes widen and shoot up to mine. I click my tongue and wink, her only response is a hitched breath. Zombie Doc announces the session is over, and we can either go get snacks and drinks or head to the art room. I look at my sweet clover one more time and creativity strikes. Art room it is.

People with BPD say it feels like: An exhausting and frustrating trap that I can't escape.

10

Sloane

I'm sitting at a table surrounded by colorful paper, mini canvases, colored and lettered beads, frail string, glue sticks, crayons and fat tipped markers. The more dangerous items, like pliers, craft wire and hot glue guns have to be requested for supervised use. At the end of the table to my left is the quiet woman in the wheelchair and Thumper is to my right. Apparently I did something to piss off Karver... again. I couldn't begin to guess what the fuck I did. Him and his goons decided I have the plague and chose to sit at the table furthest from me. Mad enough to stay away, but not enough to keep their fucking eyes off of me. Witnessing him effectively dismiss me makes me more aware of the transition that takes place in my body. The further he got from me, the more I felt the numbness seeping in again. The buzzing tingle throughout my body that made my heart race slowly faded to nothing.

Calling myself a succubus before was just an offhand comment, but now I'm starting to think it's *very* real. Every moment without him, every bit of distance has me craving him so I can feel again. Maybe Corbin was right. I do belong here. I'm pathetically latching on and depending on a man I don't even know to help me feel alive. Let's just add codependency to my list of issues. Awesome. I look around the table, hoping to find charcoal to use. Unable to find it, I get up from my seat and pause when the air changes and I notice *everyone* is watching me. Awkward. Ignoring the stares, I walk over to Leeba, who's watching over the more dangerous supplies. She looks up from her seat and smiles at me as if I'm a long lost friend. "Hi, Sloane. Everything okay?"

I try to return her smile and fail. "I wanted to see if you had any charcoal art supplies, and use the hot glue gun."

"You're in luck. We do have charcoal. Also, Nurse Regan is already at your table to supervise you with the glue gun," she says with a genuine smile.

"Oh, joy." While she's moving things around to find the charcoal, I notice one of the pencil sharpeners at the end of the table. I zero in on it and quickly check if she's looking. I place my hands down on the table, my right one directly over the sharpener. I pull my hands back, the sharpener in my grasp and bend down like I'm messing with my sock. To make it seem normal, I gripe while pushing the sharpener in my shoe. "God, I hate these socks. Leeba, do you know when I'll be getting the rest of my clothes? I really need my regular socks, these ones suck."

She looks over the table and frowns. "It should be soon. I'm sorry they're bothering you."

I smack at my shoe like I'm truly annoyed and stand up. "Hopefully sooner rather than later."

"Have fun, Sloane," she says as she hands me everything.

I wave with the supplies in hand. "Thanks, Leeba."

I plug the hot glue gun in, making sure to not get the cord stuck under the woman's wheelchair. I take a seat and place the charcoal down in front of me. I look over at the stoic woman with long, braided gray hair and wonder if she truly doesn't know what's going on around her or if she does but is so locked in the prison of her own mind, she can't let anyone know. I look back at Thumper coloring a picture of a rabbit, whistling a tune I can't place. "Hey, Thumper?"

His hand halts and he looks over at me with a smile. "Yes, darling girl?"

I nod back towards the woman. "Does anyone ever talk to her? Or do they all just leave her be?"

"Now that you ask, no. I don't think anyone says anything to her. Honestly, I don't think people really even acknowledge her existence."

"That seems really lonely. What if she's in there just screaming to talk to people, to just be noticed?"

His eyes move over to the woman and his smile falters. "You know what? You could be right." His eyes move back to me and adds, "I knew you were a sweet girl. I may be a man who's not right often, but I know I was right when I told that boy you'd be good for him."

I look in Karver's direction and find him already looking. His eyes drop the moment ours connect. "He talked to you about me?"

Thumper goes back to coloring and chuckles. "More like I talked to him about you and he threw a tantrum. Don't let it bother you, though. Life dealt him a shitty hand, and he deals with it the only way he knows. It's all a mask."

I grab a mini canvas, darkening the edges with charcoal and murmur, "Wish he'd drop it." After filling in the edges, I smudge it towards the center of the canvas.

I drop the charcoal and am met with darkness swallowing the silhouette of a crying woman. I pick up the hot glue gun, squeeze the trigger of it and place a thin horizontal line over the woman's mouth. I then add vertical lines to create stitches. I put the glue gun down to the left of me and pick up the charcoal again to add shadows to the stitches. I pick up the canvas and lean over to place it in front of the woman. "I made this for you. I'm sorry people don't include you in anything."

Her face remains frozen, but a single tear falls down her cheek. I pull back to start a new project when my wrist touches the heated part of the glue gun and I hiss. Yes. There it is. Lost in the fact that I'm feeling something, I don't pull back. I leave my wrist there to burn. The moment is shattered when Nurse Ratchet squeals, "Oh my God! What have you done, Sloane?!"

I look at her and then at my wrist to look at the burn mark. Leeba runs over. "What happened? Sloane, are you– oh my God! We have to get some burn cream on this right away. Nurse Regan, I'm going to call someone to stay here with you while I go help Sloane with this, okay?"

"Of course, of course. I've got her."

Leeba walks away and Ratchet kneels down in front of me, still holding my wrist. She looks up, her concerned face now replaced with a lifted brow and a sinister smile. She tsks me and says, "Such a shame *nobody* saw what happened sooner. Could've avoided such a nasty burn. You poor thing."

I yank my wrist from her hold and stand up. "Go find a cock to ride. You get real bitchy when your cunt is deprived."

She winks up at me, "Oh, honey. I don't discriminate. I love me a nice warm pussy to play with, too." What the fuck? I can feel Karver's stare, and as much as I want to get the fuck away from this bitch, I refuse to look in his direction. I can avoid you, too, asshole.

People with BPD say it feels like: It's hard to know who I actually am versus who my BPD wants me to be.

11

Karver

The plan was to separate myself from her. As much as I want to be near her, no, *need,* to be near her, I have to protect myself from the inevitable. I know it doesn't make any sense, fucking believe me, I know. But when you've learned that everyone fucks you over, and everyone leaves, you always, always, prepare for it. Plus, if she sees me as an asshole, then in my mind it was *my* choice for us to be apart, not hers. Fucking self-sabotage. Does it ever end?

Speaking of, what the fuck is Mousey screaming about? I look up and find her holding Sloane's wrist. The new orderly, Leeba, runs over there frantically. I grip the edge of the table to keep myself from going over there. I watch the scene unfold and realize what's happened. What have you done now, sweet clover?

I finish up the floral wire clover I've been working on and pocket it, along with a sky blue marker. Unable to wait any longer to check on her, I get up from the table to find her.

Axel and Decker start to move and I stop them. "No, just stay here."

Axel meekly whispers, "Okay," and sits down.

Decker whines like a child as I walk away. "Duuuuude, no fair."

I peek into the rec room and find only the security guard there. I then head to the room where they do strip searches and find the door open but the room empty. Where did you go, Clover? I reach our room and find the door shut. I open it to find Sloane is in the corner of the room shirtless and with her back to me, but I hear the gasp that falls from her lips when she realizes she's been caught. I shut the door and take slow steps, letting the anticipation build. I pick up a mask from my bed and slide it over my face. I close the gap between us and press my front to her back. "What are you doing, sweet clover?"

"N-nothing," she whispers, hunching in on herself.

Taking advantage of my height, I peer over her shoulder and see the blood trickling down her stomach. I drop my chin to her shoulder and bring my hand around her waist, causing her to jump. Her ass rubs against my hardening cock and I groan. "*Fuck.*"

Her heavy breaths fill the space as I slide my finger through the blood and smear it around her navel. "Hmm. This doesn't look like nothing, sweets. So I'll ask again. *What. Are. You. Doing?*"

Her chin falls to her chest as she says in a defeated tone, "I was trying to feel something. I figured this would be the best way. My body is already ugly, so it's not like this could make it any worse."

I growl at her words, pissed that she doesn't see herself the way I do. I slide my finger through more blood and make a crimson trail up to her breast. I reach her nipple and feel it harden as I rub the blood around it. "You mean the way you only feel things when you're around me?" She tries to move away from my hold, but I quickly wrap my other arm around her and pull her closer to me. "Ah, ah. Answer the question."

Her whole body starts to vibrate. "*Fuck. You.*"

"Oh, sweets. That can be arranged."

"Wha–"

Her question is cut off with a yelp when I spin us around and bend her over the edge of the bunk bed. The upper half of her body lays across my mattress, while her ass is in the air. I run my hand up her spine and grip the nape of her neck while I fumble with the pocket of my scrubs for my knife. It's not as good as the one I lost, but this was the only one I left hidden in my mattress last time I left. "Don't move." Her head turns against the mattress and she tries to look back. I bring my hand down to her ass and her yelp morphs into a moan. "I said, don't move. Be a good girl and listen, Clover."

She presses her mouth to the mattress and moans as I watch her writhe, seeking the friction she desperately needs. I slowly slide her pants down, revealing her plump ass. I leave them just above her knees and bring my hand down against her bare ass. I watch as it jiggles from the slap and I bite back my groan. "Do you have any fucking idea what seeing your body does to me? How do you not see how fucking sinfully beautiful this body is?" I slide my hand down and bring it between her slick thighs. She arches her back more as I rub two fingers up and down her dripping center. "You're already this wet and I've barely even touched you. How soaked do you think this pussy will be when I'm finished with you?"

I punctuate the sentence by shoving my fingers inside her and pumping them in and out. I flick the knife in my free hand and she gasps at the clicking sound it makes. "Wh-what are you doing?"

I run the tip of the blade up her spine with a barely-there touch. "You want to fucking feel something, *sweetheart*? Then I'll continue to be the only one who makes you fucking feel. You come to me when you're numb, I will be the one to bring you back to life. I better not ever catch you doing this shit, or fucking calling your body ugly ever again."

I push the blade harder into her shoulder blade, angry that she sees herself as anything less than she is. Blood blossoms around the blade, her loud moan is muffled by the mattress. Her hips rock, riding my hand, "That's right. Ride my fucking hand, sweets." I make a vertical line on her shoulder blade and start on the next line. Before I've finished the third line, I feel her pussy pulse and tighten around my fingers, her thrusts falter as she soaks my hand. I pull my fingers from her pussy and watch as her juices drip down my hand to my wrist. I stick my tongue through the mouth of the mask and suck my fingers. I squeeze my eyes shut and my cock twitches. I pull my fingers out with a pop. "Fuck, sweets is spot on."

I rub my hand and wrist all over my mask, followed by the bloody blade, mixing her blood and cum all over it. I fold the blade in and rub it around in the blood that covers her back, bringing the knife back down to her pussy to rub it up and down. She jolts at the touch of metal to her pussy. Turning her head again, her wrecked voice attempts to shout. "What the fuck are you doing, Slasher?"

"I'm giving you what you need, Clover." I grip the knife tight and push it inside, slowly moving it in and out. "Clamp down, sweets. I'd hate to lose my knife in your perfect cunt." I feel her squeeze her pussy around it, whenever I pull back, there's resistance. "There you go, that's a good girl." I pump the knife in and out and she starts riding it on her own. With my free hand, I squeeze the meat of her hip, hard enough to leave my mark. Unable to stop myself, I slam my hips against her to give my deprived cock what it needs.

"K-Karver, I'm- I'm gonna cum."

I barely recognize my voice when I growl, "Wait."

I step back and pull the knife out, her fist slamming down on the mattress. "What the fuck, Karver?! I said I was gonna cum, why did you fucking stop?!"

I ignore her angry questions and lick her blood and cum from the knife and drop it on the mattress beside her. I pull the blue marker out of my pocket and pop the cap off with my teeth. I bring the marker down to her ass and she startles from the cold, wet tip of the marker. Her ass shakes with the jolt when I write, '*perfect*', on her right ass cheek. I put the cap back on and shove it back in the pocket before pulling my scrub pants down and rub my hand through her soaked thighs. I rub the blood and cum mix around my cock and stroke it twice. Sick of edging myself, I don't take it slow or gentle. The moment the head of my cock notches at her entrance, I thrust forward and she moans, "Fuck, fuck, fuck. Just like that, please, please, please."

I grip her hips tight and unleash on her pussy. I'm going to make this feeling last for her days after it's done. Every move she makes, she'll feel the imprint of my cock in her pussy and my fingertips engrained along her hips. "What do you feel, sweet clover?"

"Y-you. E-everything."

I take a deep breath and tilt my head back. "That's fucking right. You won't know where I begin and you end. Without me, all you'll know is withdrawal. You'll crave my very existence, sweets." I run one hand up her spine and wrap her hair around my fist. I pull her back until she's arched into a u-shape. The all-familiar zip starts in my toes and runs up my body. The feeling travels to my cock like little sparks, I'm so fucking close. "Cum for me, Clover." I pull back until just the head of my cock is all that's left inside her and then slam forward while pulling her hair. She shouts to the ceiling as her pussy clamps down on my cock. I look down and watch as she squirts and covers my thighs.

"Fuck, fuck, fuck." My thrusts stop as my cock pumps her full of cum. With the last twitch of my spent cock, I shiver and pull back. The moment of bliss is shattered when panic sweeps in.

You're not good enough. You'll never be good enough. You're a fuck up. She will leave. Fuck. That. I'll leave first. I have to go. Now. I blink away the sweat falling into my eyes and pull out. I planned on spreading our cum and blood on the mask, but I can't. I have to go. I quickly pull my pants up and shove my knife in the pocket. I rip my mask off and walk to the side of the bed. She looks at me, her face a war of emotions. I can't stand it. I can't look at it. I lean down and put the mask over her face.

On my way out the door, I hear her broken, muffled voice ask, "Where are you going?" Fuck, I made her cry. *No. Fuck her. She was going to leave. I'm leaving first, dammit.* I run out of the room and before the door shuts I hear her shouts. "Are you fucking kidding me?!" I'm sorry, sweets, I have to. You know this. You have to know this. This is what's best.

People with BPD says it feels like: Lashing out at loved ones, followed by guilt and fear that they're upset with me.

12

Sloane

You know that feeling when you've gone a while without a cigarette, and the first one after all that time hits you like a Mack truck? You start to sweat, your stomach turns and your body shakes. That is how I've felt this whole week since Karver fucked me senseless and tossed me aside like his dirty fucking cum rag. He's been cold and distant, well, as distant as one can be while sleeping 4 feet away from each other. He was right, I do feel like I'm in withdrawal without him close to me. My body is in this constant limbo of getting just enough of a buzz when he's in close proximity, while simultaneously feeling like complete shit in his emotional absence. He was right when he said he'd leave his mark. The soreness in my pussy every time I move has only recently started to fade. Hell, even the marks he carved into my back sting less and less every day, and I never had a chance to see what the fuck he did to my ass. All that remains is the burn mark, which reminds me of how that day started. How fucking poetic. My incessant need for him is like an itch I can't scratch. You learn so much about a person while observing them. It's the only reason I haven't completely gone over the edge.

When this all happened, I tried to act completely unfazed. I realize that sounds ridiculous after my reaction when he walked away. But then I decided if he was going to try and knock me down a peg, I was going to be a petty bitch and knock him down by two. So instead of ignoring him whenever I feel his eyes on me, I come up with fun ways to stare directly at him and flip him off. I'll scratch a phantom itch with my middle finger, pretend to apply lipstick with it, turn my head and hold my hand over my ear with my middle finger pointed his way. My favorite one, however, is when I lean over his bottom bunk every night and kiss my middle finger, finishing it with a finger wave before climbing up to my bunk.

I stare up at the ceiling, twisting the blanket in my grasp over and over. I'd say the dead of night is silent, but not here. In this room alone there's three men snoring; Axel whimpers in between snores, Decker giggles and Karver grunts. Even in sleep he seems pissed off at the world. Then there's everything that happens outside of this room. The static beeps of the guard's walkie-talkie, the click of their boots on the linoleum, random shouts and sobs that echo off the walls. I lift the blanket and wipe the drips of sweat falling down my temples.

Unable to lay still anymore while sleep eludes me and my stomach turns, I throw my blanket against the wall. I sit up and cringe when the bed creaks, causing one of the boys snores to shutter. I hold my breath and sit still to see if I've woken anyone up. Since everything remains silent, I flip to my stomach and slowly slide my legs to dangle off the bed. I squeeze my eyes shut and let go, my feet slapping against the floor when I land. I watch as the sun and moon drift past each other in a quick hello and goodbye, casting just enough light in the room to see. I tip-toe over to the dresser Karver and I share, and open one of the drawers. If the situation didn't piss me off so much, it would almost be comical how fucking domestic this is for two people that are anything but. I look down and realize that the light through the window is not enough to see inside the draw-ers. I blindly dig through and feel for my facility-approved bra and underwear, a pair of joggers and a shirt. The one good thing about wearing dark clothes is I don't have to worry about picking an outfit with clashing colors. I tuck the clothes under my arm and slowly shut the drawer. I slide my feet into the rubber sandals and leave the room.

I make it halfway through the hall when a bright light hits the side of my face, followed by a deep voice. "Hey, what are you doing?"

I look over at the guard and raise a brow. "You have got to be bored. We've done this song and dance every day for the last week. You know what I'm doing. It's pretty obvi-ous. Can I go now?"

He gives a half-hearted shrug and smiles, waving his flash-light towards the bathroom. I walk towards it and mouth the words, "Be my guest."

I walk into the bathroom and shut the door, the buzz of the yellow lights above my only option for a shower playlist. Every step further from Karver, the feelings of withdrawal fade away and are replaced with the familiar emptiness I've always known. I glance one more time at the door and focus on the doorknob. I wish there was a fucking lock. The majority of this confined bathroom is an open shower where the middle of the floor dips with a few drains for the water to go down. Along one side of the wall is an old, battered bench which is bolted to the wall and has a stack of towels on the end of it. In the far corner of the room is a toilet and a small sink hugging it, both with rubber padding wrapped around them. I kick my slides under the bench while tossing my clean clothes on one side of the bench. I peel my clothes off, shoving my bra and underwear inside the scrub pants. I throw them down beside my clean clothes and turn to start the shower. I stretch as far away from the showerhead and turn the hot and cold knobs on, the water shooting out in a jet stream with a hiss. I bite my lip to hold back a shout when the freezing water reaches my body, goosebumps erupting along my flesh. When the water is tepid, I run my fingers through my hair and tilt my head back to let the water cascade down. I hiss when the water hits directly over the slashes on my back. After quickly washing my hair and body with the minimal amount of 3-in-1 the locked dispenser allows, there's a loud knock on the door followed by one of the female orderlies shouting, "SHOWER CHECK!"

Fuck. Leaving the water running, I run over to the bench and grab a towel, quickly wrapping it around my body. Right as I'm tucking the towel in, the door opens and she peeks in with a blank expression. I lift my arms and twist them around to show there aren't any cuts or injuries. I do the same with my legs, do a spin and then pat the towel down so she can see that no blood is soaking through. She gives me a clipped nod and as she steps back, says, "Don't take too much longer."

She's out the door before I have a chance to salute her and throw in a "copy that."

After turning off the shower, I dry off and pull my clothes on. As I drop the black shirt over my head, I immediately realize something is wrong. The telltale scent of coconut and musk fills my nose. Karver. Fuck, this is Karver's shirt. I slide the shirt further down and hold the shirt just above my nose. I look around, so no one catches me being a fucking creep. I shake the thought away. This is the closest I can get to him, so just for a second and then I'll take it off. I feel my heart race and my eyes tear up at the thought that this really could be the closest we'll ever be again. How many times am I going to sit here and wish to feel something, but feel so incredibly pathetic seeking it out?

Lost in my own world, I don't hear the door opening or the slapping sound against the flooring. The moment is shattered when Karver's growl fills my ear. "I told you you'd crave my very existence, sweet clover."

My eyes shoot open and my startled gasp turns into a whimper at his words. I release the shirt and it falls below my chin. My chest heaves with quick breaths and I stutter, "I-I didn't... I wasn't... it's not-"

"You didn't? You weren't? It's not what, sweets? Hmm? You didn't take my shirt to feel closer to me? You weren't sniffing my shirt like a bitch in heat? It's not what it looks like? What lie is going to fall from that pretty little fuck hole?" There's an inferno building within me, and I can't tell if it's anger at the words he spewed, or the fucked up part of me that is panting and soaked for him. He's right, though. No matter how much it pisses me off. I did technically take his shirt. I was sniffing it. And it's exactly what it fucking looks like. Fucking asshole. I squeeze my eyes shut and take a deep breath. I clench my jaw and look at him. "Ahhh, there she is."

I grip the hem of the shirt in my fists and yank it up. At the same time I say, *"Here,"* he grabs my wrists and growls, *"Don't."*

I try to step back and shake off his hold to no avail. "Let. Go. I'm trying to give you the fucking shirt back. I didn't take it on purpose!" I may have stomped my foot like a child, but I'll never tell. He holds on to my wrists as he leans forward and drags his nose along my jawline. I shiver from the contact, my body trembling and thighs clenched when he pushes his face between my shoulder and neck. His scruff scrapes against my skin and puffs of breath drag against my neck.

"I *hate* you for making me want to drop the mask with you." The loss of him is immediate as he pulls back and stomps out of the bathroom.

"I hate you, too," I whisper, feeling a tear slip down my cheek.

Signs and Symptoms of BPD: Frantic efforts to avoid real or perceived abandonment.

13

Karver

Fuck. Fuck. Fuck. I said too much. Did I? Maybe I didn't say enough. How the fuck did this woman seep so far inside of me and coil her goddamn clovers all around my ribcage, gripping the bones with the vines. Jesus, Karver, get a fucking grip. She's just a woman. She's nobody. Fuck. No, she's everything. How? I walk across the hall and knock on the door to signal the boys to get up. I shove my hands in my pockets, squeezing one hand in a fist and fiddling with my knife in the other. Mmm. My knife. Memories of it dripping with her blood and cum makes my cock stir and I drop it like it burned my palm.

I walk into the rec room after Mousey cut me off in the hall to take my meds. I sit in my usual spot across from Thumper and watch as his clouded eyes look out the window. Today must be a bad day. Decker and Axel take a seat on either side of me. As usual, Decker is obnoxiously loud, not even his antics stir Thumper from his thoughts. Out of the corner of my eye I catch Axel leaning in as he timidly whispers, "Umm. She-she's not going to sit here. She, umm, she's sitting with the quiet lady."

I tilt my head a little and murmur, "Tap the table every time she looks, Ax."

He brings his shaking hand over the table and whispers, "Okay, Karver."

Bring it on, Clover. You want to fuck with my head and my heart, my very fucking existence? I'll do the same. She may have found her way in, but I'll consume every bit of her. She'll know what it's like to have every thought be of me, just as my every thought is now of her, how she is and what she's doing. Axel taps the table and I look over my shoulder. Her eyes grow when she realizes she's caught in my trap and she can't find a way out. Our tables are close enough that I know she hears me when I say, "Just can't stay away from me, can you, sweets? Far enough to make it seem innocent, but close enough to get what you need from me, hmm?"

She crosses her arms over her chest and scoffs. "You fucking wish, *Slasher*." Fuck. I turn in my chair and adjust my twitching cock. This fucking woman, I swear.

Sloane

I swear this man has eyes in the back of his fucking head. Every time I can't stop myself from looking, he's right there turning and looking right back at me. He's been doing his best to piss me off, and I'll admit, at first it was. Until I started paying closer attention. Not only does he run his thumb along his bottom lip when lying, but I've recognized a pattern with the names he calls me. When he grits his teeth and spits my name or sweetheart out in disgust, I know he's actually upset with me. For what? Who fucking knows. I'm so fucked. I'm starting to hate my own name when I hear it fall from his lips. I love it more when he calls me sweets, clover, or sweet clover. And *that*, I know, is when he's not actually upset with me, he's pretending to be. I just wish I knew why.

Breakfast is announced and I look at the woman in the wheelchair. I wish someone would tell me her name. I lean forward and whisper, "I'm not sure if it's something you can do, but if you can, please blink once if you're okay with me walking you to breakfast." I hold my breath, widening my eyes to watch for any sign that she'll respond. Just when I think I can't keep them open a second longer, I watch as her eyes slightly shift in my direction and she slowly blinks. I smile at her and whisper, "I knew you were still in there. I wish you could tell me your name. Blink if I can give you a nickname?" I look at her gray, braided ponytail and smile, realizing exactly who she reminds me of. "Can I call you Sophie?" The side of her mouth twitches and she blinks once. When her eyes open again, a look of terror flashes in her eyes. She quickly schools her features, and I look behind me to see Nurse Ratchet walking over. Not this bitch.

I get up from my chair and she closes in, trying to grab a hold of Sophie's chair. I quickly place myself between the back of the wheelchair and the bitch's clutches. She leans in closer and her chest brushes my arm. I back the wheel-chair up, purposely running into her.

"Excuse me. What do you think you are doing, Sloane?"

I sneer at her over my shoulder. "A better job than you, obviously. Sophie and I are going to breakfast." I chance a glance at Karver and see him and his henchmen closing in. "Oh goodie, your boy toys are here to keep you company." She bats her eyelashes and the once fiery expression morphs into one of a desperate seductress. I shake my head and snort. "There she is."

Karver

I've spent the whole day trying to get under her skin, and everything has failed. She seems unfazed in every meal, art therapy, group therapy and smoke break. If anything, she's giving it back just as good. She tried to ignore me at first, and then I watched as she steeled her spine and started hitting back. Instead of shying away, she smirks in my direction. Or her new favorite, which just makes me want to bend her over and turn her ass red, is the many ways she finds to flip me off. Middle finger up to scratch her nose or brow, rest her hand on her head with her finger up, or the one that really gets me… acting like she's putting lipstick on with her finger.

It's almost time for lights out and we're all in the room getting ready for bed. I watch as she kicks her slides off next to our dresser and then climbs up to her bunk. I wait until she's settled to stand in her line of sight. I reach behind me and grab my shirt to pull it off. My necklace gets caught while pulling it off and it slaps back down to my chest. I wad the shirt up and throw it into the yellow mesh hamper. When I look up, I catch my not-so-sneaky clover checking me out. Her eyes slowly lift until she reaches the necklace and then shift over to my flatline tattoo with 143 underneath it. I watch as she can't decide which one she wants to look at, her eyes flicking back and forth between the two. I run my fingertips down my sternum and watch as she follows the trail of my touch. My thumb catches on the top of my scrubs and I slowly start to peel it down. Her breath picks up and eyes widen as she watches to see what I do next. I start to push the rest of my hand in my pants when Decker claps and chants, "Yes! Take it off! Take it off! Give us a show!"

I pull my hand away and watch as Sloane snaps her head in his direction and then over to me. I wink at her and she growls in frustration. She rolls over to face the wall, keeping her back to me. I walk over and kick my slides off next to hers and then crawl into bed. Decker climbs up to his bunk and collapses to the mattress with a heavy sigh. "I can't believe you're depriving all of us of a show."

"Shut up, Deck. Go to bed." I look at Axel on his bunk as he curls up the best he can to keep his legs from dangling off the edge. He has the sheet bunched up under his chin, leaving his legs and feet completely uncovered. "Get some sleep, Ax." He quickly nods and closes his eyes. I walk over to mine and Sloane's bunk and stop before climbing into mine. I watch the steady rise and fall as she breathes. Unable to stop myself, I reach up and drag my finger down her spine. Her body tenses just before a full body shiver dances across her body. I smile at the reaction and then pull my hand away, crawling into bed and throwing myself down on my back.

Sleep is the last thing on my mind. The lights have been out for a while, the moon shining now through the window. I slip my hand between the bed and the wall, my fingers fumbling around the stitching. I find my other hiding spot and reach inside. My fingers wrap around the plastic bag and pull it out of the mattress. The moon is bright enough that I can see the letter inside the bag. I open it up and carefully pull out the rough, crinkled paper. I unfold the letter, squinting at Nana's faded handwriting. I've read this letter so many times over the years, but now, the end of it hits harder than it ever has before. She's talking about my sweet clover.

I don't want you to live this life all alone, but you must be careful. I want the best for you, and you'll have to fight through life to get it.

Don't let just anyone in. Do not give yourself or your heart freely. When you find the one, you'll know. They'll make you feel alive, light up a room and take your breath away just by looking at them. They're the person you would live, die and kill for. There will be trials and tribulations, as there is in any relationship. But if you two can make it through those, you can make it through anything together. You'll find yourself as obsessed with them as your Pops and I were with each other. When you find that… that is when you know they are the one who deserves your heart. They will be the one who deserves every piece of you, every beat of your heart.

The sound of a groaning bed has me shoving the letter in the baggie and back into its hiding spot. I look over and see

Axel sitting up and holding his hands over his bouncing knees. He's chewing on his lip and looking at me with an apologetic expression. "What's wrong, Ax?" I whisper.

"I gotta piss, real bad."

"You'll be okay, man. Everybody is in bed, and the guard and night orderlies are doing their rounds. This is the perfect time to try going by yourself."

"But, what… what if…"

"What if you don't try? You'll never know, man. Just give it a shot. The bathroom is just across the way. We're all a shout away." He looks towards the door and slowly nods his head. Rubbing his hands across his thighs, he takes a deep breath and stands, the bed creaking with the freedom of his weight. He walks over to the door and stands frozen in place, his breathing picking up. I heave a sigh and get out of my bed. "Alright, Ax, let's go. Maybe next time."

Sloane

I jolt awake with the sound of Axel's panicked voice, "Karver! Oh no! So bad! It's bad! This is bad! Karver, Karver, Karver! I don't like it! I don't like it!"

I watch as Karver stands in front of him and Decker is sitting on his bed, kicking his feet back and forth. "Ax, look at me, look at me. What happened? Just take a breath and tell me what happened, man."

Axel paces back and forth, muttering against his fingertips. I have no idea how to help, but I know I need to try. The poor guy is petrified. I climb down from the top bunk and as I take a step forward, a blood curdling scream echoes through the halls. My head whips to the door, following the shouting and heavy footfalls. "What the fuck?"

I run out the door and hear Karver shouting behind me, "Sloane, don't! Deck, stay with Ax!" At the end of the hall, I see nurses and orderlies running around frantically.

A guard runs out of a room and as I get closer, I realize it's Sophie's. No. The guard kneels down in front of a night orderly who's rocking back and forth on the floor. Tears streak her cheeks, her eyes are wide and unfocused. I faintly hear her murmur, "No, no, no."

I ignore the shouts of everyone around me, including Karver. I run into the room and skid to a stop at the sight before me. Sophie is face down on the floor, surrounded by a growing pool of blood. On the edge of her dresser are flecks of skin, blood and strands of her gray hair, high-lighted by a glint of light bouncing off it. Is this my fault? Have I done this? Caused this? First my mother, now Sophie. Who else will meet the same fate because of me?

Signs and Symptoms of BPD: Intense mood swings lasting hours or days.

14

Karver

After finally getting Decker to keep an eye on Axel, I run after Sloane. Damn woman doesn't listen for shit. Every room I pass, residents hover in their doorways, sneaking peeks at the chaos unfolding. One of the guards is hovering over an orderly who seems to be in shock, and I notice him continuously looking back at one room in particular. Fuck. Other than Thumper, this was the one person that Sloane had really started to warm up to.

I walk into the room and find Sloane standing there, frozen in place. Just past her is the older woman lying face down on the floor. Sloane doesn't acknowledge my presence as I walk up right behind her. It isn't until I press myself against her back that she gasps and melts against me. I wrap my arms around her as she whispers, "Is this my fault? I think this might be my fault, Slasher."

I shush in her ear and start pulling her back. "Come on, sweets."

She pulls away and shakes her head. "No. I can't leave her. She's all," her breath hitches and she barely pushes out, "alone." Her body crumbles in my arms as she starts to fall to the floor. "I-I can't… I c-can't breathe, Karver."

I hold on as tight as I can and turn her so she's facing me. Her lip trembles and tears well up in her eyes. "Look at me, sweets. Just look at me. I've got you. Everything is alright."

She shakes her head, her hair whipping us both in the face. "No, no, no. I did this. I did this. This is all my fault."

I keep one arm around her as I push her hair from her face. "Shh, shh, shh. Come on, we have to go." A single tear falls before she starts to turn her head to look at the woman again. I grab hold of her chin and turn her face back to me. She places a hand over her heart as her chest heaves, her panted breaths hitting my face. A full sob leaves her mouth and I realize I'll have to take her back to the room. I grab her by the back of her thighs and pick her up. She wraps her arms around my neck, bringing her face against it. Heavy sobs rack her body as she tightens her arms and legs around me. I keep one arm under her ass and the other rubbing her back as I carry her away from the incoming stench of death that one can never forget. Every step feels like torture, as if I'm taking in every bit of pain and anguish she's feeling. Fuck, I never want to see her like this again.

Who the fuck am I kidding? There will come a time… many times… when I'll be the one to bring this out of her and I'll relish every bit of it. I avoid the looks of everyone we pass by and notice Axel's panicked rants coming from our room. Crashing noises come from the room, followed by Axel shouting, "You're not listening. Nobody is listening.

I know what happened. I know it, I know it, I know it! Why won't you believe me?!"

Decker slides out of the room and laughs before he shouts, "A little help down here! Ax is about to put the ax in axe murderer!" When I hear boots stomping and the rapid clicking of shoes, I squeeze Sloane closer and move aside for them to get in the room. Decker walks over to stand next to me and grimaces. "Yeesh, what's going on? Everyone's losing their shit."

"I can't tell you what's up with Ax, but the lady in the wheelchair is dead. It's bad, man."

He rubs his hands together. "Do tell. How bad? Is it gruesome?"

"Deck, I honestly don't give a fuck what you do. Just go do it somewhere else."

He throws his hands up, waving them around while he walks backwards. "Okay, okay. Geez, everyone is so sensitive. Have a little funsies."

I kiss Sloane's temple while I watch the staff drag a sedated Axel out of the room. As they pass, I can hear him mumbling, "I saw. I saw. I saw."

I step in front of one of the orderlies trailing behind, their shoes squeaking against the floor in their abrupt stop to avoid running into us. I have no idea why this guy works here. He looks like he's seen a ghost, sweat pouring from his bald head. "You guys are only taking him to solitary for the night, right?"

He rubs the sweat from his eyes with his forearm and starts to nod, then shakes his head, ending on a shrug. "Depends on him, I guess." He sidesteps us, quietly saying, "'Scuse me."

I carry Sloane into the room and start to put her down. She whimpers and squeezes her body around me tighter. "Alright, sweets. Watch your head." I put my hand over her head to protect it the best I can, while I sit on the edge of my bed to lay with her. She spreads her legs so they're not underneath me and snuggles in as close as she can.

I feel her lips brush the side of my neck and I shiver while gripping her tighter to me. "You have to stay. Please, please, please," she begs as she brings her hands down to my chest and presses kisses down my neck with every word.

"What are you doing, sweet clover?"

She sniffles and with a shaky breath, continues her path down my body, straddling my hips in a crouch to avoid hitting her head on the bunk above. She runs her fingers under the hem of my shirt and scrapes her fingernails along my stomach, making me groan. She pushes it further up and commands, "Off."

I sit up a little and pull the shirt the rest of the way off, throwing it to the floor. She leans down and licks a trail from one hip bone to the other, making me thrust towards her mouth. Running her fingernails along my sides, she kisses her way to my tatted pec. She swirls her tongue around my nipple, clamping her teeth around it and biting until I hiss. She kisses her way to my other pec and gives it the same treatment. My whole body feels like a boiler ready to explode.

I grab a fist full of her hair and wrap it around my fist. I pull her down to guide her where I need her and she follows along with kisses and sucks to my stomach. My muscles tighten with every suck. "Take my cock out, Clover." She yanks my pants down to my thighs the best she can with my grip on her hair. With my cock free, it slaps against my stomach, her eyes following the movement. "Don't act shy now, sweets. You took me so well last time."

She gulps, her voice raw already from crying. "I think my throat is going to find new meaning to your nickname, Slasher."

I reach up and caress the front of her throat. "Mmm. Maybe so. But we both know how much you love when I leave a lasting mark on you."

I hiss when she wraps her hand around my cock in a tight grip. She looks up and glares. "I could say the same for you."

She licks around the crown, and then flicks her tongue through the underside. I try to push her head down and she growls around my cock, the vibrations making my head spin. "Jesus, Clover."

Wrapping her mouth around the head of my cock, she sucks hard while swirling her tongue and sliding her hand up and down my shaft. I just about buck her off when she brings her other hand around my cock, and starts stroking and twisting both hands up and down in opposite directions. She's good at this. *Too* fucking good. Fuck, that pisses me off. I yank her head back and her mouth pops off my cock while she squeals from the pain in her scalp. "What the fuck, Slasher?!"

Ignoring her, I throw her onto her back. "Grab the bunk, *sweetheart*." She reaches up and grabs hold of each side of the bunk. I rip my pants the rest of the way down and kick them off my feet behind me. I crawl up her body and place my knees on either side of her head. A noise by the door catches my attention and I duck my head to look. I catch sight of Decker hovering by the door with his hand down his pants, a wild grin on his face. I fist my cock and spit on it, slowly stroking and watching as Sloane bites her lip in anticipation. "Show me what a good cockwhore you are, Sloane." I tap her lips with the head of my cock until she opens up. I sink inside the heat of her mouth and grit my teeth. I thrust until my cock hits her throat and she gags, her eyes welling with tears. I nod towards Decker. "Now look at what you've done. Look at what you're making us do."

She tilts her head back and sees Decker. Her jaw slackens on a gasp and I shove my cock down further. I place my palm against the top bunk and grip her throat with the other to feel my cock filling her throat. My thrusts pick up in speed and I watch as she grips the bed tighter. I throw my head back, listening to the sounds her throat makes every time I shove my cock deeper. Every time she attempts to swallow the spit dripping down her throat, it squeezes my cock, making it twitch. I bring my hands to her hair and grip the roots as I push her head back and forth while thrusting. She moans around me, and I start to feel lightheaded, my whole body tingling. I feel my cock expand in her throat and growl, "Fuck, fuck, fuck," as I cum down her throat. The last spurts make me shudder. I slowly pull back and look at her face, satisfyingly drenched with sweat, tears and drool, "Don't swallow, yet."

I sit back on my heels and drag my thumb down her bottom lip, "Open wide. Let me see that perfect cum dump." She opens her mouth, a few drips pouring out of the corners of her mouth. I tsk, "Don't be wasteful, sweets." I capture my cum and slide it back into her mouth. "Swallow it."

Without hesitation, she swallows my cum and I hear Decker panting, "Yeahhhhhh, fuck."

Ignoring him, I make my way down to her pants and start to pull them down. She attempts to slam her thighs closed, my body stopping her. I look at her and tilt my head in question. She bites her lip and looks away, ashamed. The fight leaves her when I continue to pull on her pants and she releases her hold on me. I pull them under her ass and see that she's soaked. Fuck, she came while choking on my cock. I push her knees down to the mattress and lick her cum from her trembling thighs, my scruff scraping along her sensitive skin with every move. She squirms and moans while I shove my face against her soaked pussy. I clean every drop of cum and devour her slit.

"W-what are you doing? I already... you know."

I lift my head. "You already came with my cock down your throat? Yeah, I noticed. That's fucking hot, sweets, but I'm not done with you."

Her eyes flick over to Decker and back to me and she whispers, "He's still watching."

"I think you like it when he watches," I say, as I glare over at Decker and add, "which is *all* he will be doing." I drop my face back to her pussy and swirl my tongue around her pulsing clit. She giggles when I run my hands up *my* shirt. I pull her bra down and her big tits fall out. I grab a handful of each and squeeze, thrumming her nipples until they're hard peaks. Her hips buck against me as her moans and pants echo around the room while I suck on her clit. I pinch both nipples and twist while I bite down on her clit. She shouts, "Fuck!" as she cums on my face. I release my hold on her and lick down to her entrance, shoving my tongue inside and flicking it up and down while suctioning my mouth to her.

"W-wait. I can't. Not again."

"One more, sweets. You're doing so fucking well."

I bring my hands to her hips and yank her pussy as close to my face as it can get. I suck and lick her entrance as I circle her clit with my thumb. My touch starts off light and then I gradually put more pressure against her clit. She grabs my head and starts to push and pull as if she can't decide what she needs more. More or less of my tongue, my touch… me. I feel her pussy pulsating against my tongue and I know she's close. My girl likes pain, so I pinch her clit as I suck harder and flick my tongue faster. She fucks my face like a woman possessed. Cumming in my mouth, I swallow it down, her taste making my eyes roll back. She flops to the bed breathing heavily. I pull her pants up and hover over her. She looks at the top bunk in a daze and I bring my lips to hers. I can't tell if I'm breathing life into her or she's doing so to me.

Decker's shout breaks the moment and I rip my mouth from hers. "Time for bed, sweet clover."

"Mhmm. Just… just a minute… I think I live here now."

I chuckle at the state I've left her in. I walk over to the dresser and pull out the blue marker. I climb over the top of her and write on her stomach. "Mmm. What are you doing?"

"Shh. I'm working on a masterpiece here."

Quietly she laughs, "I'm sorry, Slasher, but your handwriting isn't a work of art."

I lean down and bite her, causing her to jolt and yelp. "I wasn't talking about my handwriting, smartass. The masterpiece is your body."

The words give me inspiration and I scrawl, '*work of art*', across her stomach. I shove the marker in the same spot as Nana's letter and grab the blanket as I lay on my back next to her. I pull on her until she rolls herself to lay most of her body on me. She snuggles against my chest and I feel as her breathing slows down. I think she's fallen asleep until she softly whispers, "Karver?"

I rub circles on her back and kiss the top of her head, "Hmm?"

She crawls up my body and brings her lips to my ear. "Tell me something true."

I push her hair behind her ear and whisper back, "Like what, sweets?"

"Anything. Just something that nobody else knows about you. A hidden truth."

I tense beneath her. "What's spilled in the dark shall never come to light."

"Is that a poetic way of saying you don't cum during the day?"

I drop my hand to her ass, the soft slap echoing in the quiet space. She jumps and giggles in my ear. "Fucking smartass. I was just saying whatever we say at night, is not something to discuss during the day. I want to know you and I," breathing in deeply, I continue, "I want you to know me, as fucking terrifying as that is. Honestly, depending on the time of day, that could change in an instant. But I feel like these are things that should just be ours and ours alone."

Signs and Symptoms of BPD: Impulsivity and/or risky behavior.

---

1 HOUR AGO...

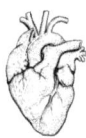

How easy it is to fool everyone here. The gift that keeps on giving in a podunk town. Trustworthy people and an understaffed hospital. How ironic that everyone sees me, yet I fly under the radar. Maybe it's the mask theory. You wear enough masks and nobody knows the truth that lies beneath.

Nobody will ever understand this need inside of me. Every moment spent in normalcy, the bloodlust crawling through my veins grows. I'll never forget my first kill, and I hope it will be a while before my last. The feel of blood drenching my hands, and the stress-ball texture of a heart is better than any sexual release.

The halls are quiet and clear. I fucking love shift change. The lady in the wheelchair may seem like an odd target, but there's a method to my madness. A plan. I step into her doorway and lightly knock on the door. She won't look. She won't respond. But she's aware of my presence. I watch her lying on her back in bed, staring up at the ceiling. I look around the room and formulate a plan. This must look like an accident. I will erase every trace of my presence... except one.

I zero in on the wooden desk next to her bed and eyeball the distance between the two. Bingo. I walk to the end of her bed and place my hand on top of her foot. Her body doesn't react but her eyes do. They widen and look down her body as far as she can. I slowly slide my hand along her body as I walk to the head of the bed. I only have one shot at this. I grab a hold of her under her armpits and lift. I test the weight and notice how light she is. This bitch is just a bag of fucking bones. I cradle her under my arm and pressed against my body as tight as I can. Her legs stay draped on her bed as I hold her upper body against my side, excitement running through me. With my free hand, I grip her hair tight at the scalp and pull it back. 3, 2, 1, SLAM!

Her temple slams against the corner of the dresser with a crack, followed by a gushing squish. Blood pouring from the wound onto her head and the floor makes me smile. I bring her head further back and watch as life leaves her eyes and one pupil blows while the other slowly shrinks. I check her pulse and find the slowing thud dissolving to nothing. I lift her again to let her free fall from the bed to the floor and watch as the blood pool expands. As desperate as I am to feel the sticky liquid coat my hands, I need to leave. I can only leave one thing behind. I lift the back of my shirt, pull the item from my waistband and toss it under the bed. With one last look at my art, I slowly leave the room.

15

Sloane

I soak in the feeling of Karver's embrace while he sleeps, one hand clasping my throat, the other splayed across my stomach. God, I wish he would listen when I say it's embarrassing for him to be grabbing my stomach. Of course, it just makes him do it more, because supposedly I'll learn to love my body as much as he does. The memory of our whispered secrets in the dark makes me smile. I try to savor this moment for as long as I can because I know reality will set in once I open my eyes. You would think I would be used to it after a week of waking up this way. Ever since Karver and I have gotten closer, I'm practically drowning in a pool of feelings and emotions. I went from feeling nothing to everything and it's been hard to handle. I mourned my mother and Sophie's deaths at the same time. Well, LeeAnn Doyle is her name. That's what they told me, anyway. She'll always be Sophie to me.

I slowly peel my eyes open and just as expected, poor Axel is sitting on the edge of his bed in a daze. It breaks my heart to see him like this. I know he was a quiet and timid gentle giant but now he's just a shell of who he once was. On one hand, it must be nice that he isn't living in a state of constant fear and paranoia, but is the alternative any better? I start to get up and check on him when Karver grunts and squeezes me tighter to him. I shiver when I hear his delicious morning voice in my ear. "Just leave it be, sweets. We just have to let him ride it out."

"What if they did to him what they did to Sophie? What if he's trapped in his own body and we're leaving him there all alone?"

Karver scoffs and pulls away from me. "Good. Everybody ends up alone. Better to learn that now."

I look over my shoulder and see him crawling out of the bunk. "What the fuck is that supposed to mean? I'm literally right fucking here with you."

He angrily pulls on his clothes and shakes his head. "For now," he spits out.

I climb out of the bed and slap my palms on his chest. He stays silent as my palms keep hitting him. "Fuck you, Slasher! Last time I checked, every time there's distance between us, *you're* the one to create it."

He grabs my wrists when he realizes I'm not going to stop. From the other bunk a sleepy Decker's voice grumbles, "I don't like it when mommy and daddy fight so early in the morning."

"Not now, Decker!"

Karver takes that moment to yank the drawers open and pull out his clothes. I walk over and try to block him from putting his slides on. "Running away again? Really? Please, do me a favor, Karver. Next time you decide you want to whine and bitch about somebody leaving you... *don't*. All it does is make you a hypocritical asshole."

He slams the drawer shut, the sound echoing in the room making me jump. He pushes his body onto mine until I'm backed against the wall. His face is so close to mine, I'm reminded of the moment in the back of the police car when I thought he was going to kiss me. His jaw clicks as he glares down at me. "That'll never change, *sweetheart*. Life made me this way. It's all I've ever known, so figure out if you're here for this fucked up ride or if you're ready to fucking bail." I open my mouth to tell him that I'm not going anywhere, but he quickly steps away, holding his hand up. "Spare me the lies. I already know what you'll choose in the end."

Karver

I storm out of the room and plow through the bathroom door. She doesn't understand. Why doesn't she understand? Nobody fucking does. Fuck. Why does it have to be this way? Why am *I* this way? She didn't even fucking do anything but show compassion to Axel. And what did I do? I let my insecurities take over and blow up in her fucking face, as if she's the one who caused this.

I use my shower to wash away my inner turmoil and tamper down my demons. The longer I was in there, the more I realized that I fucked up... again. I change and walk out of the bathroom, skidding to a stop before running into Decker and Axel. I lift a brow, "Wha-"

"This is as far as the big guy would go without you." I walk around them and walk into the room. I find Mousey standing there with the med tray just under her tits, as if offering them up. I shudder at the thought and quickly take my meds.

I feel Sloane's absence immediately. *You have to show her you're all in. You're not running away. You can do this.* I open my drawer and dig around for the clover I crafted from floral wire. I tear away all the green tape, revealing the wire beneath it. I pull my lighter from my pocket and flick it on, releasing the lever and watching the flame disappear as Decker chuckles in a sing-song voice, "Oooo, you're supposed to turn those in when you're finished smoking, Karrrverrr."

"If you're gonna stay in here while I do this, at least make yourself useful, Deck." His slides slap against the floor as he runs over, giggling.

I look at him, pulling off my shirt while he rubs his hands together. "I thought you'd never ask. What kinda dirty things ya wanna do to each other, Karvy?"

"Just shut up and do what you're told. Hold my shirt. When I tell you to, press it against the clover. Can you handle that?"

He pulls my shirt from my hand and rolls his eyes. "Psh, you ask like it's supposed to be hard," he pauses and his shoulders shake with stifled laughter. Unable to hold back any longer, he bursts, "THAT'S WHAT SHE SAID!" A shadow to my right catches my attention, where Axel hovers in the doorway.

"Jesus Christ, Deck. You sure you can handle this? 'Cuz you couldn't even handle keeping an eye on Ax. Pretty sure

126

he's not supposed to be standing around forever while heavily sedated, ya fuck."

I walk over to Axel, waving my hand in front of his face. "Ax, you need to sit down. Let's go." I reach up to push on his shoulder, but unable to reach, I grab his elbow and gently pull. "Alright. Sit down, bud, watch your head." He starts to lower without ducking completely, so I push on his head to guide him. The bed protests under his weight, and once his head is cleared from the top bunk, I walk back over to the dresser.

I pick up the clover and lighter, flicking it on. I burn every bit of metal, no piece left unmarred. I hiss as my hand shakes with the force to not drop it when the heat travels down to the stem of the clover. I bring the clover close enough to my chest where I can feel the heat radiating from it. I hover it exactly where I want it and nod to Decker, "Now."

He steps towards me and shoves the shirt over the clover, pressing it into my chest. I lift my head and breathe through the pain. It's deserved, and well worth it. *She* is worth it. If only I could convince my fucked up brain to agree with that at all times, rather than this back and forth twisted bullshit. The initial burn dissipates and I step back from Decker, the shirt and clover fall to the floor between us. His eyes grow, a smile creeping along his face. "Whoaaaa. That's so fucking sweet!"

"Thanks, Deck. Why don't you go hang with Thumper a bit before group therapy? I'll catch up with you."

He shakes his head and walks away. "Damn. Are you ever gonna let me play?"

"No, ya fuck. Get the fuck out of here." I look down at the red, inflamed clover that now connects to my flatline tattoo. I run my thumb along the edge of it and imagine my sweet clover laying her eyes on it for the first time. Will she see how much she's burrowed herself inside my chest? Can I tell her how I truly feel? Will she even believe me when I can't even seem to get my shit together? Fuck you, brain. Fuck you, parents. Just... fuck everyone that made me this way. If not for them, I could be someone else for her. Someone better. Someone she deserves.

Signs and Symptoms of BPD: Unstable, intense relationships.

16

Sloane

Fucking asshole. How do we always end up back here? We're caught in a beautifully tragic dance, and I'm not sure who will end up bruised and bloody in the end. I feel a nudge to my side and look over to see Thumper's crinkled smile. I give him a tight-lipped crooked smile in return and he points to my leg. "The way you're bouncing your leg, you're looking more like Thumper than me, my darling girl."

I place my hand on my knee to halt the movement. "Sorry... just... dealing with-"

"Karver?"

I look down and pick at my fingers. "That obvious, huh?"

He pulls a silver pocket watch out and opens it, revealing an old, faded picture of a young couple. He looks at me and smiles. "That's my bunny. And it may not be obvious to everyone, but I've only seen a love like this once."

Love? Is that what this is? He closes the pocket watch, kisses it and then puts it away. "Be patient with him. Us men tend to really fuck up when we meet our match, a woman far better than we deserve. I'm so glad I get to witness your love blossom. It'll be like reliving my life with my bunny. Thank you for that gift."

"I… I don't think that's what's happening, Thumper. The way you describe it… that sounds beautiful and pure. A dream come true. This. This is something different. Don't get me wrong. When it's good, it's sooo good. But when it's bad…. it's pretty fucking bad, Thumper."

"Oh, I promise you, my darling, it wasn't always sunshine and rainbows. I was just a shitbag shipmate, and she… she was enchanting, but a force to be reckoned with. She did a better job of putting me in my place than my Senior Officer. She loved all my broken pieces, and I was obsessed from the beginning. I truly believe that you're Karver's bunny, or his clover, if you will."

I open my mouth to respond, stopping when the sound of a chair squealing steals my attention. I look up and find Karver gripping the back of the chair he just pulled out. I tilt my head when I notice his hair is mussed and there's burn marks on his shirt. He looks down at his shirt and then back at me with a guilty expression. "Can we talk, sweets?"

There's a part of me that wants to cave and say yes, but I can't do that. I can't be that bitch who just crumbles when he comes crawling back. He needs to know that regardless of what his brain chemistry causes him to do, it doesn't mean that I have to roll over and take it. He needs someone that will not only be there, but will also hold him accountable. "Slasher, I l-... I'm not leaving, but you need to know that some of the shit you do and say isn't okay. So, during group and art therapy, I think it's best if we had some space. When you aren't taking shit out on me that I don't deserve, I know you give a fuck. So please remember that when I ask you to really sit and make a plan on how we can work on things. I'm not your verbal punching bag, even when your brain tells you otherwise."

I hear a crashing noise followed by a "FUCKING BULL-SHIT!" I look past Karver and see a man throwing his arms towards the television and continuing his shouts. "I'll get you, motherfuckers! You'll pay for what you did!" He kicks his fallen chair and stomps out of the room, an orderly following closely behind him.

Karver shakes his head. "Blake is always fucking quiet... until he's not."

I dismiss Karver's comment, unsure if it's an attempt to rope me into a conversation. I look over at Thumper and place my hand on his forearm. "Thank you for sharing your bunny with me. I look forward to hearing more about her another time."

Ignoring Karver's stunned expression, I walk over to the door, which buzzes to let me outside. I make sure to sit on the inside of the square at a table opposite the one I usually sit with Karver so I can keep my back to him and I'm not as tempted to look in his direction. I hear the buzzer on the door and the sound of Decker's giggles lets me know it's them. I can feel his eyes on my back like daggers. *Don't look, don't look, don't look.* The therapist looks around the group with furrowed brows. "Does anyone know if Jack is opting out today?" I look around and everyone stays quiet. A few shrugs are given, but the therapist is otherwise ignored.

Everyone's words pass over me during therapy, lost in the wind. I decline when it's my turn to speak. What am I going to say? My… whatever the fuck he is, who happens to be in this group, is being a dick? We have some push and pull thing that has my head a mess? I finally mourned the loss of my mother and Sophie but it hits me in waves only when he's around? Fuck that.

When it's time for the boys to talk, Decker just giggles away with random facts. Who knows if they're true. I hold my breath knowing it's about to be Karver's turn. The buzzer sounds and a few of us look to see an orderly running out, frantically waving his arms. Whatever the orderly is relaying has the therapist bringing his hands to his head and looking up to the sky. The orderly stands by the door and crosses his arms as the therapist walks back to us with his head down. He looks around at everyone, as if memorizing each face in the crowd. Exhaling his deep breath, he says in a defeated tone, "I have some unfortunate news, everyone. Our friend, Jack, is no longer with us…" What the fuck? "…My door is open if anyone would like to talk about this outside of their usual one-on-one therapy. We can all still talk about the loss of LeeAnn as well. Whatever you need. At this time, we'll need each room pairing to go in one at a time. Karver, Sloane, Decker and Axel. Your room is the last one in the hall, so will you please go first?"

I kick my leg over the bench, and walk to the door. With every step, I feel like I'm walking in a narrow tunnel. Maybe I should've talked to him. Would it have made a difference? As fucked up as it makes me sound, he seemed so unapproachable. I never knew if he didn't give a fuck about anyone as long as they left him alone, or if he wanted to kill everyone to wipe them from his existence. Now I realize he wanted to remove himself from the equation.

One of the orderlies guides us through the door after we're buzzed in. My three shadows are behind me and we step aside as Corbin pushes a gurney out of Jack's room. My breath catches when Karver runs his finger up and down my back in a caress. Corbin's eyes lift at the sound, and he stops as well. With a sad smile, he says, "Hi, Sloane. I'm sorry I haven't visited in awhile. I just thought you needed the space to truly work on things. I think... I think with everything that's happened recently, maybe I should resume visitation. Would that be alright with you?" Is it bad that I haven't even noticed his absence? I'm not sure what the proper response is here, so I just nod with a sad smile and continue walking to our room.

I walk into the room and kick my slides off by the window. I turn around and can't help but smile at the sight of Karver helping Axel sit on his bed carefully. That. That is why I love him.

Bitch, what? Pump the fucking brakes. I shake my head and climb to my bunk. I roll over to face the wall and hide my face in the pillow. If they weren't in here, I'd be screaming my fucking head off into it. Thumper is getting in my head. His story. The things he said. That's all this is. The bunk starts to squeak and I feel the mattress dip, my body shivering at feeling Karver rubbing my back in soothing circles. He moves my hair from my face and I feel his lips on my temple in a barely-there kiss. "Can we talk, sweets?"

The urge to say yes is almost more than I can stand. "Slasher, I don't think you're going to do a one-eighty in just a few hours' time. Let's just sleep on it, okay?"

With a heavy sigh against my temple, he says, "I was going to talk today… in group. I've never done that before. I was willing to do that for you."

I scoff at his attempt to sway me. I roll over and give myself as much distance as I can muster. "That's a fucking lie. All you do is talk during group. The problem is, you spew more lies than truth. You're not as deceiving as you think you are, by the way. I know there is some truth to your stories, but not quite as much as the lies you spill."

He runs a hand down his face, "You're right. It's what I've always done, Clover. As you said, it's not something that can change in a few hours. But I really was going to try and do things differently. You seem to think you can read me so well already. So, tell me. Am I lying or telling the truth right now?"

He knows I wasn't paying close enough attention to give him a proper answer. Ugh, dick. I sit up and cross my legs, pressing my back to the wall. My eyes flicker back and forth between his. "Tell me again."

He mirrors me, looking deep into my eyes. "I was going to talk during group today." Truth. "I was going to try, for the first time ever, to speak truthfully." Truth. "To tell real stories. To voice what I'm thinking and feeling to the best of my ability." Truth.

I pull my knees up and rest my chin on top of them, barely whispering, "Thank you for telling me the truth, Slasher." He claps his hands together and in one swift movement, smacks his lips to mine, his scruff scraping my face deliciously. "Oomph."

Speaking against my lips, he asks, "Can we go to bed now, sweet clover?" I blow air into his mouth and he pulls away, shocked. "Wha-"

I roll my eyes and lay down with my back to him. "Fine. I'm sure you'll just keep me up all night pestering me until I cave in. I'd rather just get that done and out of the way now."

He quietly laughs and scoops me into his arms. With one hand squeezing my hip, he gently holds the front of my throat. "Keep pretending this isn't exactly where you want me, sweet clover." Fuck me sideways, the asshole is right.

I've had my eyes shut for less than a minute before Karver starts tapping his thumb on my hip. I wait it out to see if he'll stop, but he continues tapping to some sort of beat. I huff and attempt to look at him, but he tightens his grip around my throat. "What, Karver?" I squeak.

He leans in and softly blows down my neck. "Tell me something, Sloane," he mutters almost imperceptibly.

"Tell you what?"

"Anything. Tell me something real."

Without overthinking it, "I love watching Studio Ghibli movies," falls from my lips.

His next words have me tensing in his arms, "I know."

"The fuck you mean, you know?"

I hear him mutter, "Fuck," before dropping his head to my shoulder. I twist around in his hold until he lets go and fully roll over to face him. "Speak. Now."

He whispers again and I can't understand him. "Oh, don't go quiet now. You wanted to talk, so fucking talk."

"I watched you," he confesses, lifting his eyes to pierce me with his gaze.

I look down in confusion trying to think of what he's saying and then look at him again. "Watched me? When?"

His voice cracks. "If I tell you, you'll leave me."

"What's spilled in the dark shall never come to light, right?"

Signs and Symptoms of BPD: Self-injurious or suicidal threats or behaviors.

---

4 HOURS AGO...

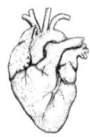

I watch the silly fucker's retreating form down the hall and notice there isn't anybody else around. Showtime. I'm veering from my list of targets, but I can't pass up this opportunity. This mopey little fucker is ready to go, I'm just going to help move things along is all. I peek into his room and notice all of his roommates are gone. He sits on the edge of his bed, fiddling with the sheet in his hands. I notice that he has it twisted and tied off around his neck. Perfect. He slightly tugs one end as if testing the resistance. I knock on the open door and he looks up, his eyes briefly widen before narrowing at me. "What the fuck are you doing—"

With quick strides, I slap my hand over his mouth just before he starts swinging wildly at me. I dodge his hits and yank the sheet backwards. "Shut up. I'm here to help you. I really just needed to do this for myself, but I guess I'll be helping you as well."

I yank on the sheet as I walk backwards, his spit and hot breath converge in my palm as he continues to shout nonsense into it. He attempts to throw punches and I turn him into a puppet, controlling every move with the sheet. The perfect advantage is everyone underestimating my strength. "Stop it. Don't act like this isn't exactly what you were going to do before I walked in. I'm just helping you, Jack." I briefly pull my hand from his mouth, and as soon as he opens it a crack, I slam my hand down on him again. "Not. A. Word. Nod if you understand."

He glares at me, but the resolve is there. The weariness has fully settled and his decision is made. He's ready for the end, just not for someone to push it along. For someone to witness his demons winning the war raging inside. I imagine he doesn't feel the satisfaction of his death being on his own terms anymore. The pretend fight in him melts away as he accepts his fate.

I tie off one end of the sheet to the bar of the top bunk. I tie the knot securely and yank on it to test how tight it is. I toss the longest part of the sheet on the top bunk and without pause kick the back of Jack's legs. The sheet yanks tight against him, his face and neck turn shades of light pink and darken the more he struggles. Natural survival instincts kick in and he starts clawing at the sheet. His eyes bulge and water as the blood vessels start to pop. Fuck, I wish they would burst more. Such a shame there isn't any blood to play in. Veins pop in his forehead. I can't decide which part of his face I want to stare at more. This is fascinating. His kicks slow down and his arms drop, essentially speeding up the process of his death. Drool and snot drips down his face now that his tongue is out, his bulging eyes open and vacant and his body completely still over his own urine and shit. Enjoy your eternal slumber, Jackie boy. I toss my calling card under the bed and stroll out of the room.

17

Karver

I didn't realize such a normal thing would bring me so much joy. I'm sitting next to Sloane, mesmerized by the clovers she draws on the mask I painted green. I watch as her tongue just barely pokes out of her mouth while she concentrates. She pauses and looks over at me, holding the mask up. "How do you keep track of all your masks? I swear you have a lifetime supply in random places all over the room." I bring my fingers across my lips in a zipper motion and she rolls her eyes, going back to painting.

Axel's quiet voice and meaty fingers on my arm break the moment. "What's up, Ax?"

"Do you think she would make me something, too?" I open my mouth to answer, but stop when Sloane reaches across, her hand inching closer to Axel and I snatch her wrist.

"No. Touching."

"Calm down, cave boy. It was meant to be in comfort. Anyways. Axel, I would love to draw something for you. What would you like?"

He chews on his fingers as his eyes flick around the room. He sucks in a breath and whispers, "Something to look at when things get scary. O-or too much."

"I can do that. Is there anything in particular that calms you down? Maybe somewhere you visited as a kid?" Fuck. He starts shaking his head and rocking back and forth.

"No, no, no, no."

"What's wrong? What did I say?" Sloane asks in a panic.

I lean over and whisper in her ear, "Parents are not a good topic for him."

"Fuck, I didn't know. Let's switch spots, Slasher."

I narrow my eyes at her. "The fuck you mean switch places? You're not sitting next to him when he's upset. He'd never hurt you on purpose, but he's a big guy."

"Karver, move your ass and stop talking about Axel like he's not here. Being upset doesn't mean he doesn't under-stand what's happening around him." She slides her art supplies in front of me and pushes on my shoulder.

"I hear compromising is important, sweets. This is mine."

"Wha-" her question is replaced with a yelp when I wrap my arms around her and yank her down on my lap. She grabs one of my hands from her waist and lifts it to her mouth. The soft kiss turns into a sharp bite and I groan as the feeling shoots straight to my twitching cock. A surprised gasp escapes her when I grind my cock against her ass.

I fist her hair and pull her back to me, growling in her ear. "Keep marking me like I'm yours, sweets, and I'll make sure everyone here fully understands it by bending you over and fucking you over this table."

Unable to bite back her moan, people look over at us. Some ignore it and some giggle at the display before them. One of the orderlies walks over in a huff. "Listen, I don't give two shits if y'all are fucking. Patients fucking and 'oopsies', not doing paperwork on it, or patients dying and obviously having to do paperwork for that. Pretty easy choice there. At least try to keep it somewhere private. You do it here and I will obviously have to do the paperwork. Don't fuck up my day and I won't fuck up yours."

I laugh at his attempt at showboating his authority. "If you think this is fucking, you might need to go get yourself laid. It's obviously been a while." The orderly sighs and walks away, muttering something as he goes.

Sloane pushes a piece of paper between her and Axel and starts lightly outlining a picture. She smudges the pencil lines and then grabs a pile of crayons. She fills the picture with vibrant shades of blues, yellow, green, orange, pink and purple. She pushes the crayons away and then grabs markers with the same colors and marks different areas with it so some areas pop with color. Fuck, she's amazing. It takes me a minute to realize why the picture seems so familiar. This is a scene from one of the movies she would watch over and over. While she was mesmerized watching it, I was mesmerized watching her. I listen to Sloane explain the art piece to Axel and rub her side. "This is from one of my favorite movies. I changed it up a bit, but I was thinking when you look at it you could imagine that this person is you. Think of your most cherished thing and hold onto it. Imagine yourself being surrounded by all these shooting stars and make wishes on them."

Axel runs his big hand across the picture and smiles. "Thank you, Sloane. I love it," he whispers in awe.

"Of course, Axel. Let me know if you ever need more pictures." Mousey walks in, searching the room. I watch as she glares daggers at Sloane and then looks up at me, quickly schooling her features and sending me a wink. I bring Sloane closer to me and kiss her temple while glaring back at the mousey little bitch. She acts unfazed, but I don't miss the way her eye twitches.

Walking over, she stands behind us. "Sloane, it's time for your one-on-one therapy. I'll be walking you there."

I squeeze her hip when I feel the way Sloane's body tenses. Beside us, Axel shakily picks up the drawing and keeps muttering, "I'm okay, I'm okay, I'm okay."

I step in and tell her, "That won't be necessary, we'll walk her there."

I pat Sloane's hip. "Come on, Clover. You too, Ax."

Decker gives an exaggerated gasp as they both stand. "You're just going to leave me here?! All alone?!"

He breaks into a rendition of *All By Myself*. When he pauses, I glare at him. "If you were paying attention, I said WE are walking her there. I'd think by now you would've figured that meant all three of us, ya fuck."

He giggles and skips to the door. "I know."

Sloane

The triple shadow that once followed me is now reduced to two while Karver walks beside me hand-in-hand. With every step, his thumb swipes the top of my hand. I try to enjoy the warmth of it wrapped around me, but I'm plagued with the memories of every time he creates distance between us. I find it confusing that I'm not more upset with him for fucking stalking me. Like who the fuck just sits there and goes, *aww, how sweet*. Oh, right. Me.

My head also swirls with the all-consuming thought that the deaths surrounding me are somehow my fault. I haven't had much to say during my solo sessions with Dr. Bart, but this is something I think should be discussed. I need answers. Maybe he'll have them. We reach the door and I start to pull away from Karver.

He grips my palm tighter and pulls me into his embrace, murmuring in my ear, "I'll be right here if you need me, sweet clover." He drops a kiss to my lips, which ends all too soon. I think I'd rather stay here than go have this therapy session. I hesitantly pull away, he squeezes my hand once more and slowly lets go. I knock on the door, opening it when Dr. Bart hollers, "Come on in, Sloane."

I walk in and shut the door behind me, my eyes widening when I realize this won't be a one-on-one session. "Uh... Corbin? What are you doing here?"

He huffs a nervous laugh and grabs the nape of his neck. "I actually talk to Dr. Bart quite often about... uh... your mother, and I did tell you I planned on visiting more, right?"

I cross my arms. "Yeahhh, for visits. This is *my* therapy session. Like you said, you come and talk to Dr. Bart often, so I'm sure you can discuss things during your time. I actually have some things I would like to discuss today. I can't really do that if we're focusing on whatever it is that you're here for today."

Dr. Bart points to one of the chairs in front of his cluttered desk. "Please, have a seat, Sloane. We can discuss whatever it is you wish to talk about and then go over what Corbin would like to share. Is that something you would be comfortable with? Or would you like to talk about it without him, and then have him come back in?"

"Sorry, Corbin, but I usually don't have anything to say during these sessions, and now that I do, I would prefer to focus on that first. I've learned that sometimes you need to put yourself first, especially when healing, so I would like to take the leap and do that."

Corbin puts his hands up. "Of course, Sloane. I'm happy to hear that you're taking this seriously."

I take a seat as Corbin walks to the door but before it even shuts, there's a bellowed, "Noooooo!"

I jump from my chair to check it out when Dr. Bart shouts, "No, Sloane."

I look at him as he picks up his phone and frantically punches numbers in. Shouts continue outside as the doctor says, "Code Bart, source unknown. I repeat, Code Bart, source unknown." He slams the phone down hard enough that it falls to the side before running out the door. The door remains open a crack, and I can hear panicked shouts from Axel. Ignoring the command I was given like a dog, I run out the door and see Axel pacing and pulling at his hair, muttering, "I saw, I saw, I saw." I see Corbin and Nurse Ratchet standing against one wall, Karver against the other wall, and Dr. Bart standing with his back to me, attempting to soothe Axel. Just behind him, I notice Decker with his hands on his gleeful face. I walk over to Karver and tug his arm. He looks down at me with a sad smile. "Where's his picture, Slasher?"

Understanding crosses his eyes and he walks over to Decker, slapping him upside the back of the head. Decker rolls his eyes and sticks his tongue out, pulling the folded picture out of his pants pocket. I stomp over there and pull it out of his hand before Karver can. I get in Decker's face and seethe, "I know you like to have fun and joke around as some sort of coping mechanism," a flicker of hurt flashes in his eyes, "but maybe don't be such a fucking dick and do it at Axel's expense!"

I unfold the picture and step in front of Axel, holding it up as high as I can. He's so tall, the picture barely reaches his chest. He stops pacing and looks down at the picture. The grip on his hair lessens, and he repeats between breaths, "I'm okay, I'm okay, I'm okay."

I nod with him and take deep breaths in and out, trying to get him to mirror the movement. "That's right, Axel. You're okay. You're safe."

Another orderly walks around the corner, syringe in hand. Dr. Bart catches Axel's attention when saying, "Not yet, just a moment."

Whatever Axel sees or hears sets him off again and he again begins shouting while throwing his fists up and down in the air. "Nooooo, I saw, I saw, I saw!"

Dr. Bart waves a hand and the orderly with the syringe, who steps up behind Axel and jabs the needle into his ass cheek. I watch as two orderlies step in to grab either side of him as his body starts to slump. A third orderly holds on to the back of his clothes as his panicked shouts turn into quiet mumbles. The rest of us watch as they practically drag him away.

"Sloane, shall we?" Dr. Bart asks. I know I told them I needed to put myself first, but I'd rather get this done as fast as possible to try to figure out what the fuck just happened with Axel.

I look at Corbin. "Can we just go talk about what you needed to tell me? I think I'd like to wait for what I wanted to talk to Dr. Bart about."

Corbin looks over at the doctor in question, who responds with a clipped nod. "Of course, Sloane, these are your sessions. Come on in, Dr. Moriarty."

I turn and look at Karver, and he tilts his head towards the wall. "I'll be right here, sweets." I smile at him and then walk into the office. Nothing could have prepared me for the information Corbin shared behind closed doors. At least I know these deaths aren't my fault now.

Signs and Symptoms of BPD: Acts of self-sabotage.

18

⎯⎯∿⎯⎯⎯⎯⎯

Karver

I kick off the wall to meet Sloane as soon as the door opens. She walks out looking like she's seen a ghost. What the fuck happened in there? I step in front of her to stop her and she attempts to step around me. I grab her wrist and pull her against me as she fights my hold. "Don't walk away from me. What the fuck happened in there?"

In a barely there whisper she pleads, "Not here, Slasher, please."

Okay, it's not me, she's not mad at me. If she was, she wouldn't have called me Slasher, right? I let go of her wrist and put my hand to her back. She moves from the touch. My touch. What the fuck? She walks quickly through the halls. We reach our room, she looks around, refusing to look at me. "Where'd they take Axel?" she asks.

"Really? That's the first thing you want to ask? What the fuck is going on? You leave that office looking like something freaked you the fuck out. You don't want me touching you. What did they say in there? Were you talking about me?"

She spins around and throws her arms out, "What? No?"

"That, no, sure sounds a hell of a lot like a question than an answer. What the fuck did you talk about in there, Sloane?"

What is she so upset about? What did they say to her? Does she know? Fuck, what if she knows? She rubs at her temples and takes a deep breath. Slowly releasing it, she looks at me with tears in her eyes. "No, Karver, we weren't specifically talking about you. More like… this person is an unknown right now, but they're close. Too close."

"You're talking in fucking riddles. Just spit it out!"

"Fine! None of the deaths that have been happening were accidental or suicide! THEY WERE FUCKING MURDERED! At this point, my stepdad will be locked away in here with us cuz these murders are making him lose his mind and saying he saw someone outside our house the night my mother died. So now he's convinced she didn't kill herself, but this mystery person killed her! What the fuck am I supposed to do with that information, Slasher?! Either my stepdad is losing his mind with his grief and conjuring up things that never happened or," she starts pacing back and forth with her hands on her head, "or some fucking psycho was outside our house, snuck in and murdered my mother while I was lost in my art a floor above! And if that's the case, is the same person who murdered my mother the same one who murdered Sophie and Jack? That would mean it could be anyone here! It could be a new patient, an orderly, a nurse, doctor, security guard. That doesn't exactly leave it simple to narrow down.

Does that mean they're going to keep killing people around me and come for me last? Keep me so on edge I won't know who to trust or what to believe?"

Don't react. She can't know you were there. Please don't ask if that was one of the nights I was there. Fuck, fuck, fuck. I have to distract her. I step in front of her, placing my hands on either side of her face. "Hey. Look at me, Clover. I'm right here. Nobody will ever fucking hurt you. I will keep you safe, okay?"

She abruptly pulls away from me and scoffs. "Really, Karver? How the fuck am I supposed to believe that?"

"What the fuck is that supposed to mean?!"

"Oh, gee, I don't know. Maybe because you treat me like some fucking toy of yours. You don't give a shit about me. You spend more time distancing yourself from me than actually being with me. Fuck, for all I know, I'm just a wet pussy to stick your dick in when you're fucking bored. Sprinkle a few sweet words in my direction to keep me hooked and you're fucking golden, right? If you actually gave a shit, you'd... you'd... I don't fucking know. Touch me more. Kiss me more. It would be like the movies or something."

Is she fucking serious right now? Oh fuck this. I rip off my shirt and slam my fist against the clover burn over and over as I say, "Does this look like something a person would do if they didn't give a shit? Do you think I would really sear your fucking brand into my flesh, next to the most important tattoo I have, if you were just a hole to fuck? No! It fucking isn't. Trust me, Sloane, if I wanted just a hole to fuck, we both know that mousey little bitch would bend over anywhere I fucking told her and take my cock."

149

Tears stream down her face as she shouts, "Fuck. You."

I wrap my hand around her throat and back her up against the wall, her body hits it with a thud. "No. Fuck you, Sloane! Fuck you for not seeing, for not feeling, for not fucking knowing the depths of what I fucking feel for you. Just because you're incapable of them without me around, doesn't mean you don't recognize it in other people. You've always picked up on things with people. I've fucking seen it. You did it with Sophie. You did it with Axel. Why the fuck can't you wrap your head around it with me?

You're right, what we have isn't what you see in the fucking movies. You know why? Because movies are fake fucking fairytales. It's all fucking make believe. What we have is fucking real and it's fucking raw. There is no sunshine and rainbows here. I'm fucked in the head, sweets. Don't you get that? I'm going to make you fucking miserable. I'm going to push you away, and sometimes it'll be in the most vile, fucked up ways. Ways that I know will fucking cripple you. Break you. Because in my fucking head, I have to ruin you. I have to give you a fucking reason to leave me. So then, and only fucking then, will I be able to tell myself that I made you do it instead of you deciding to leave me on your own like everybody else in my fucking life.

There will be days that I will fucking ruin you. There will be times that I fucking hate you, hate your very existence and wish nothing but the absolute worst for you. But in between those moments, I will love you with every fucking thing I have. My love for you will fucking consume every piece of me until it seeps into you and consumes every bit of you. All you will know is my love. My touch. My scent.

Don't mistake my love for white picket fences and romance, sweets. I'm not built for that. Am I obsessed with you? Yes. Will I protect you? With my life. I'd fucking kill for you if it meant keeping you safe. Keeping you happy. You want me to die for you? Just say the word. You want me to fight through the shit in my head and live for you? I'll try my best until I can't fucking try anymore. Hell, this clover on my chest is just the beginning. You want my knife to carve your fucking name on every inch of me?"

I pull my knife from my pocket and shove it into her hand. I step back and put my arms out. "Go for it, sweets. I'd do just about anything for you, but I can't give you that fairy-tale shit. We can have moments of greatness which will surpass any fucking love story. So what do you say, sweet clover? Will you walk through hell with me?" Tears cascade down her cheeks, her eyes make a trail as she looks repeat-edly between my face and the clover brand.

What the fuck is going on in that head of hers? Why isn't she saying anything? What is she thinking? Is she all in? Will she run away? "Goddammit, woman, say something!"

"Y-you love me?"

Isn't that what I've been saying this whole time? Words aren't getting through, obviously. I take slow, calculated steps towards her. I watch as her chest heaves, her breathing picking up the closer I get. I place my finger under her chin and lift so she's looking into my eyes. Our lips are a breath away. I nod and our lips brush together as I breathe, "You're my 143, Clover," sealing the words between us when I press my lips firmly to hers.

I hear my knife clatter to the floor beside us. She moans into my mouth and I swallow it down. I bite her plump bottom lip and take advantage of her moan to slide my tongue inside, flicking my tongue against hers. I growl into the kiss when she latches her soft mouth around my tongue and slide my hands down her sides. I slip them to the back of her thighs and grip tight as I lift her. She yelps and wraps her legs around my hips. I thrust my hard cock against her as she grinds her pussy against me, whining for more. I break the kiss and carry her to my bed, tossing her down and she opens her mouth to protest, I'm sure. I cut her off and point, "Don't fucking move."

I pick my knife up from the floor and walk back over to her. I pull my pants down and kick them aside, relishing in the way her eyes eat up every inch of me on display. I flick my knife open and she bites her lip, watching the motion through hooded eyes. I stick the handle in my mouth and reach down to curl my fingers around the tops of her pants. She jumps as I yank them down to her ankles and rip them off, throwing them behind me.

I pull the knife from my mouth and grab the collar of her shirt. I slice my knife through the front of it, her shirt and bra fall to the sides in pieces and I see a path of blood pooling to the surface where the knife nicked her. I toss the knife beside her and lean down, licking the drops of blood from her navel up to her chest. I hiss as I squeeze my cock tight to keep myself from cumming too soon. The fucker is ready to make this as quick as possible like I usually do, but I'm trying to take my time with this… with her. I slide into her and grit my teeth as Sloane's moans shoot straight to my cock. *Don't cum, don't cum, don't cum.* I shake my head, "You'll be the fucking death of me, sweet clover. I'm barely fucking hanging on here."

She squeezes her thighs around my hips and grabs the chain around my neck pulling me closer to her. She slams her lips to mine in a bruising kiss. Barely pulling back from the kiss, she whispers, "Show me what it means to be loved by you. Mark me, Slasher. Don't let me ever forget what this moment felt like."

I start to ask her how she wants me to mark her when I feel the blade of my knife against my neck. I push my neck further against the blade until I feel trickles of blood. I slowly slide my cock in and out of her dripping pussy while asking, "You want me to finish my carving on your back, sweets? Or do you want something new?" Her eyes look up towards the bunk and she bites her lip. The hand holding the knife to my neck slowly drops to my chest. I pull back until only the head of my cock is at her entrance and slam my hips forward, the tip of the knife punctures my skin, making me grunt. Her eyes bulge as she sees what she just did. She starts to pull the knife back, gasping when I hold her hand in place. "I-I didn't mean to."

"So quick to forget I just told you to carve your fucking name all over me, sweet clover. Why would this be any different? Any mark will do as long as it comes from you. Now, be a good girl and tell me how you want me to slice this pretty fucking skin of yours."

She tugs on my hold and I let go, running my hand down her side, leaving a trail of goosebumps. With a shaky hand, she taps the knife over her heart. "N-name. I want your name, here. If you get to have a clover on your chest, then I want you to give me your name."

I pull my cock out and step back. She starts stammering, "I-I, you don't have to if you don't want to. I just… I just thought. Nevermind."

She starts to pull the sides of her shirt together to hide her body from me. "Stop," I demand. She looks up at me, tears filling her eyes. "Don't do that, sweets. I'm not walking away. I just wanted to change positions for this." I crawl into the bunk and sit up, patting my thighs, "Crawl to me, sweet clover."

She gets on her hands and knees, her tattered shirt falling open and giving me the perfect view of her tits swinging as she moves. She climbs into my lap and wraps one arm around me, bringing the knife between us with the other. I grab the knife from her grasp. "Your pussy is soaking my thighs, sweets. Put my cock inside you. Ride me while I leave my mark."

She grabs my cock in a tight fist, stroking it twice. I hiss and grit my teeth. Hovering over my cock, she whispers, "Kiss me, Slasher."

I bring my lips to hers, shoving my tongue through her lips and roughly taking her mouth. She slowly slides the head in and then drops down. I swallow her shouted moan while our tongues swirl and slide against each other. She abruptly pulls away from the kiss, gasping, "I-I'm so close. Mark me, please."

I wrap one hand around her throat, and carve the first letter, blood bubbling and dripping down her chest. With every cut, I flex my hand around her throat, her moans with every slice and squeeze filling the air. I finish carving my name and watch as a drop of blood falls perfectly over her nipple. I lick the blade of my knife and then lean down, following the trail of blood up until I latch onto her nipple, sucking it into my mouth. She starts riding harder and faster, panting my name while I bite down. "F-fuck, Slasher, Slasher… I'm, I'm cumming!"

I release her nipple with a pop and grab her cheeks, "Open up, sweets." Her mouth falls open and I spit the blood into her mouth. Her eyes roll back and she shouts, her head thrown back in pure pleasure, "FUCK!"

Blood spills from her mouth and down her body. My eyes fall on my name carved on her chest as I grip her hips tight and pound up into her pussy the best I can in this position. "Look at me, Clover. I want those earthy blues on me when I cum."

She drops her head down and looks deep into my eyes, pleading, "You love me?"

My thrusts falter and I nod. "Yeah. Yeah, I fucking love you, Sloane."

She grabs the chain around my neck and demands, "Then fucking cum for me, Slasher."

I wrap my arms around her and press her as far down on my cock as I can as spurt after spurt of my cum shoots inside of her. "Fuuuuuuuuuuck."

I drop to my back with her sprawled across my chest and pant, "Tell me something real, sweets."

She snorts against my neck and I twitch at the tickle. "What's left to tell that you don't already know? Might as well call you Stalker instead of Slasher."

I squeeze her hip. "You could tell me the most important thing."

She snuggles in closer and sighs. "What's that?"

"Your birthday."

With a scoff she asks, "How is *that* the most important thing? That day doesn't mean shit." I growl as I smack my hand against her ass and squeeze. She yelps, "What the fuck was that for, asshole?"

"Don't fucking talk like that. And it's the *most*," I squeeze her ass again and she moans into my neck, "important, because it was the day my reason for existing was brought into the world. The only cure I'd ever find."

She pulls her head from my neck, lifting up just enough to look into my eyes. Tears pool as she whispers, "Cure for what?"

I grab the back of her head and bring her lips to mine in a soft kiss. I slide my hand from the back of her head and run my thumb along her jawline, then across her bottom lip. I close my hand in a fist, tapping it over my tattoo and the clover brand. "It only beats for you."

Signs and Symptoms of BPD: Chronic feelings of emptiness.

19

Sloane

I can't seem to drop the smile from my face. I woke up to Karver between my thighs, devouring me. Talk about a fantastic wake up call. Of course it didn't end there. After dealing with Nurse Ratchet handing out meds, we headed for the showers, where he picked me up and pinned me to the wall, fucking me until I was just a bag of bones. I practically begged Karver to tell me what he meant when he called me his 143 while I towel-dried my hair. I spent more time whipping him with it every time he tickled me than actually drying it.

I stop in my tracks, Karver slamming into me from behind with an "Oomph." On instinct, he grips my hips to keep us from both falling. I lift my head to meet the guard's icy gaze.

"Listen, with the information that came to light from your stepdad, we're having to crack down the best our limited staffing will allow. A lot of changes are coming. Now get your asses to the cafeteria."

He looks over my shoulder and narrows his eyes. "Try not to rock the boat, Karver. We're already rowing up shit's creek with no paddles, please don't add holes to the boat."

"I don't think-"

Karver rubs my arm. "Come on, sweets. You won't get through to him. He does it on purpose."

I nod my head. "Oh," as Karver pushes me along down the hallway.

Droplets of water from my hair perfectly land over the carving in my chest, the fabric scraping against it with every breath. I bite the inside of my cheek from the mix of pleasure and pain. I find myself hoping this takes longer to heal than the K etched on my back. Karver stops me and whispers in my ear, "Adding this to my list of favorite things to see."

I look up at him confused, "Huh?"

He kisses each cheek and then my lips. "Your smile and the dimples that appear when you do." I drop my chin to my chest when I feel the flush rising in my cheeks at his words. He lifts my chin with his finger and kisses my cheeks again. "Mmm, how far down does that blush go, sweets?"

I swat at his chest and walk away. "Knock it off, Slasher."

His bark of laughter is like music to my ears. He catches up to me before we enter the cafeteria and wraps his arm around my waist, squeezing me closer to him. He kisses my temple and coos, "Aww, don't be like that, my sweet clover."

I glare up at him. "Shut it, you."

Karver

I hate knowing that my brain and actions are going to fuck this up. I'm doing my best to just be present and enjoy this with her, but there's this constant gnawing in my brain that knows it will all blow up again. The options are endless. She could fuck it up. I could fuck it up. *Anyone* could blow up this perfect moment between us. I may be able to mask things, but I can't shut off the endless chatter in my brain.

I look around the cafeteria and find Decker across the table from Thumper, who's glued to his open pocket watch. Axel sits beside Thumper with an orderly hovering over him. I can practically see the drool falling from his mouth as he nods his head closer and closer to his food. I wish they'd stop doing this shit to him. Just get him calm enough to stop freaking the fuck out and then leave him alone. It's disgusting how they overdo it and have him like this for far longer than necessary.

I look around the cafeteria again and can't help but wonder why there isn't extra security. If these deaths are murders, then why the fuck don't they have more people watching over us?

Sloane and I get in line and grab our food trays and thick, wooden utensils that are rounded out to leave no sharp points. We move our way down as they slop lumpy, yet watery oatmeal on the tray. They point to our fruit options of bruised bananas, apples or canned fruit cocktail. Sloane can't hide her face of disgust as she weighs her options. With a sigh, she points to the banana and I opt for the fruit cocktail. Getting to our drink options, she opts for apple juice while I pick the tiny milk carton.

I follow behind her as she makes her way over to our table. She passes Axel and Thumper and then sits right beside the old man. I can't yet tell if he's having a bad day, or if he's just stuck in a memory while looking at his watch. Do I know that it's wrong to take advantage of this moment and finally scope out what he's looking at? Yes. Do I give a shit? Fuck, no. I step behind him and peer down at his open watch and the faded photograph perfectly fitted inside of it.

No. All the air is sucked from my lungs and I faintly hear the crashing sound of my tray clattering to the floor. No, no, no. This isn't real. That can't be true. Like I always say, everybody lies and everybody leaves. The proof is right fucking here, staring back at me. I reach around him and snatch the watch out of his wrinkled grasp. The move must have pulled him out of his daydream, because he sharply turns in his seat, seething. "Give that back, you little shit!"

"Karver, what are you doing? Give that back to him." Sloane pleads. I hold the watch in a tight grip, surprised it hasn't cracked from the sheer force. My whole body is vibrating with barely contained rage and everything feels hot. I focus on the picture and then look at Thumper. "Why the fuck do you have this picture? Where the fuck did you get it, old man?"

His bushy eyebrows furrow as he reaches out for it. "That's mine. That's my bunny. You give that back to me now, boy."

I snap it shut and hold it to my chest. "This is not your

bunny! This is not your picture! These are my grandparents, you fucking thief! How the fuck did you get this?!"

The orderly next to Axel closes in on me and I step away with my palm out to him, growling, "Don't fucking touch me!" I toss the watch down on the table and he grabs it as quickly as he can, cradling it to his chest. I jab my finger in his direction. "Start talking."

He opens his watch and stares fondly at the picture. "This is my bunny, Cordelia. My name is Karwyn Murphy. I don't know why you think we're your grandparents, son. We never had a grandson, as much as I wished we had."

"That's bullshit! *I'm* her grandson. *Your* grandson. Your piece of shit daughter and son-in-law named me Karver after her father, *you*, Karwyn. I had my sperm donor's name until Nana Cordelia found me abandoned by their drug-addicted asses. I wanted nothing to do with them or their name, so I changed my last name to Murphy. Because what better name to have than that of my amazing grandparents? What the fuck do I know, though? How stupid of me to think like that? Because here we fucking are. You all abandoned me. I wish I could say the Nana I knew would *never* keep us hidden from each other, but I guess I was fucking wrong." I pull my hair at the roots, my nose burning from the feeling of incoming tears threatening to fall.

I feel Sloane tugging at my elbow, and I glare down at her. I ignore the sadness in her own eyes. What the fuck is she so upset about? It isn't her life that just imploded in front of everyone. Fuck. What if she isn't even sad? What if she's just pretending while she devises a plan to fucking leave me like everyone else?

Holy fucking shit. I pull from her grasp and step back. That's exactly what she's fucking doing. She starts to follow me and I shake my head. "Don't you dare fucking follow me, Sloane." I spin around and storm out of the cafeteria, heading to the rec room. I reach the door that leads to the courtyard and shout, "OPEN THE FUCKING DOOR!"

I shove through when the door buzzes, scrounging in my pocket for my smokes and lighter. I pace back and forth while lighting my smoke, my head swimming with flashing memories of everyone who's ever left me. The memories morph into visions of Sloane doing the exact same as they all did. I have to do something. I... I know she's going to leave. I need to make it my doing. I need to give her an actual reason to fucking leave me. If I don't, I'll never truly understand why she's doing it like everyone else. What do I do? I need to know what to do. How do I take control of this situation?

The door buzzes and I spin around, ready to yell at whoever the fuck followed me out here. I open my mouth to scream and notice that it's the mousey bitch. I narrow my eyes at her. What the fuck does she want? I catch sight of Sloane heading this way and my plan unfurls in seconds. Just wait, bitch. Now you'll have a real reason to leave me. This was my choice, not yours.

Mousey saunters over to me, her hips swinging in the most ridiculous way that she seems to think is sexy. Her brightly painted red lips smile big and I see the stain on her teeth. I suppress the shudder that threatens to leave me. Fuck, I don't want to do this, but I know I have to. *Stick to the plan, Karver, don't be a little bitch.*

She closes the distance between us, her chest pushing up against me. She tilts her head with an over-exaggerated pout, "What's wrong, Karver baby? Do you need," she looks me up and down like a piece of meat, licking her bottom lip, "*help* with anything?"

I try to discreetly look past her and see how close Sloane is to the door. She's standing there, seething and shouting. I can't make out what she's saying, but my guess is it's the same as what I shouted earlier. I place my hand on Mousey's hip and slightly turn us so Sloane can see us better. I rub my thumb across my bottom lip and then slowly lean in, her breathing picking up the closer I get to her. She starts to pucker her lips expecting a kiss and I swerve towards her ear. She's so lost in the moment, she doesn't even acknowledge the buzzer releasing Hurricane Sloane. I whisper the last thing she expects. "Don't ever fucking come near me again. I'll make your life a living hell, you desperate fucking slut."

A gasp falls from her lips and she attempts to pull away from me. My grip on her hip tightens until she whimpers like a kicked fucking puppy. Even in rubber slides, I can hear Sloane stomping over to us. I can see how close she is out of the corner of my eyes and then she shouts, "Get the fuck away from him, you fucking skanky bitch!" When she attempts to turn this time, I release my hold on her hip.

She spins around and starts to say, "Excuse m- ahhhhh!"

In a move I did not see coming, and clearly the mousey bitch didn't either, Sloane punches her in the face. She falls to the ground and I barely step out of the way from her crumbling body. She brings her shaky hands to her bloody nose, crying hysterically. Sloane climbs over her, swinging wildly.

My cock hardens at the sight of Sloane losing her absolute shit on the bitch. Fuck, I love her. No. *No, dumbass. She's going to leave you. Stick to the fucking plan.* When I pull myself from my thoughts, I watch as two orderlies come barreling in to pull Sloane off of her.

Even as they drag her away, she continues to thrash around, screaming. "You stupid fucking bitch! Stay the fuck away from him! Nobody wants your stretched-out, stanky ass pussy!" I recap her words in my mind. Did this just backfire on me? Is this a fucking trick? Fuck.

Signs and Symptoms of BPD: Inappropriate, intense anger and rage.

20

Sloane

My head is swimming and I feel sick to my stomach. I stare up at the ceiling... am I staring up? I don't feel so well. Am I in a boat? Why is everything rocking back and forth? Am I rocking back and forth? Why do my eyes feel so heavy and burning? I'm tired, so very tired. *Darkness.*

I open my eyes and smack my mouth, attempting to stave off the cotton-like feeling. I rack my brain on where I'm at and look around the room. There's a cold feeling around my wrists and ankles when I attempt to look at them. Unable to move far, I look down and see that I have leather cuffs around my wrists and ankles with straps that connect to the bed. Is this where they take Axel? Why am I... oh. As much as I hate that this is where I ended up, that skanky bitch deserved every bit of my wrath and more.

I can't figure out if I'm actually surprised at my reaction. In any other situation, this would be completely out of character for me. Her antics would never faze me or come close to registering on my radar. But she involved Karver in her bullshit and all I saw was fucking red. Red like that bitch's stupid fucking crispy hair. Red like the blood that stained her face and my hands.

It wasn't enough. I wanted more blood. I wanted that bitch laying in a pool of her own blood that I spilled. I imagined stabbing that bitch in her chest and carving her fucking heart out. I wanted to rip her hair from her head. Tear her fucking face off. My throat feels like sandpaper and I try to clear my throat a few times. With a raspy whisper, I question, "H-hello?"

Fuck, nobody is going to hear me right now. I need to get the fuck out of here. I need to check on Karver. On the outside looking in, I should be pissed at him. I should be just as mad at him as I am with the nurse. But I'm not. Does that make me fucking stupid? Maybe. I know he was just lashing out because of everything that happened with Thumper. Not only that, but I don't think the asshole fucking realizes he gave himself away. He was fucking scheming. It was all a lie. An illusion. I saw the flick of his thumb over his bottom lip. Even his body was screaming, 'THIS ISN'T REAL!'.

I twist my wrists and ankles the best I can in the restraints. Fuck, how long do they plan on leaving me here for? I look up to the ceiling, my vision blurring while focusing too long on one spot. I notice little divots in every tile and start counting each one. After counting the divots, I imagine connecting the dots to form a picture. I remember my art pieces of Karver and how much I miss drawing them.

Every picture I conjure in my mind is every expression I've ever seen from him. The good, the bad, the dark.

There's a clicking sound at my door pulling me from my invisible art and I drop my eyes towards the door. Dr. Bart peeks his head in and he smiles when he sees that I'm awake. He walks in and trailing behind him like a kicked bitch is Nurse Ratchet. She keeps her head down until Dr. Bart asks, "Sloane, is there anything you'd like to say to Nurse Regan?" With his back turned, he misses her sneering at me. I can't help but smile in return seeing her bruised and cut face. My eyes slide over to the doctor and I see as he lifts a brow and then slowly turns to look at the nurse. She quickly changes her expression to one of pained sorrow. Looking back at me, he questions again, "Sloane?"

"I'll be honest, doc, you really don't want to hear what I have to say in this situation. I'm calm now, so can I please get out of here?"

He sighs and puts his hands in the pockets of his pleated khaki pants. "Under one condition. We need to set up an emergency one-on-one therapy session. Yesterday you displayed behaviors that are extremely out of the norm for you and it's quite concerning."

I attempt to shrug and my wrist jerks in the restraint. I glare at the leather cuff as if it will magically fall from my wrist and then look at the end of the bed at the doctor. "I have a condition of my own."

He nods and waves a hand towards me. "Of course. Within reason."

I jerk my chin. "I'll do it as long as she isn't there. I'm willing to move on from this shit if she learns to just do her job and keep her pussy in her skirt. Her behavior is desperate and disgusting." She throws her hand to her chest and gasps. "Why do so many people fall for that act? I saw right through you from the beginning. If you want dick so badly, why not just become a prostitute, or hell, even a stripper who dresses up as a naughty nurse. You sure know how to act like one. Is that how you got the job here? Sucked a supervisor's cock?"

"Sloane, please," Dr. Bart says.

I look at him and laugh. "What? It's true. Her job here is to be a fucking nurse, not a nurse who fucks. All she does is follow the males around here like a bitch in heat. Suggestive looks, swaying her hips, shaking her ass, showing extra cleavage," I glare at her and add, "*propositioning* them."

She sniffles as if crying. Not a tear in sight, her eyes are dry as the fucking Sahara. "I can't believe you would accuse me of such horrible things, Sloane. I don't understand why you hate me so much. I've never done anything to you."

Dismissing her, I look at the doctor again, doing the best sad face I can muster. "Dr. Bart, please. I will do the therapy session. But I would really feel more comfortable if she left."

He closes his eyes and slightly bows. "Of course, Sloane." He takes his hands out of his pockets and walks around her to the door. Opening it up, he waves a hand out of the door, "You heard Ms. Flanagan, Nurse Regan. Please respect her wishes."

Before turning to leave she slowly mouths, "I'll kill you."

I wink at her before she stomps her foot and spins around. Once she's cleared the door, Dr. Bart pushes the door shut with a click. He walks to the end of the bed and unclasps my ankle cuffs. He moves on to take care of my wrist cuffs and then pulls a chair up to sit next to the bed. He pulls a compact tape recorder out of his pocket and waves it. "Not the same as the one in the office, but I'll need to record this session as well."

I rub my ankles and wrists to soothe the ache. I scoot further up on the bed and bring my knees to my chest, the best these damn tits will allow. He clicks the red record button and I hear the tape rolling inside. He places the recorder down on the bed next to my leg before saying, "This is Dr. Bart, I am here with Sloane Teagan Flanagan for an emergency therapy session. It is currently May 21, 2024 at 10:33AM. Sloane, do you give consent for me to record this emergency session?"

I start to nod my head and then correct myself. "Yes."

"Thank you, Sloane. Now, can you explain what led to the incident that took place yesterday?"

"I pretty much said it all while she was still here. She doesn't know how to do her job properly. All she does is flirt and proposition the males and treat the females like shit. But she'll only do it when people can't see or hear it. She took advantage of a bad situation, a bad moment that Karver was having, and I wasn't going to stand back and let her do that."

"I see how that could be bothersome. What were you thinking leading up to that moment?"

"Before I went outside? Like in the cafeteria? Or?"

He shrugs a shoulder and waves his hand. "All of it. Start from the beginning. What did you feel in the cafeteria, on the way outside and then right before the incident?"

I close my eyes and focus on the moment in the cafeteria when Karver's world imploded. "I... I felt... a mix of confusion and concern when Karver took Thumper's watch and started freaking out. Then as everything came to light... my heart broke for him. For both of them. Thumper's memories are a part of a whole different life before Karver. But it seems more like Karver was just forgotten and abandoned, which is something he's struggled with his whole life. So at the same time, my heart broke for Karver. He was having to relive something like this all over again. When he stormed out of there, I felt worry... maybe... anxiety or fear. I'm not sure. I just felt... sick to my stomach and my heart was racing. It was almost like having the flu, but worse. And then when I saw what was happening outside, I felt... hurt. But only for a moment. And then as I walked outside all I felt was rage. Like I was clawing at a cage to get out. Rabid almost."

"That seems like a lot. Especially all at once, and even more so for someone who isn't used to those types of feelings. Two things. One, we will have to keep a closer eye on you for the time being. With these murders that have been happening and your new behavior, we have to stay vigilant. Second, I have a question for you. Do you believe it is safe for you to be out of solitary confinement?"

I fidget with the fabric of my scrub pants. Keep an eye on me? Do they think I'm the fucking killer? Seriously? I'm not the fucking killer, I just needed to teach that bitch a lesson.

How do I explain that I'll behave? I need to get the fuck out of here. But if that bitch doesn't tread lightly, I will fucking snap... again. Just lie, Sloane. You need to get back to Karver. I look up at Dr. Bart, and see that he's holding his chin waiting for my response. I nod my head with a small smile. "Yes. I think it's safe for me to be let out of here. I'll… I'll behave."

Signs and Symptoms of BPD: Dissociation and feelings of detachment.

21

Karver

Why did she do that? It was a trick, right? Pretend to give a fuck, so she can rope me back in and make sure she's the one to leave on her own terms? She wouldn't do that. Of course she would. Everybody else lies and leaves, why the fuck would she be any different? I continue to twirl my knife in my hand ignoring Decker's obnoxious laughter and shit jokes. I can feel Axel staring at me from the edge of his bed. I already feel on edge with everything that's been going on. The room feels like it's closing in with these two filling up the space. I shove my knife in my pocket and climb out of my bed. I go to open the door and stop when Axel speaks up. "You already missed breakfast with us, Karver. A-and I haven't had my shower yet. C-could you... w-would you maybe stand watch for me?"

I grip the door tightly, and huff through my nose. "Decker will do it."

Refusing to listen to anymore of his whining, I stomp out of the room. I shove my hand in my pocket and slide my thumb back and forth against my knife. I miss the times when this action felt calming. Now all I feel is anger inside me ready to fucking explode, the impending doom of her leaving me looming over my head. After yesterday, I know she's fucking done with me. Good riddance. Obviously I'm better off on my own. Always end up alone, anyway.

I walk through the rec room and hear Thumper. "Karver. Karver, can we please talk, my boy?"

My jaw pops from the pressure of clenching my jaw and I walk to the door for the courtyard. I hear the sound of a chair scraping against the floor and look over my shoulder. Oh, fuck no. I watch as Thumper pushes himself up out of his chair and his eyes glued to me. I dismiss him again and turn back to the door, slamming my hand against it.

The door buzzes and I push through, speed walking to the furthest picnic table. I step on the bench and drop my ass to the table and watch as Thumper stands at the door. I light up a smoke and glare in his direction, letting him know with my eyes that he better not come near me. His face draws down almost in a pout and for a second, he almost looks like an older version of Axel. He drops his head and turns away, hobbling back to his table. I finish my smoke and crush it against the table to put it out. I pull my knife out of my pocket and flip it open. I bring the blade down to the table and start carving.

5-years-old

While Nana bakes, I walk to the garage and open the door. I look around and see Nana's car and Pop's truck. This thing is so cool. I hope I get to drive it when I'm all growed up. I look around the walls and see a big sign that has what Nana calls the Navy emblem. Below it is an American flag in the shape of a triangle. I've never seen one like this or in a picture frame. Weird.

I walk over to the area where my Pops played with wood. I grab the bench and chair, pulling myself on top of it. It starts to fall and I quickly drop on top of it.

Whoa. The chair starts to spin me away from the bench and it makes me laugh. I push off of the bench and let myself spin and spin. Everything looks funny and goes by super fast. My body starts to feel shaky and my stomach feels weird. I throw my hands out to catch the bench and stop myself. I finally get myself stopped but still feel like it's spinning around. I rub my stomach. Yuck, I hope I don't throw up. I see three of everything and it slowly goes back to just one.

I look above the bench and see a calendar with a girl not wearing a shirt. Why isn't she wearing a shirt? Isn't she cold? I look at her chest, or what my mean dad called tits. I've never seen them without a shirt over them before. They kind of look like those funnel things Nana uses when she bakes. I climb on top of the bench and flip to the next page. "Ahh!" I drop the page when I fall back. "What was that?" I lift the page a little bit at a time. I look at the picture again. Eww. Why does this lady have some kind of furry animal on her privates? I don't think that's a very good idea. What if it bites her and she gets an owwie? I drop the page again and shake my head. Girls are weird.

I climb down to the seat again and pick up one of the tools. It has a big handle made of wood and rectangle metal sticking out of it. At the end, the metal looks more like the end of those garden tools Nana uses. I push the end of it into the wood and watch as pieces of wood turn into small twisty pieces. Coooool. I keep pushing it against the wood until Nana's hand covers mine. I look up and see her smiling at me.

"Oh, hi, Nana."

"What are you doing, my darling Karver?"

I push my shoulder up. "Playing."

"I see that. Pops would be so happy to see you out here. He would've loved to teach you how to make beautiful things out of wood."

The thought of him not being able to teach me things and being gone makes me very sad. My eyes and nose feel funny and I rub my arm under it. It's hard to see Nana when I look at her as I start to cry. Stupid tears. "Why isn't he here, Nana? Where did he go? Why did he leave like everyone else?"

She wipes away my tears and pulls me in for a hug. I hold on to her as tight as I can, hoping that it will keep her from leaving, too. She rocks me side to side. "Shh, shh, shh. Don't cry, my darling boy. Pops didn't want to leave. He's in a better place now."

I wipe my nose on her and pull back. "Why wasn't this the better place for him? Didn't he love us?"

"Of course, Karver. Sometimes we don't have a choice when we have to leave our loved ones behind. And those of us that are left just have to find a way to push through each day. Some days are harder than others. Some moments are harder than others, but we have to push through, Kar-"

"Karver!"

I suck in air and everything comes into focus. I can hear the breeze through the trees and the annoying ass birds chirping. I scowl at the picnic table when I realize I've spent this whole time carving fucking clovers into it. Are you fucking kidding me? I stab the knife into the table in anger. Always fucking there. When I love her. When I hate her. When I'm mad. When I'm happy. She's just constantly *there*. My mind is a never ending loop of Sloane, Sloane, Sloane.

I look up when I hear panting and see Decker bent over with his hands on his knees. "Wooo. I. Am. Out. Of. Shape." He sucks in a few more ragged breaths and then stands up to put his hands on his head. "Didn't you hear me calling you? What were you-" He stops when he looks at the table to find the ridiculous amount of clovers I carved into the table. "Ohhhhh. Missing your boo thang, huh? Well, that's what I'm here to talk to you about. She's back, man. They finally released her from the cage of doom."

"And? She's not my anything. Go find someone else to fuck with, Decker."

He crosses his arms and he gives me one of his signature smiles which mean mischief. Oh boy, here we go. "Sooooo, what you're saying is I can have a go at her then? Ya know, cuz she's not your anything." Motherfucker. I yank the knife from the table and walk over it to the bench on the other side. I hover above him and hold the knife to his neck. He pushes into it and giggles when drops of blood fall. "That tickles, Karver. Why do you always tease me?"

I grit my teeth. "Don't. Fucking. Touch. Her."

He drops his lower lip to pout. "But you said she's not your anything. So why would it matter if I got myself a taste of that sweet, sweet pussy."

I slam my face into his and he falls back to the ground. "Oomph." He smiles and I see the blood pooling in his mouth and staining his teeth. "I love it when you get rough with me."

177

I rub the sore spot on my forehead and glare down at him. "When the fuck are you going to realize I'm not fucking around? That I mean what I fucking say? Keep your shit up and I'll fucking kill you."

I kick him in the side and he grunts. I close my knife and pocket it. I storm over to the door just as one of the guards and an orderly are running out. I throw my hands up and move aside. "Listen. It's done and over with. He's fine. Everything is cool."

The guard puts his hands on his hips and sighs. "Why? Why do you do this shit? You're lucky none of the head honchos were walking by and witnessed that shit. Do you know how much pap-"

I cut him off. "Yeah, yeah. I just heard this yesterday. You guys don't want to deal with the paperwork. Got it. Can I go now?"

He narrows his eyes at me and then waves the orderly away. "We're done here. Get your shit together, Karver."

I give him a mock salute and walk by. I smirk and then mutter, "Aye, aye, 2.5."

"Dammit, Karver!"

Signs and Symptoms of BPD: Trouble trusting others.

22

Sloane

Dr. Bart escorts me to the rec room and I look around, my eyes falling on Thumper who's sitting at the table, looking defeated. The doctor taps my shoulder and I look over at him. He smiles at me and says, "Thank you for speaking with me, Sloane. It's good to talk things out and refrain from aggression. I know we're working on you with your feelings and emotions and aggression is a part of it, but it's not a healthy coping mechanism." He grimaces and whispers, "Also, the timing is awful. I'm not kidding when I tell you, this could make you look like a suspect, Sloane." I curl my lips in and smile with a nod.

I start walking towards Thumper and briefly stop when I look outside and see Karver. I shuffle my feet towards him and back to Thumper, unable to figure out which way to go. A flash of movement catches my attention and I see Decker skipping over to me. He slides to a stop in front of me, clasps his hands in front of him and bats his eyelashes.

"Hiiii, Sloaneeee. Did ya break yourself out of the cage of doom? Naughty, naughty."

I bring my finger to my mouth. "Shhh, it's a secret."

He gasps and shakes his finger at me. "We gotta keep our eye out on you, huh?" We? The only eyes I want on me are Karver's. My eyes shift towards him and well up with tears. I shove my sweating hands in my pockets and curl them into fists. Decker gently shoulder checks me, there's a tiny glimmer of sadness that passes his features and then he smiles big at me. "Don't worry, I'll go push his buttons. He'll be ready to run from me and straight to you. I gotchu, girl."

"Tha-" I watch as he runs off before I can thank him. I pull my hands out of my pockets and run my fingers through my hair, heading towards Thumper's table. I sit across from him and smile when he looks up.

His face lights up. "You remind me so much of my bunny. What's your name, darling girl?"

My smile wavers at his confusion. "H-hi, I'm Sloane."

He brings his arm over the table and holds his shaking, wrinkled hand out. I clasp my hand in his and he gently shakes it. "Hello, Sloane. You can call me Thumper," he holds my hand a little tighter as he leans in and whispers, "that's my Navy name, but you can call me Karwyn."

I smile at him and squeeze his cold hand, whispering back, "It sounds like your name is a secret. Why are you trusting me with it?"

He looks around and scans the room like there's an incoming enemy. Leaning in further, he whispers, "The enemy is always near. You never give up information to them." He gives me a quick nod, which I return, and then pulls back. There's a twinge in my heart that I only recognize when shit blows up with Karver. I grimace and pat my chest. He's not near me and this is happening. Why? Did that sedation flip a switch in me? Change my brain chemistry or some shit? "What's wrong, Sloane?"

I flinch at his voice. "What? Sorry."

"You look like you're confused and in pain. Is everything okay? Should I holler for someone?"

My tongue feels thick in my mouth and I work it around. I clear my throat. "No, no, I'm okay. I think. Just trying to figure things out is all."

Ready for the attention to be off of me, I shake my head and give him the best smile I can muster. "How about you tell me all about your special lady."

Somehow, his smile grows and I swear there's a fucking twinkle in his green eyes. I can't believe I missed it before. His eyes are the exact shade of green that Karver's are. He starts to speak when the sound of stomping boots has us both turning to look.

I see the direction they're heading and my heart starts to pound. I can hear it pounding in my ears and it almost feels like everything is warped and slowed down. Oh god, Karver. I whip my head around to search for him outside and find him standing over Decker. Fuck. I watch his interaction outside and he walks through the door smirking. He looks over at us and immediately his smirk falls and morphs into a sneer. He quickly turns away, kicking a chair while stomping out of the rec room.

Karver

I sit at my table alone and push my food around the tray. I watch as Axel and Decker start walking towards my table but I shake my head and nod towards Sloane and Thumper. They can all have each other.

I can't help but look at their table and search out Sloane. I watch as Nurse Leeba sits down across from her and they start happily talking like old friends. How does she do that? Everyone just falls all over themselves for her. Including me. She just has this way about her that brings a smile to everyone's face. How can someone who has struggled their whole life with feelings and emotions bring so many out of people so effortlessly? Who am I to question any of this? I can't even get a handle on my own fucking bullshit. The only difference between us? Where she lacks feeling, I feel it all. Sometimes I wonder what it would be like if we could swap places. Even for just a day. I wonder if she thinks about that, too. Or me? Does she think about me like I think about her? Fuck, does my brain ever shut the fuck up?

Maybe I should freak out like her and Axel did. Let them sedate my ass and get a vacation from my fucking thoughts. I need to get the fuck out of here. Maybe go to bed early. I stand up and grab my tray, walking it over to the trash can and dumping it before dropping off the tray and heading for the door. The hairs on the back of my neck stand and I look at the corner of the room.

I find Mousey glaring over at Sloane or Leeba, maybe both. I smile at the blooming bruises and cuts on her face. She must feel my stare and looks at me. Her breath hitches and she's unsure of what to do. She starts looking back and forth between me and Sloane. She adjusts her uniform and messes with her rock hard hair. I snort and shake my head as I leave the cafeteria.

Sloane

Leeba is in the middle of sharing a hiking story when Nurse Ratchet stomps over. She refuses to look at me and leans down to Leeba, loudly whispering, "We have paperwork to do. Now."

Leeba looks over at her, surprised. "Oh. Umm. Okay."

She looks at me and smiles. "Sorry, Sloane. We'll catch up during my next shift, yeah?"

I watch as she leaves and look at the guys. "Since when is paperwork *that* important? Has anything new happened? I mean other than the obvious," I wave my fork around at the guard and orderly in the room, "extra eyes everywhere."

Decker shrugs and shoves a mouthful of food in his mouth. I look at Axel and his eyes flick back and forth. Falling on me, he quietly says, "Not since... you know...." He points his fork around his face and nods at the door the nurses went through. I do my best to bite back a laugh at him dancing around the topic of me beating Nurse Ratchet's ass.

"What about you, Thumper?" I look at him as he quickly shuts his pocket watch and shoves it in his pocket.

"Huh? What?"

A shrill scream startles me and I immediately look around the cafeteria. I don't see anything wrong in the room, other

183

than a guard and orderly running out to the doorway to look down the hall. Where did that scream come from? They keep looking down the hall and in here, unsure of what to do. Makes sense. Check on the danger out there, or chance something dangerous happening here with everyone. I stand up on shaky legs and wipe my sweaty palms down the front of my pants. "Guys, let's get somewhere against the wall. If people start freaking out, I don't want any of us getting trampled."

I look up at Axel's hulking form and snort. "Well, those of us that aren't the size of a shit brick house."

He looks down at himself, covering his face with his shaggy hair. "S-sorry. I wish I wasn't so big."

I lean down and do my best to make myself seen through his curtain of hair. "Hey, Axel?"

I wait for him to lift his head and look at me before continuing. I offer him a kind smile when he does. "I didn't mean anything bad by it. Promise. Would you be willing to help stand by Thumper? Keep him safe if people start running around?"

Thumper scoffs and stands against the wall crossing his arms. "I'm a goddamn Navy sailor, I don't need some *civilians* looking after me."

"Alright, calm down there, muscles."

I swing my head to the door when I hear a loud banging. One of the guards is standing there slamming his flashlight against the door. "Listen up! Just like we've done before, we're going to have you take turns filing out of here and heading to your rooms. There will be no showers tonight, only bathroom breaks when needed. You will call for assistance at your door and wait for someone to escort you there and back. First up, as usual, last room in the hall. Sloane, Axel, Decker. Let's go."

I look at Thumper. "You good?"

His scowl turns into a small smile. "I'll be just fine, my darling girl."

Petulant BPD: Unpredictable mood swings, passive-aggressiveness, and a need to feel in control.

23

Karver

I open the door to our room and the blood curdling scream makes me stumble into the door head first. Pain blooms on my forehead and I clasp my palm over it, trying to rub the ache away. "Motherfucker."

I look in the direction of the scream and one of the orderlies points and shouts, "Back to your room, Karver!"

My head throbs and I walk back inside muttering, "Whatever." I pace the room, rubbing my head in the hopes it will push the headache out.

After a stupid amount of pacing, shouts halt my movements. "NOOOOO!!! LEEBA!!!!" Sloane. I run out of the room and watch as Axel tries to guide Sloane away from the room she's looking into. She thrashes away from him. "DON'T TOUCH ME! DON'T FUCKING TOUCH ME!"

Axel visibly shakes while he whispers in her ear. She looks behind her to see an orderly walking up behind them. She takes a few steps back from the door with her hands up. "I'm fine, I'm fine. I'm not going to do anything." She jabs her finger towards the open door and shouts, "I KNOW IT WAS YOU, BITCH! YOU WERE THE LAST ONE WITH HER!" She takes a deep breath and walks towards our room. I glare at the hand she placed on Axel's arm as if she'll feel the burn of my stare and remove it. They look at each other while walking, and I hear the end of the conversation when she says, "Really, Axel. Thank you for trying to keep me out of trouble. I'm sorry for yelling at you, I don't know what came over me. I'm not mad at you, I promise."

"What the fuck is going on?" She freezes at my voice and I watch as she slowly inhales.

She glares at me and in a lifeless tone says, "Leeba is dead," as she brushes past me into the room. I look down the hall and see everyone shuffling about, different patients filing to their rooms. Dr. Dead comes running through, his hair mussed and adjusting his tie. He slides on a pair of rubber gloves as he steps into the room and out of sight. God, Karver, pull your head out of your ass. You're sitting here fighting with everyone over your own issues while people are dropping like fucking flies. What if they're next? What if Sloane is next? Do I really want our last memories to be her catching me with that skank? Me avoiding her and being a dick? Fuck no.

I walk back into the room and find Decker kicking his dangling feet off of his bed while Axel is cornered on the other end of the bed to avoid getting kicked in the head repeatedly. I look at Sloane's bed and find her curled up in a ball on her bed. I grab the edge of her bed and pull myself up to stand on mine. I stand there frozen in place. Do I reach out and touch her? Apologize? Why is everything so fucking complicated? "Sl-" my voice cracks and I clear my throat to try again. "Sloane?"

With a heavy sigh, she mumbles, "Not now, Karver."

I reach out to touch her and my hand hovers over her hip. "Can we j-"

I pull my hand back as she flips over and seethes. "I said not now, Karver! Go get your dick wet with the skank. This pussy is fucking closed for business!"

I reel back at her words. I don't fucking want that mousey bitch. Fuck. Of course she doesn't know that. I shake my head back and forth. "Sloane, I don't want her."

She throws her head back with a dark laugh and glares down at me. "Maybe you should put one of your masks on permanently, Karver. Does a better job hiding your bullshit than your fake mask does. That shit might work on everyone else, but it doesn't fucking work on me. Newsflash, I can fucking read you. And I honestly can't decide what's fucking worse. If you actually wanted to fuck that bitch, or the fact that you pretended to just to get under my skin and hurt me."

She can read me? Nobody can fucking read me. Fuck, this is confusing. I don't even have a good answer for her. She's right. Both options are completely fucked. I stutter trying to form a response, "I... you..."

She holds her hand up. "No. Oh no, Karver. I think you've done enough talking, enough hiding, enough lying. It's my turn to talk, and you're going to shut the fuck up and hear me out for once. I know your fucked up life has given you enough leeway to be fucking selfish, but it doesn't mean every fucking moment of your life. It doesn't mean dish it out to those who don't deserve it. Take some fucking accountability. I know your brain is a fucking dick, but maybe, just maybe, reach out for help when that happens. Just because your brain is a dick to you, doesn't give you the right to be one to those that don't deserve it.

Thumper did nothing wrong. Maybe sit down and fucking hear him out. For fuck's sake, the man is a fucking Vietnam vet and we've all seen the signs. Dementia is coming in hot for the poor man. You treat Axel like fucking shit when you're in a mood, and he's never done anything to deserve that."

She looks down at Axel and the anger turns to pity as she whispers, "Please don't be mad at me for what I'm about to say, Axel."

I look at him and back to her. Wait, apologize for what? She looks back at me and curls her lip. "He fucking worships the ground you walk on, and in return you give him shattered glass and piss to crawl over for you." He. Worships me? Why? Tears fill her eyes. No, sweets, don't cry. Her voice breaks when she points to herself, "A-nd me?" With a watery laugh she shakes her head and the tears start to fall. "Me? You've been punishing me from the very beginning. You convinced yourself I had done you wrong before we even knew each other. Every issue we've ever had is about things you make up in your own head. You think if you push me to the breaking point and *make* me leave, then you'll be a little more comfortable with it, so you can say that it was your doing."

My heart races with every word falling from her lips. How the fuck does she know me and see me better than anybody in my entire life? "I've *never* done anything to you but fucking fall in love with you. Who the fuck knows why at this point. You leave me begging for fucking scraps from you. You know just what to say and do to hook me back in, to have me grasping for any lifeline you'll throw my way." There's a knock on the door and it's slowly pushed open. A tired looking orderly looks around and in a bored tone says, "Room check." Without another word, he quietly shuts the door.

I look at Sloane as she sighs in exhaustion and flops on her back. "The prettiest lie you ever told me was that you loved me," she mumbles.

I'm totally going to get kneed in the dick for this, but I'm at a loss at what else there is for me to do. She doesn't want my words. Fine. I'll fucking show her how much I love her. I dig my hands into her mattress and pull myself up. She stares down at me and grits her teeth. "Don't. You. Dare." I ignore her demand and crawl over her. I feel her shift underneath me and I smirk, quickly straddling her hips. I can see it in her eyes that her resolve is already breaking, but she keeps the fight going. She glares up at me and seethes. "Get the fuck off of me, Karver."

"No." She's quicker than I give her credit for when my head whips to the side and my cheek burns from her slap, the coppery tang of blood heady on my tongue. I slowly look back at her and flick my tongue across the cut in my lip. I swiftly wrap my hand around her throat and squeeze, a choked gasp leaving her. "How quickly you forget how much we love to hurt each other."

She slaps at my arm and digs her nails in, crescent moon cuts left behind from each one. "*You* are the one who gets off on hurting me, asshole. Fuck you!"

"Your lips are dripping with venom for me. What else can I make drip, sweets?"

Her breath hitches and she stares at me, her eyes tracing every inch of my face. "Don't do this, Karver. Not now."

"Don't do what, Clover? Love you? *Show* you everything rather than telling you?" More tears fall from her eyes and I lean down and lick them from each cheek, the salt stinging my lip. She tries to turn her head away and I grasp her chin and make her face me. She shakes her head trying to fight my hold. "Let me love you, sweets."

She spits in my face and it drips down to my lips, making me groan. I slam my lips to hers, smearing her spit between us. She refuses to kiss back and I bite her bottom lip until the taste of blood bursts in my mouth. Her mouth falls open on a gasp and I shove my tongue in, coating her tongue with her own blood and spit and sucking it back into my mouth. She moans into my mouth and I swallow it down, our tongues sliding against each other. I reach into my pocket and pull out my knife. I grip the blade in my palm until blood cascades down my hand. "Take it." Her shaky hand reaches between us as she grabs the handle of the knife. "Slice me, sweets."

She pulls the knife from my hand, deepening the cut. I reach back and pull my shirt off, throwing it to the floor below. She brings the blade of the knife to the clover brand on my chest and traces the outline of it. She points the tip of the blade against the stem of the clover and seethes, "I hate you."

I press further into the blade, a drop of blood trickles around the blade and down my chest. "Show me how much." She drags the knife down in a quick motion, slashing the end of the stem. I hiss from the sting and bite my tongue, trying to force myself to take this slow.

I push the bottom of her shirt up and she tries to cover her stomach. I grab her wrists with one hand and look at her. "Stop. Use that knife all you want, but don't you dare keep me from loving every fucking inch of you." She drops her hands to her sides and I watch her grip the knife tighter. "Do it, Clover. Don't hold back. Give me every ounce of that venom." I continue pushing her shirt up and kiss across her tits and down her stomach, leaving nothing untouched. With every suck, she gasps and with every bite, she moans. I slowly bring her pants off and kiss each knee, trailing kisses and bites along each thigh. I pull my pants off next and my cock slaps against my stomach. "Look at what you do to me. Only you, sweets."

I drag my hand through the blood dripping down my chest and stroke my cock with it. Her breathing picks up as she watches every stroke. I look down at her pussy and smile when I see that she is, in fact, dripping for me. I line my cock up and thrust to the hilt in one go. She moans and squirms with the knife in hand, slicing down my chest. I groan when the movement makes her pussy grip me tightly. I ball up my fists and drop them next to her head. I pull my hips back slowly and give her short, slow strokes. She huffs in frustration. "This sure seems like you're still trying to punish me for something. What the fuck are you doing, Karver?"

I look at her and wink. "You know what to do if you want more, clover. Hurt me. Hurt me I like I hurt you." She sits up and grips the hair on the back of my head. Before I can blink, she drags the knife down my left cheek and the surprising move has me thrusting forward fast and hard. Her hand pushes further into my cheek and I feel more blood pouring from the cut. I grit my teeth, "Again!"

I thrust harder and faster, our sweat-slicked bodies sticking together, her breathy moans in sync with the slashes she gifts me with. Her pussy clamps impossibly tight around my cock and she drops the knife between us as she cums. I watch as her eyes roll to the back of her head and it's my undoing. "Guh, fuuuuuck." I drop my lips to hers and rasp, "You're my 143, sweets."

The moment is broken when Decker whoops. "Damn, who needs porn when I have you two as roommates? I just came in my pants."

Sloane slaps her hands over her face and giggles. "Oh my God, we are assholes for roommates."

She drops her hands from her face and rolls her head to face me. "Are you ever going to tell me what the 143 is, Slasher?"

I check that Axel and Decker aren't paying attention. They're both laying with their backs facing us, so I hold a finger up. I crawl down from the bunk and grab Nana's letter and the blue marker from inside my mattress. I hold it to my chest and take a deep breath. Fuck, why is this so hard? I climb back up and she watches as I sit back on my heels and grip the letter tight. She sits up, concern etched on her face. Jesus, just hand it over. I start to hand it over but I pause with my hand frozen between us. "Just. Please, be careful. It's a really old letter. Delicate."

She gently wraps her fingers around it and opens the plastic bag, slowly pulling the letter out. I watch as she slowly and delicately unfolds it and begins reading. Her eyes flick back and forth, and a tear falls from her eye. I can't handle watching the emotions that cross her features as she reads. I was going to wait to use the marker, but I need to distract myself. I pull the cap off and bring the marker down to her chest. She looks down, "Wha–"

I refuse to look at her and whisper, "Keep reading."

I write 'K143S' over her heart and shove the marker under her pillow. I look up just as her face crumples and a sob leaves her. She crawls into my lap and holds me tight, her voice cracking. "Y-ou're my 143, too, Slasher."

Discouraged BPD: Fears of being abandoned, neediness, emotional mood swings.

3 HOURS AGO...

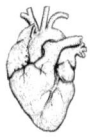

I check the hall to make sure everything is clear and then walk into the exam room, following behind Nurse Leeba. I silently watch as she starts unlocking cabinets and pulling medication out. She opens the top of one of the large medication bottles, dumping it on a tray to count. She's lost in her counting and doesn't hear me walking up behind her. When I'm within arm's length, her back stiffens. She starts to turn her head and her eyes widen along with her mouth. I swiftly clap my hand over her mouth and she mumbles against my hand, thrashing around. "Stop. I'm going to move my hand and if you fucking scream or fight me, Sloane will be next."

I feel her tremble as she slowly nods, tears falling down her cheeks and over my hand. "You don't want anything to happen to Sloane, do you?" She shakes her head no over and over.

I spin us so her back is against the counter and grab a handful of the pills in the tray. I grip them in my hand and slowly slide my hand from her mouth, waiting to see if she'll scream. A soft whimper leaves her mouth and I glare down at her. The sound cuts off and I shove the handful of pills in her mouth. I put my hand over her mouth again when she gags at the taste of the pills.

I look inside the open cabinet and search for some form of liquid. Rubbing alcohol. Perfect.

I pull it from the cabinet and place it on the edge of the counter to hold against my body. I carefully twist the top off, fumbling with the cap while opening it one handed. I pour all of it in her mouth bit by bit, covering both her nose and her mouth to help push the pills down her throat. Liquid pours through my fingers as she coughs and gags at the burn and the bubbles forming in her mouth. Eventually, her body starts to slump and I let her go, watching as she falls to the floor, convulsing and clawing at her mouth and throat. I let her struggle on the floor as I wipe my prints off of everything. I can hear the taps and squeaks of her shoes on the floor quiet down. After taking care of my fingerprints, I toss my calling card on top of the tall medicine cabinet and look down at her. Her eyes stare vacantly across the room, bubbles and blood frothed around her mouth. I flex my hand at my side with the effort of restraining myself from painting her skin with it. Goodnight, Nurse Leeba.

24

Sloane

Before I open my eyes, I feel Karver wrapped around me. I usually find so much comfort and security when he holds me like this, but right now... I'm mad at myself. I'm mad at him. I was supposed to keep as much distance as I could between us for him to figure his shit out. I told him everything I've been thinking and feeling and I was supposed to push him away to think about it. But what did I do? I let him back in. I let him consume every piece of me. And I love it. I love that he finally opened up and shared something so personal with me.

A piece of my heart broke for him while reading his Nana's letter for the little boy that lost the most important person in his life. But the soothing balm of it all, was realizing what 143 meant to him. To them. I know he made an effort by sharing with me, but can that really be the end all, be all, fix all? I really don't think so.

I was so lost in him, in us, that I didn't even think about Decker and Axel being there. Axel. Fuck. Does this make me a horrible person? I've literally just pieced things together with how he feels for Karver, and I fucking threw it in his face. I called him out and then let Karver fuck me stupid right in front of him.

I know I was laughing when I called us assholes, but it's true. I need to apologize to him. I won't apologize for loving Karver, for picking him even in the darkest of times, but I should apologize for doing something so intimate in front of him. I pull at the hand that's cradling my throat, and he grunts while squeezing in protest. I claw my nails down the back of his hand and he thrusts his hips forward, pressing his hard cock against my lower back.

"Mmm, good morning to you, too."

"It won't be a good morning when I shove your ass off this top bunk."

He slowly peels his hands from my body and sits to hover over me. He tries to meet my eyes but I keep them focused on the wall, trying to figure out what to say, what to do. I need space. Time to think without him clouding my mind.

I scoot down to the end of the bed. "Where are you going?"

I ignore him and climb off of the bed. I shiver when my feet hit the chilled floor. I grab my discarded pants and slide them on, stumbling like a newborn fawn. "Sloane? What are you doing?"

I look to see if his loud ass voice has woken the other two. When they don't make a move or sound, I glare up at him. "Shh."

The confusion marring his face turns to unveiled humor. "Did you just shush me?"

I run my fingers through my hair and huff as I stomp my feet over to the dresser. I rip it open and pull a change of clothes out, muttering, "Space. That's what I need."

"What, sweets?"

So much for not wanting to wake everyone up. I slam the drawer shut and seethe. "Shut the fuck up, Karver. I need some fucking space. Is that okay with you?"

He opens his mouth and I shout, "No! Don't answer that. I need space. We both do. You need to take time to pull your head from your ass, not act like you're going to long enough to fuck me stupid, purposely making me forget before you even pull your cock out. Maybe take this time to fucking apologize to those who deserve it."

I walk to the door and open it, finding one of the orderlies standing there like a statue. His eyes slowly shift my way and he nods. "Your room is up first for showers, go ahead."

I step out of the room and a thought crosses my mind. I turn and look at him, ignoring the sad expression on his face. "While you're at it, go fucking listen to what Thumper has to say. We both know in a moment of clarity, you're going to feel like shit if you don't hear him out. Nobody lives forever, Karver. Especially around this fucking death ward."

Karver

All during breakfast, I watched as Sloane sat away from me with Thumper. I know she felt my stare, but refused to spare me half a glance. Everywhere we walked today there were workers running around, messing with lights and doors. The place looks like a mad house with so many people running around. I snort at the realization that we are quite literally in a mad house.

Never far from my mind, I start thinking about the things Sloane said this morning. Space? She wants us to have space? First of fucking all, isn't now the time to be together? She literally had to remind me that people are dying around us, and then has the audacity to say we need fucking space from each other. Not only that, but there's no such thing as space now that those on shift are always checking things out and I have two goons shadowing me everywhere I go. Fuck it. I'm on a mission to make my woman happy. I'll show her. I can do this. We can get through this. I'll figure my fucking shit out. I have to.

I stop and watch as police and investigators shuffle around the room where Leeba was killed. The police tape is torn and dangling down one side of the door frame. An investigator with a notepad stands in front of Mousey asking her questions. She holds a tissue to her nose and sniffles, not a single tear shed during her recant of events. I scoff and head towards the rec room. I take a deep breath before turning the corner. I rub my sweaty hands down the front of my pants.

Jesus, Karver, quit being a fucking pussy. It's a conversation. Hear the old man out. See what the fuck happened. Where the fuck he's been? No. Stop. Calm the fuck down. You're supposed to listen. Do shit differently for fucking once. I crack my neck and knuckles. Dude, fucking chill. You're not prepping for an MMA fight with the old fuck.

I don't look anywhere else, I know he'll be in his usual spot. I find Sloane sitting beside him with a hand on his forearm and nodding along with whatever he's saying. I stand there and watch the exchange as he pulls his pocket watch out and opens it. He smiles big and shows her the picture of him with my Nana. He furrows his bushy brows for only a moment and shakes his head. Sloane musters up a smile for him and looks my way before swiveling back to Thumper and she pats his arm. I watch as she stands up and slowly walks over to me. There's my girl. Yes. She knows I'm trying. Unable to stop the movement, I bounce on my toes in excitement.

She quickly clocks the movement and bites her cheek. Her eyes plead with me before she even speaks, "Please be nice to him. Today," she takes a deep breath and glances back at him for a moment, "today is a bad day for him. I don't know how to explain it. It's like a computer that randomly goes into sleep mode and then you push a button and it wakes up. He'll be with me in a conversation and then, poof, disappears somewhere else. He's been doing it all day."

I look at him and the confusion on his face makes sense now. I shift on my feet and scratch the scruff on my face. "I was going to talk to him... ya know... about... things." Panic grips me when I realize this could keep her from me longer. "Does this mean I have to wait? What about..." I look around and lean in to whisper, "What about us, sweets? I'm trying here. Are you really going to punish me for something out of my control?"

She starts to slowly back away. "Funny you should ask. Isn't that exactly what you keep doing to me, Slasher?"

Fuck. I chuckle and follow after her like a fucking lost dog. There's those fucking thorns of hers. Thumper looks up as I pull the chair out to sit. A war of emotions crosses his face, unfortunately the flicker of clarity is snuffed out by confusion. He looks around the table and sees Sloane getting ready to take a seat. He jumps up, the chair slamming against the wall. He stands up as tall as he can and bows to Sloane. "Miss. Allow me."

He grabs her chair, pulls it out and then waves an arm for her to sit. She curtsies. Yes. Fucking curtsies and takes her seat, allowing him to push her chair forward. He looks at the three of us and glares. "You're lucky there's a lady present or I'd have a few choice words for you civilians and your lack of manners. Maybe you three should enlist. Do you lot some good. Learn some manners and get all that hair squared away."

Decker giggles obnoxiously at the scene playing out before us and I backhand him in the gut. "Ugh. Oww, Karvy."

I side-eye him and grumble, "Knock it off."

I hear Thumper righting his chair and watch as he takes a seat. He looks at me and freezes, his eyes blinking rapidly. "Who's your mama, son?" He tilts his head and stares at me, waiting for my response. How am I supposed to respond? Do I play along or tell the truth? Fuck it, truth it is. Turning over a new leaf and all. Dammit, Clover.

I put my hand over my chest. "I'm Karver. Karver Murphy."

He starts to shake his head and blink some more. "That. That name. Awfully close to my name. My name, my name, my name." He looks at me and squints, then opens his eyes wide. "You. You are very... you're confusing me. What's going on here? Where?" He looks around the table at everyone and then the whole room. "Where am I? Where the hell is my bunny?"

"Na- Cordelia is no longer here, Po- Thumper. Cordelia passed away 13 years ago."

Thumper slams his fist on the table and roars, "NO!" I stand up and grab Sloane, pushing her behind me. He jumps up again, losing his balance and stumbling against the wall. He starts pointing his shaky finger at everyone with tears in his eyes. "That's a lie! You're a liar! Where's my bunny? BUNNY! BUNNY!" He grips his head, shaking it furiously. "I want to go home. I need my bunny. Where is she? She's not gone. You lie, you lie, you lie. Noooo. No. No."

A few orderlies rush by us and Thumper starts swinging haymakers at all of them. "Get. Get away from me. I want to go home! Leave me alone!" They put him in a two-man hold while the third orderly pulls out a syringe, with prac-ticed moves pulling the cap off the needle and pushing it into his neck. His shouts grow quieter and meld together into slurred words. The fight leaves his body and he slumps down, the orderlies just barely keeping their hold of him with the dead weight.

I cringe at the high-pitched voice behind us. "Yoohoo. Excuse me, coming through." I feel Sloane tense behind me and if this situation wasn't so fucked, I'd say the little growl she let out was cute as fuck. Mousey moves around us with a wheelchair and locks the wheels. The orderlies drop Thumper into it and look at her.

One of them asks, "Isn't your shift over, Nurse Regan?"

She unlocks the wheels and smirks, "Oh, don't you worry about that. I'm just getting him all settled in and then I'll be clocking out." She sways her hips and whistles a tune I can't quite place as she walks away.

Self-Destructive BPD: Partaking in self-harming and abusive behaviors

---

.

25

Sloane

I stare at the ceiling with my hands clasped over my stomach. The room is cast with shadows amidst the rays of moonlight shining through the window. I can hear the rhythmic sounds of Decker and Axel's snores. Sleep eludes me while I lay here willing myself not to go lay down with Karver. I realize he's awake when I hear him shuffling around in his bed. I hear him huff, and watch as he walks to the door. The door slowly opens with a hiss, the rubber padding scratches against the floor. The buzz from the dimmed fluorescent lights in the hall fills the room. A beam of light centers on Karver's face and he puts his hand over his eyes. "I'm just going to take a leak, get that shit out of my face."

The light drops to the floor and Karver shuts the door as he leaves. I stare at the door for a moment until I'm pulled into the memory of earlier tonight. When I walked up to him in the rec room, I may have appeared calm on the outside, steadfast in my decision to make him put in the work, but on the inside I was reaching towards him.

I just want everything to be magically fucking fixed and be near him without our toxicity hanging over our heads like a heavy cloud. I hated that I had to stop his chance at talking things out by telling him what was going on with Thumper. He can be mad all he wants, but I know he gives a shit about that man. It couldn't have been easy for him to witness Thumper regressing and crumbling before our very eyes. How confusing it must be to sit there loving, hating, admiring and worrying about someone all at once. For the first time in who knows how long he was going to put in the work to make things right, only for the chance to be stolen by the war in Thumper's brain. You don't think about the demons waging war in a person's brain until it bursts free and comes to light. I didn't realize I had been holding my breath watching it all unfold until Karver grabbed me and pushed me behind him. Even in the midst of chaos and the drift between us, he still felt the need to protect me. The moment his hands were on me, I sucked in air and held onto him like a lifeline.

The door slowly opens and I hear his heavy sigh as he shuts the door. His shadowy face looks so handsome in the moonlight. His head is back against the door, and his eyes are shut. He drops his head and opens his eyes. The moonlight makes various shades of green pop from his eyes. He takes a step towards the bunks and says, "Clo-"

His words are cut off by a loud buzz and clicking sound, followed by flashing red lights and an incessant trill of an alarm. I jump up and look around the room trying to piece together what the fuck is happening. The lights illuminate the room enough that I can see Decker holding his pillow over his ears and shouting, "Well, this is new!"

I look below him and find Axel also holding his pillow over his ears, a panicked look across his face as he rocks back and forth. I watch as Karver steps towards me and then stops to look back at the door. He looks torn between checking on it or me, and I watch as the door wins with him turning back to it. He tries to open it and it doesn't budge. Spinning around, he says something, but I can't make out the words. I cup my hand to my ear and shout, "What?!"

He jabs his thumb behind him and yells back, "I! SAID! IT'S! LOCKED!"

I tilt my head and thrust my arms towards the door. "YEAH! OBVIOUSLY!" He narrows his eyes at me for a moment and then turns back to the door to bang on it with his fists. I shake my head, what the fuck does he think he's doing? I climb off the bed when his shouts start to surpass the sound of the alarm. I place my hand over his and slowly pull it from the door, the wet and sticky feel of his blood coating my palm. He turns to me and I bring his fist to my mouth and start kissing each bruised and bloody knuckle, the blood coating my lips. I look at him, opening my mouth to speak and the taste of copper explodes on my tongue. Our eyes lock as I hold his fist up and mouth, 'stop'.

The deafening scream of the alarm turns to a whistle that fades and then completely cuts off. The flashing lights slow to a blink and then shut off with a low hum and the new locks on the door click and hiss.

Axel's shaking voice penetrates the silence. "W-what was that, guys? Wha-what's happening?" His fear pulls me from the hold Karver's eyes have on me. I drop Karver's bloodied hand, wiping the blood on my palm down my pants. I walk around Karver to Axel and step in front of him to halt his pacing. He stumbles as he tries to avoid crashing into me and keeps his face hidden behind the curtain of his hair.

I lean to the side and tilt my head so I can meet his eyes through his hair, softly saying, "Hey, Axel. We're going to figure out what's up. You're safe. I- *we* won't let anything happen to you, okay?"

I guide him away from the bunks when I notice Decker's swinging feet getting too close to Axel's head. Decker whines above us. "Ughh, fun sucker."

I glare up at him. "Quit your bitchin', Decker."

His eyes widen and he claws at his chest, gasping. "Allll the painnn in myyy hearttt," he obnoxiously sing-songs.

From behind us, Karver sighs. "Not now, Deck. Stay alert. I'm gonna go find out what the fuck is going on."

I let go of Axel's arm and spin around. "The fuck you are! It's obvious why the fuck they set all this up. Which means someone is fucking dead. We don't know who the fuck the killer is, so no. Don't you dare go out there."

His steely determination is written all over his face. He's not going to listen to me. "I think you underestimate the lengths I'll go to fucking protect you, Clover." He turns, opens the door and steps into the hall once more. The dimmed lights are now shining bright and the sounds of heavy footfalls can be heard. Fuck this, he's not going alone. I rush towards the door, and without looking back, I say, "Stay here with Axel, Decker."

"When the fuck did I apply for a babysitting gig?"

I glare over my shoulder at him, "Just do it, Decker!"

I run out the door and turn down the hall. I find Karver standing in the middle of the hallway, frozen. "Karver? Karver, what is it?"

I peek around his body and watch as Corbin pulls a gurney out of one of the rooms. No. No. No. This can't be happening. Not before they could have a chance to fix things. I look at Karver as he stands there, eyes unblinking and partially open mouth. I grab for his hand and he starts to pull away from me, but I intertwine our fingers and squeeze his hand tight. "I'm right here. I'm not going anywhere. I'm so sorry, Slasher."

One of the older guards steps out of the room shaking his head, a crestfallen expression on his weathered face. He looks over at us and for a moment, I think he's going to yell at us for being out here. Looking at Karver, his expression softens and he sighs. Whispered words are exchanged between him and Corbin. I watch as Corbin pulls a clipboard out from under his arm and taps a pen against it. With his head down, he walks into Thumper's room and the guard tilts his head. "You wanna say goodbye to him, kid?"

Karver walks over and once we reach the gurney, his voice cracks, "Don't call me that." He white-knuckles the bed rail as he grabs it. "Dammit, old man. You couldn't have just left me once, but you had to go and do it twice."

He growls under his breath and pulls away from the gurney. He slowly takes two steps back, and looks down at Thumper and to his room. His eyes widen and he jumps forward. "Wait! His watch, where is his watch?" He frantically pulls at the sheet draped over Thumper and then his scrub top. "Where is it? I need it. Where the fuck is it?"

I look at Corbin and the guard, stunned as they standby and watch without a word. I snap my finger. "Guys! Help him!"

The guard walks into Thumper's room and Corbin rounds the gurney to the opposite side. He reaches into Thumper's pocket and pulls the watch out, holding it in front of him. Karver doesn't notice with his frantic search and I gently place my hand on his wrist. "Karver?" His body tenses and I can hear his heavy, close to panicked breaths. He slowly looks at me, sweat drips down his temples and the look on his face breaks my heart.

Without looking at Corbin, I reach out with my other hand for the watch. He drops it in my hand, the metal cold against my palm. I bring it between us and show him. "It's right here, Slasher." His quick breathing slows down as he looks at the watch in my hand. I grab his hand and open it. I drop the watch in his palm, gently wrapping his fingers around it. My heart breaks for us both as I pull him away from the gurney and place my hand on his back. "Let's go back to our room."

Impulsive BPD: Binging, risky and aggressive behaviors.

1 WEEK AGO...

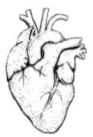

I tip-toe down the hall and keep an eye and ear out for anyone. There was a lot of commotion today, which helped me pinpoint my next target. Killing these older patients is also a hell of a lot easier, considering they get to have a room to themselves. Bittersweet. A room to themselves, away from other patients, but leaves them easy targets. His death will devastate people, hell, I'm even torn about it, but I can't pass this opportunity up. I watch as his chest rises and falls with every breath. His sedation will keep him from knowing I'm here and what's happening to him.

This will be the only kill where I show any kind of mercy. I lift his head and pull his pillow out from under him, letting his head fall to the bed and not even that interrupts his soft snores. I grip the pillow on both sides, placing it over his face. I press down as hard as I can, ensuring there's no space to provide him with oxygen. This position makes it almost impossible to keep an eye on his breathing but I look down the best I can and watch as the movement in his chest slows to a stop. I hold the pillow in place, knowing I need to wait just a little longer. I hear the sound of a door shutting and yank the pillow from the old man's face, putting it back under his head. There's no heart-beat thumping against my fingertips when I check for a pulse, so I toss my calling card under his bed and make sure I'm clear to go.

26

Karver

The last week passed in a blur. I stumble through each day, barely noticing all the new protocols put into place since Thumper was killed. It's like permanently wearing beer goggles. I can see and hear everyone to an extent, but it's all distorted. Except for Sloane. She has been with me every step of the way, the only beacon of light in the darkness surrounding me. My 143. Nobody else seems to exist but us in this new bubble I've created. Something seems to be going on with her as well, and I can't tell if it's her concern for me or something else. Then again, she could be suffering her own form of grief. She got close to Thumper in the short amount of time they knew each other. She was like the granddaughter he never had. Hell, maybe she was glimpse at what it would've been like to have a wonderful daughter, rather than the bitch that was my mother.

Her voice breaks through the fog that surrounds me. "Slasher?"

"Hmm?"

"Will you look at me, please?" I roll my head to the side and find her looking at me, concern etched across her beautiful face. Unshed tears brim at the edges and I don't know if she cries for me, herself, or every loss she's dealt with since we've met. She runs a finger between my eyebrows and the bridge of my nose. I go cross-eyed following the move and she smiles. "We have to start our day. It's almost our room's shower time. And then w-"

"I know."

She furrows her brow. "Karver, you're barely present for anything. How would you know?"

"You're all I see. All I hear. As long as I follow you, I'm sure I'll end up where I'm supposed to." She leans forward to kiss me, the salt of her tears now on my lips. She sniffles and pulls away, quickly swiping the tears from her face. She musters up a smile and pats over my clover brand and tattoo.

"Let's go." I watch as she crawls over me and walks to Axel and Decker's bunks.

Sloane

After waking Axel and Decker, we met Nurse Ratchet at the door for their meds. I felt Karver's stare as I watched her every move. I can't explain it, but I know she's the one murdering everyone. I can't even tell anyone or they'll think it's all in my head, that our confrontation is clouding my judgment. I glared at her as we left the room, and as usual, Decker whined how unfair it was that I don't have to take meds like they do. It doesn't matter how many times I try to explain the reason, he just whines more.

There's something almost eerie about this place now that we have these new protocols in place. If it wasn't for the guards and orderlies who follow us around and the nurses who go to each room, it would almost be like we had free rein of an abandoned facility. Each room has to go one at a time for bathroom time, meals and smoke breaks in the courtyard. Arts and crafts are canceled until further notice, we no longer have group therapy and are not allowed in the rec room. We are escorted everywhere we fucking go, even when we go one at a time to one-on-one therapy with Dr. Bart. Every time Karver comes back from his session, he seems more irritable than when he went there. He won't go into detail other than saying Dr. Bart keeps asking him the same shit over and over.

As much as I enjoy Karver's attention, I feel like he's been watching me more intently this week. He's definitely noticed my rapt attention of Nurse Ratchet, but I don't think he's pieced together the why. I've spent every waking moment figuring out how staff run things. I watch for who works what shift, and what they're doing as they walk with us. If we pass a room that I see staff in, I scope out what they're doing. I make more frequent bathroom trips to see who is walking the halls to escort us there and back.

I've learned that night shift would be the best time for me to sneak out of the room and see if I can find any answers in the rooms where the murders took place. I know they've been combed through by police, but I'm holding onto hope there could be something they missed. I wish the bitch worked that shift, it would be so much easier to catch her doing shady shit. Unfortunately, she works during the day, so I can only watch her in passing and when she administers meds.

Speaking of the bitch, I grip my fork tight as I watch her walk into the cafeteria. She strides in with her head held high and jabs her finger into the shoulder of Leeba's replacement. The nurse's face contorts in pain and she pulls away from her talons. They exchange a few heated whispers, the tension palpable even in the near-empty space. The new nurse juts her chin and marches out of the door. I watch as Ratchet scans the room and her eyes fall on me. She narrows her eyes and smirks, as if she's already forgotten her well-deserved ass whooping. Warmth envelops my hand and I loosen my grip on the fork. I look over and find Karver looking back and forth between me and Nurse Ratchet. I offer him what I hope is a reassuring smile. He leans in and places his lips to my ear. "What's going on, sweets?"

I pull away and meet his eye. "Nothing. Are you ready to go back to the room?" I see the wrinkle between his brows and reach out to smooth them out. "I'm okay. Let's go back to the room."

He nods and stands up, grabbing our trays to dump the leftover food. Decker and Axel follow closely behind as I look over and find her already staring at me. I curl my lip and glare in return. Game on, bitch.

Treatment is often done through DBT or other long-term intensive therapies.

27

Karver

I feel Sloane's body cradled in my arms and smile to myself. I can feel the fog has cleared, and I can finally take my first breath of air since Thumper died. I've been trapped with the demons in my head, whispering how things could have been different. Screaming at me that this is all my doing. That if I just pulled my head out of my ass sooner, then maybe, just maybe, we could have fixed the drift between us, which really was my fault. We could have shared memories of Nana. I could have told him how much I looked up to the man my Nana spoke of, even without ever truly knowing him. Hell, maybe his murder could have been prevented. Along the way, I fucked up and it cost him his life. I won't make that same mistake with Sloane. I know something is going on with her. Fog or not, I watched her every move and her obsession grow as time wears on. I need to stay vigilant and protect her, even if it's from herself. I fear her piqued curiosity is going to find her in the crosshairs of the killer.

Sloane moves in her sleep, her ass grinding against my morning wood and I grunt, "Fuck." I squeeze my hand around her throat and she moans in her sleep, grinding back once more. I pull my hand from her stomach and tug on my pants, moving around until they're down by my knees.

The movements jostle her around and in a groggy tone she questions, "What are you doing, Karver?"

"Shh." She starts to roll over and I grip her hip to stop her. I curl my fingers into the tops of her pants and pull them down. I bring my legs up to push them the rest of the way down with my feet. I spit on my hand and stroke my cock before lifting her leg and bringing it back to lay over me. I slide my cock in between her thighs and rub it along her pussy. I feel her arch back further, pushing my cock inside of her, making her moan. I slap my hand on her thigh and grip it tight. She reaches back, clawing at my arm. The bite of her scratches on my arm have me thrusting inside her hard and fast. Her moan echoes around the quiet room. I let go of her thigh and lean over her to grip her chin tight. I bring her mouth to mine, muffling her moans. There's so many things I want to say to her. Tell her how much I love her and that I hope she never fucking leaves like everyone else does. The thought of losing her sets me on edge and makes me thrust inside of her at a brutal pace, as if impaling her on my cock will keep her with me forever. Each angry thrust breaks the kiss over and over. It's all lips, tongues and teeth crashing together over and over, breathing each other's air.

Decker's pained, "Oww, fuck!" halts my thrusts.

I look behind me and find Decker rubbing the back of his

head with one hand and the other down his pants. "Dude, what the fuck are you doing?"

He pulls his hand out of his pants and steps away from the door. "Well, I was enjoying the show until *somebody* decided to bash my head in. Excuse me for having a little fun."

The door pushes open further to reveal Mousey pouting. My cock flags at the sight of her and Sloane pulls her pants up, discreetly pulling the blanket over us the best she can. Mousey doesn't see us at first and looks at Decker. "Oh no, I'm so sorry, honey."

I can feel how tense Sloane is as she mutters, "Kill me, now." I snort at her comment and it catches the nurse's attention. She gasps at the sight of my bare ass hanging out of the blanket, and in a flirtatious tone whispers, "Oh, my."

Sloane growls and throws the blanket against the wall. She crawls over me and stomps over to Mousey. She grabs the tray out of Mousey's hands and barks over her shoulder. "Boys, take your fucking meds."

Hot damn, okay, sweet clover. We run over and grab our med cups, watching as she slams the tray against Mousey's chest. She moves until she has the nurse pushed against the door. "Do you need another reminder that you're here to do your job and *nothing* else?"

Her mouth opens and closes like a fish. "I-I, y-ou, you can't talk to me like that."

"Drop the act, bitch. You can play damsel in distress all you want and try to fool everyone, but you can't fucking fool me." Sloane steps back and lets the tray fall to the floor. The crashing sound has the nurse startling and picking it up. She runs out of the room and the three of us lift our med cups to our mouths in sync. Sloane spins around quickly. "NO! Don't take those!"

We slowly drop the cups from our mouths and I tilt my head. "I never do, but why do you think we shouldn't?"

She glares at me. "Don't even get me started on that. I *know* you don't take yours. You're not as sneaky as you think you are." She nods at Decker and Axel. "But those two do take their meds. And as risky as it is for them to be off their meds, I think it's more of a risk taking ones administered by her."

I look over at them and watch as Decker looks down at his cup. A grimace slips past and he quickly corrects it by giggling. "This could be fun."

Axel's cup shakes in his grip. "This could get really bad, you guys. You think I have problems, now? It only gets worse without my meds."

Sloane walks up to him and gently pulls the cup from his hand. "I really don't want to scare you, Axel, but it could be a lot worse if you do take them. Please trust me on this. Maybe you can talk to the nurses and see if they'll start giving you your meds at night. That way you won't be off them, you just won't take them during that bitch's shift."

He longingly looks at the meds and then at her, slowly nodding his head. "Thank you."

Dinner time rolls around and we're all sitting at the table eating. I look over at Decker and Axel, and can already see the subtle changes in them from one missed dose. I don't think anyone else would notice, but I've been around these two fucks long enough to notice. Decker is his same pain in the ass self, but it's almost watered down. A few less giggles and cracked jokes. As for Axel, the extra fidgeting and hypervigilant eyes give him away.

I watch as Sloane pushes her food around. At first it looks like aimless moves, until I look closer and can see the landscape she's creating with it. My poor clover is missing her art. I hate that losing arts and crafts time has taken that away from her. I lean in and whisper in her ear, "You need to eat, sweets."

She turns her head to me and blinks a few times. "Huh?"

I nod to her food, and she looks down at it. "Oh."

She takes a bite and before she has a chance to take another, the sound of footsteps steals her attention. She drops her fork and her head shoots up to see who it is. Dr. Bart walks through the door and her shoulders drop. The tap of his loafers on the floor stops next to us and I look up. Fuck. He smiles at me and blind optimism shines in his eyes. "You're looking well, Karver. I was hoping we could go have that chat, now. What do you say?"

I open my mouth to make a smartass comment, only stopping when I feel Sloane's hand drawing circles on my thigh. I look at her and find her already staring at me, her eyes begging me to go. I playfully narrow my eyes at her and grumble, "Fine." Her eyes light up and she smiles big. Fuck. I'd do anything to keep that look on her face. I quickly kiss her temple and pick up my tray as I stand, the doctor trailing behind me as I dump my food and tray. "Alright, lead the way, doc."

He shuts his office door as I take a seat, the leather squeaking beneath me. I put a hand on each arm of the chair and drum my fingers on the wood. Dr. Bart takes a seat in his chair and lifts his tape recorder from the desk. He presses the record button with a click and brings it to his mouth. "This is Dr. Bart, I am here with Karver Damon Murphy for a check-in after loss and investigative purposes. It is currently May 28, 2024 at 5:33PM. Karver, do you give consent for me to record this session?"

The mention of investigative purposes has me gripping the wood tight until my hands cramp. "Normally I would say no, but I'm thinking I don't really have much choice, here."

With a rueful smile, he sighs. "Afraid not, Karver. I apologize. This is still your session, though. There is one choice I can give you. You can choose to talk about anything you want and then we get to the questions, or the other way around?"

Either option fucking sucks. My thoughts turn to the look in someone's eyes when death is making its call. Somehow, the thought morphs to thinking of Sloane and how I can get lost looking into hers, the way they change with every thought, every newfound emotion she discovers. Without pause, I open my mouth and words spill out.

"You always hear that you'll find all the answers in a person's eyes. They're the windows to the soul. Did you know your eyes dilate when you see someone you love?" I pause for a moment and look at him. He holds his chin in his palm as he listens intently. He gives a slight nod to my question and I continue. "It is also said that in anger, they dilate. I wonder if that's the prime example of the fine line between love and hate. In my opinion, the answer is both right and wrong, and only the beholder knows the truth deep down." I give a half-hearted shrug. "Then again, all the drugs you guys shove down our throats cause the same reaction. Maybe none of this is real. After all, we're all fucked in the head, right?" I suck in a breath, realizing how out of the norm this is for me. To sit here and ponder on things out loud, without lies tossed in between it all.

He leans forward and his brows furrow. "I love that you're willing to voice these thoughts with me." He puts his palm up before speaking again. "Don't get me wrong, we are all entitled to our own opinion. I just want to say, none of you are fucked in the head as you say. I don't see it that way. Everyone has battles in their mind, but it never means that any of you are fucked in the head. You didn't ask for these things. Nobody asks for the brain chemistry they're dealt, or the traumas that they endure. Okay?"

I nod and shrug at the same time, unsure of the right response.

"That's okay. This is new for you and it will take time to reconcile these thoughts and beliefs." The fight is evident on his face with what he has to say next and I find myself sitting up straight, unsure of where this is leading. "I'm sure you're not ready to dive into the loss of Karwyn, but part of our conversation has to do with that. Maybe we could try easing into that by just sharing a few thoughts and feelings. Did his death maybe bring up your feelings of abandonment that you've endured?" My heart races and my stomach rolls. I don't want to do this. I refuse to talk about it with him, but the damage is already done. The storm within me has begun. I feel the spiral of thoughts starting, but his next words seem to break through. "...Karver, there have been some concerns voiced about your whereabouts during the murders that have taken place."

What the fuck is he talking about? Concerns? From who? When? "The police have asked that I try to speak with you first, due to the circumstances of where we're at and all."

The police? Is this what he meant by investigative purposes? Fuck. My palms start to sweat and slip from the arms of the chair. "So, to start. Karver, what part of the ward were you at the night that Karwyn was murdered?"

"People with BPD are like people with 3rd degree burns over 90% of their bodies. Lacking emotional skin, they feel agony at the slightest touch or movement." - Dr. Marsha Linehan

---

28

Sloane

I walked back to the room with Axel and Decker a while ago. If I wasn't so worried about Nurse Ratchet trying to poison them, I'd tell them to just start taking their meds again. I didn't realize one dose would take its toll on them already. As soon as we walked into the room, they both went straight to bed and buried their heads under their pillows. I cross my arms over my chest and tuck my hands next to my body. I pace back and forth in the room while waiting for him to finally come back. I grimace at the feel of the extra skin of my arms.

I push back the thought. What the fuck is taking so long? There's no way he's actually talking to Dr. Bart. What if something happened to him? Fuck. What if... what if... no, nope, not even going there. Trying to avoid those thoughts brings my attention back to the extra weight I carry. I angrily squeeze each arm a few times and then drop my hands.

I stop pacing and look to make sure the boys are still asleep. I lift my shirt and tuck it under my chin, running my hands down my stomach and sides. I scrape my fingernails along the lightning strikes of stretch marks scattered along my stomach and sides. I wonder if I can fill these in with flesh-colored charcoal. I grab at the extra fat clinging to my sides and squeeze them tight. These really need to go. I don't want these anymore.

Without thought or pause, I find myself digging in the drawer for the blade I stole from the charcoal sharpener. I stand in front of the window and tuck my shirt under my chin again. The light of the moon guides me as I dig the blade into my right side. I grit my teeth and hiss at the first puncture from the tip of the blade. I feel the warmth from the blood spilling around the blade and dripping down. I run the blade across my skin and watch as it separates, more blood dripping and bubbling to the surface. I hear the door open as the rubber padding scrapes across the floor. Oh fuck. I slowly turn, forgetting that I've left myself exposed. I see Karver standing there, glaring in my direction and I'm frozen in place. I feel like I'm desperate for air, unable to get a full breath in. Hide it, hide it, hide it. He takes quick strides towards me until I'm pressed against the window, the blade biting into my skin again. I can see the rage boiling to the surface, but along with it, turmoil. Fear. He slowly breathes in through his nose. The moonlight showing his once bright green eyes are now a darkened shade. On an exhale, he mutters under his breath. Unsure, I ask, "What?"

A vein bulges at his temple, and I can see the rhythm of his heart pounding in the artery of his neck as he screams in my face. "YOU TRYING TO LEAVE ME, TOO?!"

My hair blows back from the force of his shout and a speck of spit hits my cheek. "What the fuck are you talking about?"

I hear the squeak of the bunks and watch as Axel peeks out, biting his nails. I look up and see Decker sitting against the wall with his knees to his chest. I look back at Karver and watch as he takes a few steps back and brings his hand to his chin. I follow the move and then watch his eyes scan my body, narrowing his eyes on the cut in my side. He swipes his thumb across his lip and sneers. "Go ahead and leave, I was fucking done with you, anyway. You were just a fucking toy to pass the time. You were so fucking easy to manipulate."

I know he's fucking lying to me but the words cut deep. My eyes well up with tears and my voice shakes. "Stop."

With a dark chuckle, he continues. "Look how fucking pathetic you are. You're so fucking desperate to feel, that you sucked up every fucking morsel of attention I gave you. All I had to do was fuck that pussy just right, throw in a couple I love you's and you were like a puppet on a fucking string." Swipe. I barely catch the motion with the tears blurring my vision.

I try to speak louder. "Stop it, Karver!"

He takes one step forward. "I hope you know that every time I said I love you, what I meant was I fucking hate you. Why do you think I lost my shit on you at the party? Because even then I fucking hated you. Every fucking thing about you. The way you talk, the way you laugh, your voice." He swipes his lip again, and looks me up and down in disgust. "*You.*"

231

My throat aches from the force of pushing my sobs down. With another measured step, I can see it in his eyes, he's going in for the final blow. He looks down at the blade still clutched in my shaking hand. "Do you think I find that attractive? Fucking look at you. A waste of skin, oxygen and fucking space. I told you to stop doing this shit, and you went and did it anyway. Next time you want to be fucking stupid, do us both a favor and cut closer to a fucking artery."

He swipes his lip one last time, followed by biting his lip hard enough that a drop of blood cascades down his chin. The words are a knife to my fucking heart. Lie or not, they cut deep and I can't hold my sobs back any longer. Tears pour down my face and I start sucking in air.

"Y-ou d-on't m-ean t-hat!" I suck in air and close the distance between us, slamming my fists into his chest over and over, "I know you fucking don't! You're lying! Why are you doing this?! I know you! I fucking know you better than anyone, Karver! Stop fucking hiding from me! Stop fucking pushing me away and blaming me for all the things that have hurt you in the past!"

He grabs my wrists to stop the blows and I feel him shaking, pushing and pulling me. "You don't know a fucking thing! I do fucking hate you! And I can't wait for you to fucking be gone! I don't fucking need you!" I shove and thrash against his chest as the tears continue to cascade down my cheeks.

"You're such an asshole. Fuck you. Why are you doing this?"

His panted breaths hit my face as he pushes my hands away from his chest. He steps back and grabs hold of his hair, pacing back and forth. "No. No. I'm not lying. You're lying. You're just like everybody fucking else! Fuck you, Sloane." He looks towards me once more and grits, "FUCK YOU!"

I look over his shoulder when I hear someone pounding on the door and shouting. My eyes widen when I notice Axel and Decker pressing their backs against the door. I nod at them and with a shuddered breath, I question Karver. "What the fuck happened with Dr. Bart?" I notice the flash of fear and turmoil in his eyes. "Just… just let me help you, Karver. Whatever it is, we can deal with it. *Together*. You're so worried about me fucking leaving, that you're trying to get me to actually leave. Does that actually make fucking sense to you?!"

He continues to ignore me, the grip on his hair getting tighter. I inch closer to him with every broken word. "Maybe I am fucking pathetic. Because here I am, still ready to walk by your side through all of this. After everything we've been through. After everything you've fucking said to me. I'm still fucking here! Stop being a fucking coward, Karver! Stop hiding. Let me in!"

He pulls his hands from his hair and I watch as the walls come crumbling down. A sob bursts forth. "I can't! I can't! I can't! I can't do it! Why do you even want me?! Why?! I'm such a fuck up!" The weight of it all brings him to his knees. I sink down and wrap my arms around him, letting him collapse against me.

People with BPD may have identity disturbances. They may try to find their identity in others or their relationships by mirroring them and feel like they don't know who they really are. Their hobbies, interests, speech patterns, dressing style change with the people around them.

29

Sloane

Karver and I lay side by side, his hand engulfing mine, our fingers intertwined. I watch as the darkness in the room is slowly swallowed by the sunlight, and roll my head to the side to look at him. His eyes are closed and his breaths are steady, but the furrow in his brow and clenched jaw tell me he's still awake. As much as I wish last night was just a nightmare, the pain in my heart and the knots in my stomach tell me it was very real.

I cradle Karver's head in my lap, running my fingers through his hair as he continues to quietly cry. Rain pelts the window, the timing tragically beautiful now that it's happening the very moment Karver's walls come crumbling down. The banging on the door briefly stops and Decker takes advantage of the moment, his goofy humor shining through. "Sorry, we can't come," he stops to giggle, "to the door right now! We're busy having an orgy and you're not invited!"

My throat feels raw from screaming and crying, and my voice cracks. "G-uys, go ahead and let them in so they can see that everything is okay." Axel shuffles to one side as Decker heavily sighs and opens the door like Vanna White.

"Welcome to our humble abode, but fuck you very much for the coitus interruptus."

The night guard and two orderlies storm through the door with flashlights, shining them around the room and I squint at the harsh light when it lands on us. Their heavy footfalls echo in the room as they walk over to us. The guard hovers above. "Everything good, here? He hurt?"

I shake my head. "N-o," I clear my throat and try again. "No. Not physically."

He lowers his flashlight and nods. With one last look at Karver, he turns around and the orderlies follow after him. They shut the door as they go and the guys shuffle awkwardly by it. "I'm sorry if we woke you. I've got it. You can go back to bed if you want."

Decker's goofy smile falls and he nods before climbing to the top bunk. Axel continues to shift from one foot to the other. "Do you need help moving him?" he mumbles.

Karver tenses, his hands gripping my thighs tighter. I look down at him and massage the back of his head. "No, it's okay, Axel. I got it. Thank you, though." I hear the squeak of the bed and watch as he crawls in and covers up. I drop a kiss to Karver's head and whisper in his hair. "Come on, Slasher. Let's get you to bed." He reluctantly pulls back so we can stand. I drop the razor into the drawer and then crawl into the bunk, Karver slowly following behind to lay side by side. He grabs hold of my hand, linking our fingers and squeezing.

With a shuddered breath, he whispers, "He knew about me. At least, young me. His mind just wouldn't let him remember." He rubs his hands down his face. "I hate my brain, Clover. Do you know that? It doesn't ever shut the fuck up. It takes whatever I'm feeling and maxes out the voltage. When I love you, I fucking love you with everything that I am. And if I can siphon more of it from somewhere I would, just to give it to you. But when I hate you, fuck, do I hate you. I think and wish for the worst of things in the moment, and I fucking hate myself for it.

Everything is too much, all the fucking time. Even at baseline, every-thing is heightened. When I'm sad, I'm fucking drowning. When I'm happy, I'm a goddamn ray of sunshine. I didn't just lose my friend, Thumper; I lost my pops. And damn near until the very end I was so fucking mad at him. Nothing was fixed. Nothing was talked about. So many missed opportunities and conversations. So now I'm left with this boiling anger at him, a mountain of confusion, and this ache inside me that feels suffocating."

As much as I want to talk, I know he needs to just let it out piece by piece, even if it takes all night. I lay there and listen to him all throughout the night, telling me how his Nana would visit Thumper while he was at school, and he wishes he could've gone with.

Then he drops the bomb that Dr. Bart had to question him about his whereabouts for all of the murders here. I watch as he rolls his head to look at me and his eyes widen, panic taking over. Before he can spiral over letting his walls down with me, I squeeze his hand.

"What's spilled in the dark shall never come to light, remember?" Relief washes over his features and he releases the breath he was holding.

Karver

Before my eyes are even open, I feel the loss of my clover's warmth immediately. I crack an eye open and the moon-light shines the perfect spotlight on her. I watch as she stands at the door, peering out the small window. I watch as she brings her hand down and starts extending one finger at a time as if she's counting something. What the fuck is she doing? She uncurls her fingers and slowly opens the door.

She peeks her head out and I quickly shut my eye as she looks over her shoulder. I hear the door shut and throw the blanket off me. I climb out of bed and walk to the door. I crack the door open and Decker pipes up, "Need back up, Karv?"

Without looking back, I shake my head, "No," and peek out the door. I watch as she tiptoes down the hall with her head on swivel. She peeks into the exam room where Leeba was murdered and slowly walks in. I walk over and press my back to the wall, listening to my surroundings. There's not an employee in sight, or that I can hear, for that matter. She must have been waiting for shift change. How fucking long has she been clocking this for?

I hear her shuffling around in the room, opening and closing cabinets and drawers. She may have planned out shift change, but she definitely didn't figure out how to be fucking quiet. She's just begging for us to get caught. I'm also fucking pissed at her for taking this risk. She has no clue who the fucking killer is and just wants to walk around alone where anything could happen. I'm shaken from my thoughts which are veering towards the worst case scenario, and hear a final drawer shut, followed by a heavy sigh. Her muffled footsteps get closer and as she steps out she looks at me eyes wide and mouth falls open. A squeak falls from her lips before my hand is smashed against her mouth, muffling it. My hand gets hot and clammy, vibrating as she talks against it. I shake my head and growl. "What the fuck are you doing, Sloane?"

She narrows her eyes and I smirk, knowing what she plans to do. Her mouth opens behind my hand and she bites the flesh of my palm. I press my palm further against her teeth and she releases her hold and I drop my hand. "Just go back to the room, Karver."

I snort. "Yeah, that's not fucking happening. You really think I'm going to leave you to walk around alone with a killer on the loose?"

She scoffs with a humorless laugh and crosses her arms. "Gee, I don't know, Karver. You sure had no problem with my death being at my own hands. So why not let the killer get the job done?"

I drop my head, ashamed at the memory of the fucked up shit I said to her. I fucking hate myself for it. I'll never forget the words I said and the reaction it caused. At the time I didn't give a fuck, it needed to be done. I needed her to hurt like I was hurting. I needed to be the cause of our downfall. Now I have no idea if I can even fix this, and if I can, I sure as fuck don't know how. How the fuck do you mend a heart you shattered? If I have to, I'll happily cut myself on every shattered piece I pick up, just so I can try to put it back together for her. And when it inevitably crumbles again, I'll start all over.

I lift my head and notice that she left me behind with my thoughts. I run down the hall as quiet as I can, whisper-shouting, "Sloane." She keeps walking without even looking in my direction. "Goddammit, woman, wait for me." I catch up to her and huff, "Seriously? Did you not hear a fucking thing I said?"

"Oh, I heard you alright. I always fucking hear you, Karver. Even without you saying a fucking thing, I'm always hearing you. I'm trying this new thing out. Ignoring you." Why is it so fucking hot when she gives me a fucking attitude? I adjust my twitching cock and groan. She looks at me and then follows where my hand is, her eyes widen.

"Really, Karver?"

I lift my hands in the air, "Hey, don't blame me. Not my fault you're sexy when you're pissy."

She rolls her eyes and starts walking again. "You're annoying."

I get as close to her as I can as she walks and sing-song, "Yeahhh, but you still love me."

"What's that saying? I will always love you, but right now, I don't like you very much."

"Hey, I'll take it. That's better than nothing, right? What are we doing here, anyway?" She spins around and I quickly stop. She mirrors my move from earlier and slaps her hand over my mouth.

"I'm getting the proof I need to prove all this shit is that ratchet bitch's fault. Just need to find out where they keep the surveillance feed at." I open my mouth to tell her that Dr. Bart said the footage was compromised, but she holds up her hand. "Now, shut the fuck up or go back to the room before your big mouth gets us-"

The creak of a door stops her mid-sentence. We slowly look at the door, and stand there frozen in place. Fuck. Dr.

Dead steps out with a smile on his face. He looks up and sees us both, his smile falling. He shakes his head and mouths, "Stay there."

He peeks his head back into the door, "I just realized we didn't reschedule. I have a date with the dead, so I'll have to give you a call to figure that out. Have a good one, Dr. Bart." He steps back and closes the door. He walks over to Sloane and attempts to hug her. She steps back and he quietly chuckles. "Still not a fan of hugs, I see."

He looks at me and I watch as he shoots a glare in my direction. His scowl is gone just as fast as it appeared and he looks back at Sloane, whispering, "What are you doing out of your room? It's not safe, you know that. Come on, let's get you back before you *both* get caught sneaking around. Wouldn't want to be accused of the murders, would ya?"

I step towards him. "What did you just say?"

Sloane places her hand over my heart and slightly pushes. "Let's just go." I stand stock still and stare him down, my fists balled tight. "*Slasher.*" I look down at Sloane and see her plea to walk away. My fingers shakily unfurl from my palms and I spin around with a huff.

On the way back to our room, we pass by the arts and crafts room and I stop. I walk backwards until I'm in front of the door and peer through the window. I try the door-knob and find the room locked. "What are you doing?" Dr. Dead questions. I look at the card reader and back at him.

"Hey, you wanna open this for us?"

He furrows his brow. "What?"

I turn to fully face him and cross my arms. "Listen. We need in there. For Sloane. It takes a badge to get in there, and *you* have a badge."

Sloane steps in between us and puts her hand on my chest. I look down at her as she questions, "What are you doing? I don't need anything."

"Yes you do. I pay attention more than you think I do. I know how much you're missing your art. So let's get you some things so you can keep doing what you love and what you're amazing at."

I look back at Dr. Dead. "All we need is for you to scan us in, and then you can go on your way and act like you know nothing about this. You care about her, right?"

A vein pops in his forehead, and he seethes, "Of course I do."

I tilt my head to the door. "Okay, so help us out."

With a huff, he yanks on his badge and the pull string groans from the forceful pull. He slaps his badge against the reader and it blinks green with a beep. The lock disengages with a click and I open the door. He releases his badge and it snaps back into place. He puts his hand on Sloane's shoulder and she shrugs away from his touch. He places his hands up. "Still hate touch, I see. Take care of yourself, Sloane." He looks at me and narrows his eyes and then back to her. "Please be careful. You never know who you can trust here."

BPD is not a trend. It is not cute or quirky. It's a debilitating condition which, without the appropriate support and treatment, can have a significant negative impact on the person's life.

30

Sloane

I stand under the showerhead with my eyes closed, the tepid water cascading over me. How the fuck am I going to find proof against this bitch? There was nothing in the exam room Leeba was murdered in. I knew there was a chance of everything being found and bagged for evidence, but dammit, I was really hoping. My backup plan was the surveillance footage and Karver said that was compromised. So now what the fuck do I do? I already follow her moves the best I can when we're allowed out of our rooms.

The door creaks open and I sigh. I wipe the water from my eyes as I step out from under the spray. Before my eyes are open, I spit, "It's not time for my shower check yet."

My eyes shoot open when I hear Karver's voice dripping with lust. "I'm sure as fuck not here to check the shower, sweet clover." He prowls towards me, stripping his clothes as he goes. My eyes get stuck in a battle of where to look.

Cock, necklace, eyes, clover, over and over. I can hear the smile in his tone when he says, "You're staring, sweets."

I continue to stare at his cock as it twitches and whisper, "No, I'm not."

I yelp when I'm quickly spun around and pressed against the wall. He presses against me and slides his cock between my thighs and I moan from the friction. It's not enough, I need more. I try to arch back and he presses me against the wall harder. He brings his mouth to my ear and whispers, "Now, you're not looking."

I can't tell if it's the chill from being out of the water or the anticipation of what's to come that has me shivering. His palm splays between my shoulder blades and he pushes forward. I arch my ass against him and he groans as his cock slides between my clenched thighs. "As much as I miss your pussy gripping me tight, we have to be quick. Are you gonna be a good girl and take everything I give you?" I'm lost in the moment and forget to answer. My yelp morphs into a moan with the crack of his hand against my ass. He squeezes the cheek tight and rubs away the sting. "Answer me, sweets. Or I'll leave you desperate and aching for my cock, while I stroke myself until I cum all over you."

I slap my hand against the wall. "Yes!"

"Good girl."

He rubs his cock along my soaked pussy and then thrusts forward. I slam against the wall with the force of it. "Ugh, fuck, Slasher."

He wraps his arm across my body and grips my shoulder to hold me in place, panting, "I'm sorry, I'm sorry."

His thrusts get faster and harder, the tip of his cock hitting my g-spot over and over. I'm so close to cumming, but my body refuses to fall over the edge. I feel his hips falter and his grunts grow louder. "Don't you fucking dare cum without me, Karver!"

He grits, "I'm. Trying. Not. To."

Pain. I need pain. "Bite me. Bite me, Karver." I feel his teeth sink into my shoulder and I gasp. His teeth scrape against my skin with every thrust. "Harder. Make me bleed, Slasher." I feel the pinch of his teeth gripping my skin. I start to feel the warmth of blood pooling to the surface as my orgasm hits me. "Fuuu-mmmm." His hips slam forward once more and he stays in place. Aftershocks hit me with every spurt of cum and I press my forehead against the cold wall.

Karver

After getting cleaned up and dressed, we walk out of the bathroom. Mousey is standing there with the med tray and a scowl on her face. Axel and Decker tower behind her, both looking down at the floor. I grab my meds and pop them in my mouth, followed by a cup of water. Without a word, she walks away and I spit my meds into the paper cup. Everyone continues to stand there and I look at Sloane, who is glaring at Mousey's retreating back.

"Uhh, guys? Let's go before we miss breakfast." They all stand still as if they didn't hear me. With a huff, I raise my voice. "Guys?!"

Their heads all shoot up and in unison say, "Huh?"

247

I throw my arms out, "Breakfast. Let's go." I grab Sloane's hand and pull her down the hall with me. I look over my shoulder to see the two of them shadowing us.

Walking into the cafeteria, I throw away my cup into the trash can and beeline for the food. Sloane shakes her hand from my hold and I glare at the empty space between us. I slowly lift my head. "The fuck?"

She shakes her arm at me. "You're gonna rip my fucking arm off, chill."

"Ugh, fine," I retort, rolling my eyes. I walk behind her and start pushing her towards the food. "There. Better?"

She swings her arm behind her, swatting me in the side. "No, not better. Why are you in such a fucking hurry?"

"Because I'm not about to be stuck in a room where all four of us are hangry. We already have one murderer on the loose, let's not add to that list." Axel whines and speeds up to walk next to me and Sloane.

Decker remains behind us and mutters, "Killers could take me out."

I look over my shoulder and lift a brow at his lowered head. I look forward and bring my mouth to Sloane's ear. "We need to get this guy back on his meds. He goes any longer, he'll be the next dead body."

I feel her body tense with my words and she spins out of my hold to look at him. "Decker?"

He slowly lifts his head, his eyes vacant. "Yeah?"

"Why don't you go first and help Axel find a spot for us to sit?"

"Okay," he replies in a monotone voice.

Sloane

I sit on the edge of Karver's bed and lean against the wall. I didn't think I missed my art as much as he said I did until I brought the charcoal to paper. Karver is sitting against the wall in front of me with his green clover mask on. I outline his form with his right leg stretched out and the left knee up. He lets his left arm dangle over his knee and the right holds his knife over his thigh. His head is supposed to be tilted for the piece, but he's spent most of the time rolling his head side to side.

"Do you need a break? I can just finish it by memory."

His head shoots in my direction and he sits up straight. "What? No. What did I do wrong?"

"If you're not comfortable down there, it's fine. You're just moving your head a lot and it's supposed to stay in one place."

He lifts his arm from his knee and waves it. "Okay, okay. I'll stop. It's fine." The door hisses as it's pushed open and I quickly shove the supplies under the bed. So much for that. I shove my charcoal-covered hands in the pockets of my pants and swivel around to face whoever has walked in. The older guard walks in with his hands on his utility belt.

A look of shame crosses his features and he sighs, "Karver?" I quickly look at Karver and then back to the guard, as two police officers step in behind him. I jump from the bed and stand between Karver and all of them.

"What the fuck is going on?"

The officers walk on either side of the guard and block his view. The one on the right looks past me. "Karver Murphy? We're going to need you to come with us."

I hear his footsteps behind me and his warmth on my back. "For what?" He asks.

"We're going to need to ask you a few questions."

Axel curls in on himself and starts rocking back and forth, his hands cover his ears and he hums to ignore what's happening. Decker watches everything unfold, but not a single smartass comment is dropped. "I already answered questions with Dr. Bart the other night. He said he would talk to you guys about it and then it would be dropped," Karver says. The guard stands taller so he can be seen over the heads of the officers.

"Dr. Bart is dead."

Quiet gasps fill the air and I'm not sure if it was one or all of us. Karver pulls me behind him and shouts, "Well, I sure as fuck didn't kill him!"

The guard pushes between the officers with his hand up in the air. "We know that. Dr. Bart killed himself. But he left a note with more questions than answers. Since the police can't talk to him directly about your conversation, they need to talk to you. Please don't make this difficult and just walk with them for questioning. Also, they're going to need to see your masks."

"Go fuck yourselves. I didn't do shit."

I watch as he reaches into his pocket, and realize he's going for his knife. Without thought, my hand shoots out and I cover his through the pocket. I move around him and wrap my other arm around his neck, pulling him closer to me. I stand on my tiptoes and whisper, "Please don't. Just go answer their questions and get it out of the way."

I pull back and look at him and the look of betrayal guts me. "You think I did this, Sloane?"

I put my hand over his heart and shake my head. "*No*. I just don't want anything bad happening if you go this route. *Please*, Slasher."

He squeezes me tight against him and I feel him nod against the top of my head. "I get to come back here, right?"

The younger officer chuckles. "Guess it depends on what you've been up to at night."

With a deep chuckle, Karver says, "Fucking my sweet clover. Something you know nothing about, little boy blue balls."

I roll my eyes and scoff. "You're unbelievable."

"Why, thank you, sweets."

I pull away from him and move aside. "Now you're on your own, asshole. Go give them *real* answers."

The guard holds his hand up. "The masks?"

Karver shrugs and walks out of the room with a sing-song voice, "I don't know what you're talking about." I watch as the door slowly shuts and feel the tug in my heart, begging for its other half to come back.

BPD: Imagine having emotions so intense that it physically disables you. Now imagine on top of that feeling shame, embarrassment and guilt for having the emotions in the first place.

To Whoever Finds Me First:

I apologize that the image of me will be one you
carry with you for the rest of your life. I
fooled myself into believing that I was making a
difference here. I really did try. Or so I
thought. My patients and staff are all dropping
like flies at the hands of one of our very own.
It is unclear if it is a staff member or patient
committing these murders.
It's been brought to my attention that one of my
patients in particular,Karver Murphy, is a
person of particular interest. A friend of mine
has voiced his concerns, almost in a frantic
sense. It is hard to tell for sure if these are
sound accusations or just the cries from a
broken man grieving the loss of his wife.
The police have mentioned they have found masks
at every crime scene, and there's only one
patient I have with these masks. Karver. The
problem is, anyone can get a hold of these
masks. It wouldn't be difficult to take some
from him, and if it's a staff member, they can
easily access such an item. I just don't know
what I'm doing wrong here. Either I have a
patient that is so far gone they've become a
murderer, or worse, I don't trust my credentials
enough to know for sure what's truth and lie.
Why didn't I see this sooner? Is there even
anything to be seen? Or is it all a ruse? I
can't handle the uncertainty. The failure. I'm
sorry I couldn't be as strong as I try to teach
my patients to be. I'm so sorry I took the out
that I fight to ensure they don't. I have failed
you all. I am so sorry.

Dr. Fletcher Bart

31

Karver

I feel dead on my feet as I'm escorted back to the room. I've lost track of how long they've been pestering me with the same fucking questions over and over. They believed I would trip up if they worded it differently. Fucking idiots. I spin around with my back to the door. "It's been fun, boys. Let's schedule a time to do this again, yeah? Preferably between the weeks of go, fuck and yourself."

I give them a salute and push back into the room. I slowly shut the door and smirk at their annoyed expressions. I squint at the brightness from the sun peeking through the window and kick my slides across the room. They smack into the dresser and fall to the floor. I pull my shirt off and crawl into my bed, finding Sloane already curled up there. I brush her hair away from her face and find her silently crying. "Hey, hey, hey. What's going on?"

I lay on my back and pull her to lay across my chest. She sniffles and I feel her tears dripping down my collarbones.

"Are they going to take you away from me?" her voice cracks.

I wrap my arms around her and rub her back. "Not a chance, sweets. They'll have to try a whole hell of a lot harder than that."

"Tell me about it. What did they ask? Why did they want your masks?"

I tap her ass. "Whoa, whoa, whoa. Slow down. It was more mind games than anything else. They just kept asking me the same things over and over, trying to trick me. It didn't work, by the way. It's fine. Everything is fine."

I feel her body tense, a question boiling beneath the surface, and my own body responds the same. I roll her to the side and hover over her. She refuses to meet my eye. "Holy fuck. You think I did it, don't you?"

She gasps and looks at me, eyes wide. "No! I just," she sighs, "what if there's enough against you? Even if you didn't do it, what if whatever they have found is enough for you to get in trouble? I mean, out of everyone here, why are you the only one they've questioned?"

Her breathing picks up, her thoughts causing her to panic. I slam my lips to hers to silence the fear spilling from her lips. Her muffled, "Mmm," vibrates against my lips. I bite her lip and her gasp grants me access to her mouth. The taste of her blood blooms like wine on my tongue as I slide mine against hers. She groans in frustration as if she can't decide if she wants to pull my shirt up or pull my pants down. I tilt back from the kiss and kneel above her. "Clothes. Off," I demand, as I yank my own shirt and pants off.

Her shirt and bra come off but she struggles to get her pants off fast enough. I slap her hands away and curl my fingers around the top and yank them down until they're off and at the end of the bed. I start to crawl over her body and she huffs in annoyance. She quickly sits up and grabs my chain, yanking me towards her and kissing me hard. In between kisses she pants, "Need. You. Now."

I wrap my hand around her throat and push her down to the bed. I line myself up and thrust forward, slamming my hips against her. Her back arches, bringing her body closer to me and I lean down to suck her left nipple into my mouth. I swirl my tongue around the bud before biting until she hisses. I release her nipple with a pop and she yanks on my chain again. Sweat drips from my forehead and lands on her cheek, sliding along her jaw and neck. I slow down and swivel my hips before slamming forward, her moans coming from the deepest parts of her. I kiss along her jaw line and down to her neck, my tongue sliding and flicking, the salt of her sweat mixes with the aftertaste of her blood and it's fucking intoxicating. The urge to mark her is all-consuming and I sink my teeth into the side of her neck. I can feel her pulse pounding against my tongue as I suck the flesh into my mouth. My fucking girl loves the pain and it shows when she can't help but thrust against me over and over while moaning. I release my hold on her neck and lick around the already forming bruise. I drop to my forearms and bring us closer together. I look into her hypnotizing eyes, the swirl of colors reminiscent of the world, and the burst of sunflowers that surround her pupils pull me in. Every inch of her is the very definition of beauty. I wish she could fucking see it for herself. Her nails dig into my chest, the burn of the cuts and blood dripping down catches my attention. "143, Slasher."

The look in her eyes and the words combined have me on the verge of cumming. "Fuck. Cum for me, sweets." I kiss her deep and bring my hand down to her tit and squeeze tight. I loosen my grip, pinching and twisting her nipple, feeling her pussy clamp around my cock. Her body jolts over and over as she cums. I follow behind and drop my weight to her, breathing heavily. "Whatever happens, 143, Clover."

Sloane

I woke up to a new mark on me. 'Beautiful' was written in small letters along my forearm. I smile at it, remembering all the times he's done it before. We probably slept about twenty minutes, if that, before Nurse Ratchet woke everyone for meds and breakfast. I glare daggers at her the whole time as if they'll deliver the final blow, extinguishing the bitch from existence. If only it was that easy. Decker lays in bed, refusing to move or acknowledge anyone. I whisper in Karver's ear. "You think it's okay to leave him here?"

Karver shrugs and grabs my hand. "His stomach will win and he'll join us soon, I'm sure."

We walk into the hall and quickly realize we're not being escorted to the cafeteria. Karver and I look around, confused, while Axel brings his fingers to his mouth and nervously looks up and down the hall. Nurse Ratchet goes to the next room as we continue on towards the cafeteria. We slow down to a stop while in line and Axel bumps into us. I start to fall forward and Karver steadies me. "Easy, Ax."

"S-sorry."

After getting our trays of food, we find a table to sit at and watch as the other patients start pouring into the cafeteria. Axel quickly gets up and speed walks to our side of the table. He sits down and presses his body against mine. His voice shakes as he asks, "W-hat's going on, guys? This isn't right. Something is wrong."

Karver drops his fork with a clatter. "Alright, alright. Chill, Ax. I'll try and find out what the fuck is going on and check on Decker, too. Okay?"

He kisses my cheek and murmurs, "You good here, sweets?"

I turn towards him, leaving a chaste kiss on his lips. "Yeah, Slasher. We're fine here."

Karver

I shove my hands in my pockets as I walk down the hall, looking for one of the workers. I stop in my tracks when I realize my knife isn't in my pocket. Dammit. Fucking thing must have fell out of my pocket when I took my pants off this morning.

Is there some sort of fucking weird takeover happening here? No fucking staff in sight and everyone is out of their rooms. Damn, maybe Sloane and I passed out fucking hard and this is a weird-ass fucking dream. I go to open the door and hear a scraping noise, followed by a crunch. I look down and find one of my blank masks crushed beneath my foot. What the fuck? I push the door open as I bend down to pick it up. I shut the door behind me as I look at the damage done to the mask. Out of the corner of my eye I catch sight of something on the floor and look up. The mask falls from my fingertips and the blood drains from my face. Decker lies on the floor, coughing up blood and gasping for air as a knife sticks out of his chest. Not just any knife… it's my knife. I run over to him and slip in the pool of blood, falling to my knees next to him.

"It's okay, Deck, it's all good man," I try to reassure him. I press my hands on either side of the blade and push down to try and stop the bleeding. More blood seems to spill around my fingers.

"Fuck. Fuck. Fuck. What did you do, ya fuck? Why would you do this shit?" Decker attempts to talk, but only his labored breathing and gurgles of blood can be heard. He grits his teeth and his eyes keep looking past me.

"What, man, what?"

I look over my shoulder and time stops.

No fucking way.

The average life expectancy for someone with BPD is 27 years old.

32

Sloane

Axel and I sit at the table, our food forgotten as we anxiously await Karver's return. I bounce my knee while Axel sits beside me, mumbling against his fingertips. While my eyes keep going to the doorway, looking for Karver, my mind drifts to one of our late night talks.

Cradled up against Karver's side, his comforting hold is like a cocoon protecting me from the rest of the world. Thoughts circle my mind and spill from my lips before I can stop them. "Slasher?"

"Hmm?"

"Do you ever wonder if we live in some other reality?"

"What do you mean, Clover?"

I sigh, trying to get my thoughts in order. "Like... as shitty as things can be here, do you ever wonder if we exist in another time and space where it's far worse and this is all in our heads to escape that reality?"

"I don't know. I mean, when things are bad, they're really fucking bad. And if this is better than reality, then I don't ever want to wake up to discover what that is. The all-consuming thoughts that scream I should kill myself in this reality are already hard enough to fight. I don't think I'd survive another possibility. And a world where you don't exist isn't a place I'd ever want to be. I'd cut my own fucking heart out just to stop the pain of not having you."

A single tear falls from my eye as I confess, "I wish you always felt that way. Not wanting to die, but not wanting to be in a world without me. I wish your love for me could overcome your demons."

He tenses beneath me and pulls his arms away. He slides out from under me and sits up. "Do you think I enjoy feeling that way? Do you think I want there to be times when I can't fucking stand the sight of you? To hear you? To know you? To wish nothing but the worst for you? Do you think I enjoy creating issues to push you away and make you leave before you inevitably decide to leave me?

I fucking hate it, Sloane. I'd give anything for this," he stabs at his temple with his fingers, "to fucking function properly. I'd love to think right, act right, feel right." I take a deep breath through my nose and start crawling out of the bed. He grips the back of my shirt, holding me in place. "Where the fuck are you going? What? You're just done with the conversation that you started?"

I look over my shoulder. "I may have started the conversation, Slasher, but you took it in a whole different direction all on your own. You're twisting my words and getting defensive. Don't start a fight where there isn't one."

He lets go of my shirt, crawls out of the bed and throws his arms out. A humorless laugh falls from his lips. "This is exactly what I'm talking about. Do you think I fucking want to? I can't help it, Sloane. Don't you fucking get that? The demons upstairs will win every fucking time. If you can't fucking handle that, then just be done now.

Seriously. Just fucking go. Leave like everyfuckingbody else. I don't fucking need you," thumb swipes his bottom lip, "I don't need anybody," swipe, "I've made it this far."

I get out of the bed and stand in front of him with my arms crossed. "Done yet?"

"The fuck you mean, am I done yet?"

"We're not doing this tonight. Your own body betrays you every time you lie to me. So get the fuck back to bed. I'm not going anywhere and neither are you."

I jolt at the heavy hand shaking my shoulder. I blink a few times and look at Axel. I place my hand over his to stop him before he throws me out of my seat. "What's up, Axel?" He mumbles against his fingers while his eyes scan the room. I tap his hand and point down. "I can't hear you through your fingers. What's up?"

He shakily drops his hand and whispers, "I gotta piss real bad, Sloane."

For a moment I'm confused. "Okay?" His eyes continue to bounce around the room. Realization dawns on me. "Oh, fuck, right. Alright, let's go."

As we step out of the cafeteria, I notice some of the staff talking amongst themselves. I start to walk in their direction to ask why restrictions have been lifted, when Axel steps in front of me, vibrating in place. His eyes are wide. "Sloane, please. Have. To. Go. Bad."

I run my fingers through my hair and nod. "Alright, let's go. Maybe Karver got some answers and he's trying to wake Decker up." Every few steps, the casual brush of Axel's arm against mine turns a little more forceful and he mutters an apology each time. He stops in front of the bathroom door and looks over his shoulder at me like a lost puppy. "Nobody is down here, Axel. I'm just going to check the room for Karver and Decker. It'll be really quick, okay? You got this."

He drops his head and starts inhaling and exhaling slowly. He lifts his head and a look of determination transforms before my eyes. "Okay. I can do this, Sloane."

"Fuck yeah, ya can. I'll see you in a minute."

I walk to our room and push the door slightly open until it's met with resistance. "Slasher? Decker?" I holler.

The door quickly opens and I'm suddenly grabbed by the arms and yanked into the room. My view of the room is blocked as I'm shaken like a ragdoll. "See?! See?! I told you! I told you!" Corbin frantically shouts in my face.

His hair is disheveled, sweat dripping down his face and an almost giddy expression on his face. "Corbin, slow down. Told me what? What is going on?"

He steps aside and throws his arms out to the carnage before me. No. Unable to form words, I fall back against the door I feel like I'm stuck in a tunnel, the only thing I see is Decker bleeding out on the floor, and Karver with his hands around the knife in Decker's chest. I shake my head. "No, no, no. What is this? WHAT IS THIS?!"

The world spins and I find myself stepping forward but freezing. I keep looking at Corbin then back at Karver and Decker on the floor. Karver's face is one of complete shock and desperation as he continues to press down on the wound. "I can't. I can't make it stop. It just won't stop. Why won't it stop?" Karver chants.

Corbin grips my upper arms tightly and shakes me. "We have to go, Sloane. We have to tell someone. It's him. It was him all along. I have to get you out of here. Come on. Before he kills us, too."

I swear I hear a muffled bellow outside the door, but nothing is making sense right now. "What? No. I... He..."

I turn to Karver. "Slasher?"

He starts shaking his head, torn between looking at me and helping Decker. "I... it's not..."

Corbin opens the door and starts pulling me out of the room. "Wait. No. Corbin, wait." I beg and plead as he drags me out of the room. My heart is breaking and I'm not sure if it's because I'm leaving Karver behind or if it's the worry that maybe he really did do all of this. No. He couldn't. He wouldn't.

Corbin pushes me down the hall until we reach the rec room. He steps in front of me and I see his mouth moving but the words don't register. His finger is in my face before leaving me standing there to go talk to one of the guards. As they talk with serious expressions on their faces, the guard's eyes widen and glance over me before looking at the direction we came from. He nods his head and then presses the button for the doors. Corbin starts waving me towards him and on auto-pilot, I follow his lead. The loud buzz on the door goes off and they automatically open to allow us through. We walk through them and I can't help but continuously look over my shoulder until we step onto the elevator.

People with BPD are emotionally volatile. They are known for expressing their irritability through angry outbursts, often directed at someone the person with BPD loves and trusts. Typically there's no explanation and no warning signs.

33

Axel

Fuck. I hate being so afraid and paranoid all the time. I feel like the shadows are speaking to me. Something sinister is hiding, just biding its time to leap out and attack. I never know if it's the darkness within, or something truly evil is waiting for me. I quickly go to the bathroom and look over my shoulder the whole time, searching every corner of the bathroom. I finish pissing and skip washing my hands so I can get back to my friends... to Karver.

I shake my head. No. Stop thinking about him that way. It's wrong. He belongs to sweet Sloane. She's good for him. I need to find someone good for me. Someone who doesn't unknowingly blur the lines.

I yank the door open and search the hall for anyone or anything that will jump out. The door is cracked open and I hear a man shouting, "See! See! I told you! I told you!"

"Corbin, slow down. Told me what? What is going on?"

Corbin? Her stepdad. Dr. Dead. My heart races and my palms sweat. I remember. I remember. Nobody would listen to me. I tried to tell everyone. I saw him. I saw him. He hurt that poor old lady, LeeAnn. I thought he was comforting her until… until he wasn't. The crack of her skull replays in my head, the sound of a wooden bat shattering when it slams into a baseball. Her blood flowed like a river. I bring my hand to my mouth and nibble on my fingers. I need to help my friends. How do I help them? What do I do?

Corbin's next words have me seeing red. "We have to go, Sloane. We have to tell someone. It's him. It was him all along. I have to get you out of here. Come on. Before he kills us, too."

I shout against my fingertips and stomp down the hall. I have to fix this. They can't put this on Karver. He didn't do this. I have to save him.

Oh no. What about sweet Sloane? Is she like Corbin? Will she be a sweet, venomous snake and betray Karver? I know what I have to do. Can I do it? Yes. Yes, I can. For Karver I can. I have to. I can't let them do this to him.

Without a second thought, my feet move me to the cafeteria. I ignore the few patients still eating in here and walk through the door to the kitchen. The staff look up at the squeak of the door opening and freeze in place. Some get back to work and others look at me in confusion. I watch as one takes the long way around to reach the phone. I use my size to my advantage and shove a staff member away from the hanging knives. I pull down the biggest one and wrap my fingers around the wooden handle. I hold it out in front of me, swiping it every which way as I walk through the kitchen. Most of the staff huddle in the corner of the kitchen and a few run towards me as if to stop me.

I pretend I'm a swashbuckling pirate and swiftly slash the first across the neck, followed by a sharp stab into the stomach. I can't tell if the red I see is all the blood, or if it's just my vision. I slip and trip over the blood and bodies on the floor. With every kill, flashes of Karver taking the fall start. As I move through the cafeteria, everyone's faces morph from blurry shapes to those of my parents. I remember every scream, every threat and malicious word thrown my way by my parents. Every hit and kick. Every missed meal. I remember it all, and it's as if I'm feeling it all again, using it as fuel to do what I need to.

Sloane

My mind spins at everything that just transpired. Corbin is practically dragging me along with him. The pull to be with Karver is almost unbearable. He pushes the door open to his morgue and I rub my hands up and down my arms in an attempt to warm up. Corbin runs around the room, shuffling through paperwork on one counter then moving to another. "Corbin, can you please explain this to me. What has happened? What do you know?"

A dark chuckle leaves him and he shakes his head, moving on to drawers. "What do I know? What don't I know? It's him. I know it's him. *I have proof.*"

My stomach rolls and I feel sweat dripping down my back. Something is off. I no longer feel the chill of the room, and press my fingers against the metal cabinets that bodies go in. Does he really have proof? I continue to run my fingers along the cabinets to feel the chill against my now hot skin. "What proof do you have, Corbin?"

"Proof, yes, proof. The best proof. The nail in his coffin. The green mask with clovers on them. He left it behind after he killed your mother. Can you believe that? What an idiot."

I stumble at his words and furrow my brow. That's not possible. We made that mask here. "Are you sure about that, Corbin?"

He scoffs at my words, "Am I sure? Of course I'm sure!" I jump at his bellow and take a deep breath. A drink. Yes, I think I need a drink. I walk to one of his fridges, grab the handle and as I open it he shouts, "NO!"

I roll my eyes at his outburst. "Relax, I'm just getting a-WHAT THE FUCK?!" I step aside and wave an arm towards the fridge. I swallow the bile rising in my throat. "What the fuck is this, Corbin?"

I watch in horror as his panic-stricken face morphs into a dark smirk, his eyes now distant as he stares into the fridge. In a daze, he whispers, "You weren't supposed to see that."

A person with BPD may react to a seemingly insignificant event, such as a misunderstanding, with very strong feelings of anger and unhealthy expressions of anger such as yelling, being sarcastic or physically violent.

BLEEDING HEARTS

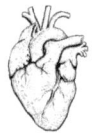

Every slice into a cadaver over the years has always felt erotic to me. I quickly learned in school to keep myself pressed against the table at all times. It even got so bad, I had to invest in wearing a cup over my cock. When I finally got the medical examiner position and had the space to myself, I got to really play. I'd make sure to lock the door and jerk off at the sight of the cadaver's cracked open chest. There came a time when that just wasn't enough anymore. I could get hard, but I couldn't cum anymore. I found it increasingly frustrating that it no longer worked.

The only time I could cum these days was after Denise was knocked out from her sleeping meds, and I'd fuck her from behind and imagine she was dead. We had a loveless marriage. One of convenience. She found support for her and Sloane, and I had the mask of normalcy with them. Win-win. Until it wasn't. My morgue is and always will be my sanctuary. Home was suffocating. She was suffocating. Things weren't too bad where Sloane was concerned. If anything, she kind of reminded me of myself, just without the mask. She was always herself, where I kept my mask on and had to act like the concerned stepdad and husband. Over time, Denise made it more and more difficult to pretend. I had to play the long game and convince her that she was losing her mind. I made a plan. Set her up to look like the woman had let her demons win, while I remained the grieving husband. I came in my pants when I ran the blade down her arms and the blood spilled around us. I had to force myself to walk away so I could prepare myself to scream, shout and cry on the phone with 911.

I stare down at my wife's dead body and replay the moment I took her life from her. My cock grows hard and I smile at the memory. I need to feel that again and again. I slice a Y in her chest, pull apart her fileted flesh and crack open her chest. I caress the heart in her chest and revel in the feel of it. I wonder...

I cut her heart from her chest and caress it in my palm. I look down at my throbbing cock in my pants and inspiration hits. I take my scalpel and cut out a circle in her heart. I pull my cock from my pants, noticing her blood all over the khaki material. I'll have to change these. I slide my cock inside the hole in her heart and groan. Yes. Oh, fuck yes. With my free hand, I grip the slab of metal she lies on. I pump my hips, thrusting in and out of her heart. Images of her death flash in my mind and I jerk my hips faster. "Yes. Yes. Fuck yes. S-so good. This is what I needed."

Remembering the look in her eyes as her life was snuffed out, I cum so hard I almost black out. I slump over, barely catching myself from falling. I have to keep this. A trophy. I grab a large specimen jar and dump the heart in, pouring formaldehyde inside of it. I can't let this be the last time. This is the feeling I've been searching for all this time. I will find my euphoria in bleeding hearts.

34

‑‑‑‑ᴧᴧ‑‑‑‑‑‑‑‑

Karver

I watch the door after they leave. This is it. It's all over.
Sloane and I are over. My life is over. This motherfucker is
really going to get away with framing me for this shit.
Decker's choked gasps bring my full attention back to him.
His eyes ping-pong around and his breathing sounds like a
slow gurgle. His eyes land on me and he chokes, "K-a-r-
ver?"

"Deck, stop talking, man. You never stop talking. Just. You
have to stop. Let me think. I'll get you help, okay?"

A tear falls from his eye and he shakes his head. He
wheezes his final words, "G-ood. L-ike. T-his. F-f-inally."

His last word is barely a whisper as he takes his last breath
and his eyes remain open. I shake his body, "Deck?
Decker? Come on, ya silly fuck. Don't be such a pussy,
come on."

A gasp by the door makes me whip my head in that direction. Mousey stands there with her mouth and eyes wide open. I pull my bloody hands from his chest and wave them as I shake my head. "No, no, no. This isn't what it looks like." I slowly stand up and she takes a step back.

"Don't. It wasn't me. It was Dr. De- Corbin. Dr. Corbin Moriarty did this."

She frantically shakes her head. "No. No, he would never. You won't get away with this, Karver."

I take another step towards her and she jumps back. "Don't fucking do it, Mousey," I hiss.

She sucks in a deep breath and squeaks, "F-fuck you!" She spins around to run away, startling me into chasing her down. I slide against the floor to avoid running into her when I see she's already ran into Axel. He's drenched in blood from head to toe. His eyes are glossed over and he pants with a sneer on his face. Mousey's gasp turns into a watery groan as she looks down.

"Ax?"

He doesn't seem to hear me, so I step around and see the carnage across the hall. I look back over at Axel, who has a tight grip on her shoulder and a knife shoved into her stomach. With robotic movements, he pulls the knife out and then continues to stab.

In, out, in, out.

Her body jolts with every stab, the only thing keeping her standing is Axel's giant form. He yanks the knife out one last time and slashes it across her throat, narrowly avoiding the blood spray as he steps away. His head slowly turns in my direction and I put my hands up. He takes a menacing step forward and I hold my ground. In a stern voice I say, "Axel." He takes another step towards me and I shout in his face as he brings his arm back with the knife. "AX!"

His arm freezes while it's still behind him and he blinks a few times, shaking his head. "Karver?" he questions in a quiet voice.

I nod, "Yeah, man. It's me, Karver." My eyes peek down the hall again and back up to him. "What the fuck have you done?"

I watch as his eyes continue to blink and he looks as if he's confused himself. He brings his arm forward slowly and checks out the blood-stained knife. He turns it side to side, and then turns his head down the hall and a puppy-like whimper falls from his lips. His head whips back in my direction. "I, you, he…" He shuts his eyes and breathes in deep through his nose. On an exhale, his voice deepens. "I did this for you."

I rear my head back. "Me? What do you mean you did this for me? Wait. So are you and Dr. Dead *both* the killers?"

He frantically shakes his head, chanting, "No, no, no, no. Well… he's the killer. I mean… I guess I am now, too." He paces back and forth and brings his bloody fingers to his mouth and muttering.

"Axel. Stop." I step in front of him to halt his pacing. "Axel. Tell me what happened here."

The hand with the knife thrusts back towards our door, "He was going to put it all on you. I couldn't let that happen. No. You're good. You didn't do this." He shakes his head and mutters again. "You're good. You wouldn't do this. I had to save you."

"Save me? Axel! This. This isn't how you save someone. I mean. Dude, they're going to put you in solitary for the rest of your fucking life. You hate solitary. You hate sedation. Why? Why would you do this, man?"

He stops and looks at me, the look of panic and confusion becomes one of despair. He mutters, "You know why." With a heavy sigh, he shakes his head and steps over the fallen bodies in the hall.

Sloane

Corbin seems lost in a memory and I know this is my chance to find something to protect myself and try to leave. While lost in thought, he slowly starts to hump his desk. What the fuck? The bile burns my throat and tongue as it rises. I look around the room to see if I can grab anything without him noticing. My heart is racing wildly as I tip-toe to the medical tray next to the table. I notice the sounds of my heavy breathing and quickly shut my mouth to muffle it. I reach the tray and just barely catch myself before tripping into the tray. I clap one hand over my mouth to keep from gasping, and the other I smack over my pounding heart. Fuck. That was close. Too close.

I look down at the tray and some of these things seem like they'd only be helpful in pissing him off unless I hit just the right spot. I really hope I don't have to use any of this, but who's to say he won't kill me, too? He's the murderer. His first victim that I know of was my mother. If he was so willing to kill her, then he obviously wouldn't think twice about killing me as well. *Focus, Sloane.*

I look at the tray and over at Corbin, still rhythmically humping his desk. All the things I never knew about him. This is the last thing I would ever have guessed. Two of the items look promising. One looks a lot like the bread knife we use for loaves of bread and bagels. The other looks like a giant knife which has a handle that almost looks like it belongs on a pistol. I grab the handle of the bread knife with my thumb and pointer finger and wince as I slowly try to pick it up from the tray without a noise. There's a slight scraping sound and I quickly lift the knife in the air, gripping it as tight as I can to keep it from slipping. I tightly wrap my fingers all the way around the handle and then go for the other one. This one is a little more difficult to get a good grip on since it's heavier. I hear the moan fall from his lips as his hips jerk against the desk.

I quickly hide the knives behind my back and try to take a few steps back towards the door. He hunches over, panting, and shakes his head. His head very slowly turns in my direction, looking very much like a possessed doll. He looks past me towards the door and then back at me. He pushes himself off the desk and turns towards me. Not a single look of discomfort at standing there with cum-filled pants. Jesus, there's only so many times I can push the bile down before this shit has me puking everywhere. He tilts his head, "Where do you think you're going, Sloane? Don't you have questions? I promise I won't do a villain monologue."

He gives the hand signal for scouts' honor. My voice cracks, "N-o. No questions."

He tsks as he takes slow, calculated steps towards me. "Even now you still don't have any feelings, huh? Now, that can't be true. I know you at least feel one... fear."

He pauses and waits for me to respond. I can't. I don't know what to ask. What to think. Feel. The only thing running on a loop in my mind is; he's a sick fuck, I need to leave, I need to get to Karver. "Always such a bitch, sucking the fun out of everything. You can't give me this one thing? I'll make it easy. Ask me how I knew when to go after the victims?" He vibrates in place, his face turning red. A vein bulges in his temple and he shouts, "ASK ME!" His scream is so forceful that his hair falls out of place and sticks to his sweaty forehead. He sucks in a breath and pushes his hair back from his face. He looks at me and smiles, "Ask me, please."

He really does belong here. He's just been on the wrong floor this whole time. I squeeze the knives tighter in my sweaty grasp as I feel them slip a little. "How did you know when to go after them, Corbin?"

He chuckles and then looks like a child that's been caught with their hand in the cookie jar. He brings his hand to his mouth. "Oopsie." He drops his hand from his mouth. "Now, I know you hated your mother, so this shouldn't bother you too much. I needed someone who could give me the heads up I needed, but dumb enough to not realize they were doing so. Who better than the needy little whore, Nurse Regan? You fill that bitch's sloppy cunt and she'll spill more than just cum.

All I had to do was text her to say I needed to see her, and she would tell me where everyone was at. That way, I could get in without people noticing. Shift change is a beautiful thing in an understaffed unit. You know what else is? When security cameras mysteriously break and they don't bother to fucking fix them, even in the midst of all the murders. Having the alarms and lights installed was as much effort as they were willing to put in."

He runs his hand down his arm like he's brushing dust off. "Plus, what better way to have another fall guy set up? Karver was the goal when I caught him at our house the night I killed your mother. I saw him in the tree like a fucking pervert. Even better, he dropped his knife in the courtyard, so I made sure to use that a few times. And of course, the masks, well, I had to make those be the killer's calling card. We both know how much that boy loves his masks. The irony. The one thing he uses to protect himself from others will be his downfall. Poetic, don't you think?"

Hearing his plan to frame Karver makes the fear leave my body, and is replaced by pure, unadulterated rage. I was ready to kill Corbin to protect myself if he came after me. But the game has changed. I'm going to kill Corbin to save Karver. To make him pay for taking away people that mattered.

Just because their brain chemistry was off, didn't mean they didn't deserve to live. They deserved the chance to fight another day against the demons inside their mind. They all did. What if they could've won the battle? What if they just needed a little more time, and Corbin snuffed it out like the flame of a candle?

I crack my neck and steel my spine. He must see the change in me, because he stands a little taller with a smirk. "Alright, Sloane. Give it your best shot."

He thinks his confidence will make me back down. Not a fucking chance. I walk towards him and slowly bring the knives out to each side. He clocks the glint of them immediately and chuckles. "Smart girl." He lunges towards me

279

and I try to duck out of the way. The damn rubber slides make me trip and I start to fall down. I yelp as he grips my hair at the scalp and yanks my head back, ignoring the knives in my hands to punch me in the face. He releases my hair as I stumble back from the blow to my eye. I keep blinking to push away my blurry vision and can already feel blood pooling to the surface, swelling my eye shut. I let the thoughts of Karver fuel me to feel everything I need to.

I feel the grief of everyone lost, the anger at Corbin for framing Karver, and the fear that I won't be able to save Karver from this. Corbin unbuttons the cuffs of his sleeves and slowly rolls them up as if he has all the time in the world. He thinks he's won. He's fucking wrong. While looking down and chuckling to himself, I charge after him with the knives at the ready. I scream as I close in on him and wildly slash the knives across his body.

"Fuck!" He holds his arms up as he stumbles back, thinking it will protect him. I can't stop. That's where everyone fucks up. I'm blinded by the blood spray but continue slashing and stabbing the knives all over him. I feel the knives slipping from my bloodied palms and grip tighter. When I feel that I'm stabbing at air, I quickly hide my face in my shirt and wipe the blood away. I'm breathing as if I just ran a marathon and my heart feels like it will burst from my chest any moment.

I huff and look down at the floor where Corbin's lifeless body lies in a spreading pool of his own blood and strewn flesh bits. If I didn't know it was him that I just killed, he would be completely unrecognizable to me. Pieces of hair, skin and an eye are missing. He looks as if a werewolf mauled him to death. I start to step away from him when I realize my work here isn't done. I strip out of my blood-soaked clothes and throw them in the biohazard bin. I clean off all the blood at the sink and then throw on a pair of Corbin's clean scrubs. I grab everything I need, including his badge to get through the doors and find my way back to Karver.

BPD is associated with different types of sleep disturbances, such as sleep continuity, sleep fragmentation, alterations in slow wave sleep, REM sleep regulation and dysphoric dreaming.

35

Karver

I follow behind Axel and everywhere we go, there are dead bodies and blood. It all matches what you would find in my favorite slasher films. Without a doubt, the news outlets are going to call this the St. John's Damascus Massacre. This is going to go in the history books as the most gruesome slaughter our tiny town has ever seen.

We reach the rec room and Axel begins to pace close to the entrance doors, muttering against his fingers. "Dude, you realize you're getting everyone's blood in your mouth, right?" He ignores me and continues to do it. I roll my eyes. "Whatever."

I watch out the small windows in the double doors, hoping that Sloane comes back. What if she doesn't? Either outcome will be devastating. Either she believes Corbin and is leaving me on her own or... or he'll fucking kill her. How fucked that my brain can't decide which is worse. The incessant tapping of his slides is driving me crazy. "Ax, please. Just… I need you to go sit down or something. I have to try and figure out how the fuck to get you out of this mess."

Lie. There's no getting him out of this. Nobody can. I stand up straight when someone steps out of the elevator down the hall. I bang on the door when I see that it's my clover. "Clover!" Bang, bang, bang. "Sweets!" Bang, bang, bang.

She looks up and a look of relief crosses her face. Her bruised and swollen face. What. The. Fuck. She starts running towards the door with a bag over her shoulder. She pulls a badge out of her pocket and swipes it at the door. I step back when the door buzzes and they open with a click and a hiss. With a sigh of relief, she walks through the doors and opens her arms for me. "Slasher. I was so-"

Her eyes widen as she looks past me. I hear Axel running and screaming, "Noooo!" As she shoves me out of the way, I stumble against a wall and watch in horror as she throws her hands up, shouting, "Axel! No!" I run towards them to stop him as the knife slashes down at her. She falls to the floor with a scream, clutching her face. Blood pours between her fingers. I spin around and crouch down before he has a chance to go after her again. I don't have enough room to run at him so I push as hard as I can against his knees, which buckle and make him fly backwards. The knife drops from his hand and clatters to the floor. I scramble over the top of him and grab hold of it. I hover above him and shout, "STAY DOWN, AXEL!"

He refuses to listen and starts to move. "No, no, no. What if she goes against you like her stepdad? I have to. I have to protect you!"

I hold the knife up, ready to use it and shake my head and grit, "Axel. Don't." Ignoring my words, he lunges for the knife in my hands and I bring it down without hesitation. I plunge the knife into his lower stomach and hold it there as he gasps and looks down. He slaps his hands around the knife and blood pouring from the wound. He starts to hyperventilate. "W-w-hy?" He starts to cry and whimper. "It hurts, Karver. I just wanted to save you."

I leave the knife in his stomach and slowly stand above him. "I couldn't let you save me at the cost of her life. Deep down, you know that. Push past all the fear, and you know it's true, Ax."

His voice cracks as he whispers, his eyes slowly blinking, "I-I understand. T-tell her I didn't mean it."

I nod my head, "I know, Ax." I turn around and rush over to Sloane as she sits up, clutching her face.

Sloane

I push myself up to sit and hold on to my cheek. The slice in my cheek feels like fire and the blood pours between my fingers. Note to self. I *only* like being slashed by Karver. Fuck, this hurts. Karver turns and rushes over to me. He picks me up and pulls at my fingers. "Let me see, Clover. Fuck, it's bad isn't it? Let me see."

I fight his pull, afraid to let go of the cut. I look past him and see that Axel is lying still on the floor. My nose burns and my eyes well up with tears. "Why did you do that?"

He stops pulling at my fingers and grips my hips, shaking his head, "He was going to kill you. He wasn't going to

285

stop until the threat was gone. In his paranoia, you were a threat. I couldn't let him do that. I can't live without you, sweets." He rubs his hand over his chest. "It only beats for you."

I'm distracted when I hear heavy bangs around the corner. Fuck. They're coming. We're out of time. Fuck, fuck, fuck. *What do I do?* The bag on the floor catches my attention and I lean over to pick it up, forgetting about the cut on my face and throw the strap over my shoulder, digging inside of it. Karver panics and grabs at my face. "Fuck, fuck, fuck. This is bad, sweets. It's really fucking bad. Fuck." He yanks his shirt off and presses it against the slash in my cheek and I hiss. He grimaces, "I'm sorry, I'm so fucking sorry. I have to. I have to. It's bad, it's so bad."

The bangs around the corner continue and then I hear shouts and heavy footfalls in the hall behind us. Fuck. I'm out of time. Tears fall profusely at the realization that I really have to follow through with my plan. Karver thinks it's from the pain and keeps chanting, "I know, sweet clover, I know. I'm so sorry. I'm so sorry."

With a shuddered breath, I steel my spine. "Karver." Like a mantra he keeps repeating himself, unable to hear me. "Karver…Karver!" I bring one hand up and place it over his and shout in his face, "SLASHER!"

He stops repeating himself and looks at me, "Wha-"

"I love you, Slasher."

He's so panicked, he doesn't even realize what's happening. In a daze, he responds, "I love you too, Clover."

I shake my hand as more tears fall. "No, no. Listen to me." I push his hand harder against my face and nuzzle his palm the best I can. "I need you to listen, please. We don't have much time."

"No. No, don't say that. You'll be fine. I know it's a lot of blood, but you'll be fine, sweets. I promise."

"Shhh. I know they always tell us that we need to get better for ourselves. But I know you. And I know you'll never do it for yourself. So, please. Please, do it for me, Karver. Try. And try again. Keep trying. Life won't be perfect, but it can be better."

"Why are you saying all of this?" I hear the police trying to break the doors down and he looks over my shoulder with wide eyes. I lean forward and kiss him; once, "I," four kisses, "love," and end with three kisses, "you. Please, remember how much I love you. *No matter what.* Please forgive me, handsome."

"For wha-" he gasps before finishing his sentence and looks down. He puts a hand over the blood dripping around the knife in his side. He looks up with shock and confusion on his face. "Why?"

I caress his face, "Because I love you." I smear the blood from my cut all over my face and hands and then collect the blood from Karver's stab as well. I reach in the bag and skip around the rec room, throwing the jars of hearts. I save one last jar and hold it in my hand as the police barge in from both entrances.

They all shout at the same time.

"FREEZE!"

"PUT YOUR HANDS UP!"

"GET DOWN ON YOUR KNEES!"

"Aww, have a heart, boys," I say amidst giggles in a child-like voice. They start closing in and I watch as Karver is pinned down to the floor. Fuck, keep going. Convince them. I throw my arms out and bat my eyelashes, "Wanna play with all my dolls? They're all wearing my favorite color. I had to make them, of course. They just wouldn't listen to me. They made me mad, mad, mad. So they all had to go bye-bye."

My arms are gripped tight and brought behind my back. I'm yanked to my feet as I feel the cold cuffs wrap around my wrists, ending with a tight bite. In a stunned voice, one of them asks, "You mean to tell me you did all this?"

I laugh again. "Of course I did, silly. Doesn't every girl like to play with bleeding hearts?"

People with BPD can have a "favorite person", who they are very attached to and feel like they can not function without this person and depend on them for their sanity.

Epilogue

Karver

It's been just over a month since everything happened. I called it when I said the news outlets would call this the St. John's Damascus Massacre. They've spent all this time trying to fix everything up as nothing ever happened. To the outside world, something horrific happened here. But within these walls, with all the blood and bodies gone, just the ghost of a memory is left in its wake.

When I returned from the ICU, the only remaining staff was the night shift who weren't here for everything that happened. The staff were run ragged as they did everything they could to get new staff. There are a few new faces, but not many. Not like they need much staff anyway. There's only four of us left from that day. I walk this floor alone; while Sloane and Axel are left in solitary and the other sneaky little fuck, Blake, hides out in his room more often than not. I visit Sloane and Axel daily. I'll stand outside their doors and let them know that I'm there. When my brain isn't twisting things, I let them know that they're not alone. But on the dark days, I find myself taunting them and spitting venom. Twisting the things they did just to make them feel like shit for how everything went down that day. I pace the halls and decide to take a seat in the rec room while I wait for my visitation time.

I sit in my usual spot and watch the television as the news talks about the massacre, and then briefly discusses murders from the Gemini Slayers. Good for them. I hope they never find out who they are. I faintly hear the sound of Blake's shouts from his room. I roll my eyes, as always, never a peep until the news has him screaming.

The entrance door buzzes and I look as the doors slowly open. A man walks in with a big smile on his face, a guard walking behind him. I can't help but notice his hair. The black dye seems to be growing out with the massive amount of light brown roots showing. I snort at the style he's rocking. The 90's called, they want their boy band cut back.

He looks around and shouts to the ceiling, "Honeyyy, I'm homeee." He looks in my direction and waves while walking over. "Sup, man! Nice digs." He pulls out Decker's old chair and sits in it backwards, his arms dangling over the back of the chair. "Sooo. Just thought I'd introduce myself. I hear you're the only one here, so we'll be roomies. We almost didn't get the chance to meet, but somebody decided to make Amissa Stella go kaboom." He throws his hands out and makes sound effects like a bomb. Jesus, he's like Decker 2.0. "Wait. You might not know it, huh? Tiny town. La Grande. About ohhhh, an hour or so away." At my continued silence, he continues, "Quiet one, huh? That's okay. You'll open up to me eventually." Not a fucking chance. He nods and taps the back of the chair.

"Okayyy. Well," he brings his palms up to his chest, "I'm Rhyatt, but you can call me Slayer if you'd like."

From behind him, the guard taps his shoulder. "Let's go, Rhyatt. Time to get all the paperwork done."

He shoots up from his chair with a mock salute. "Sir, yes, sir!"

He looks at me once more and wiggles his finger at me. "I know how to crack eggs like you. You'll see. We'll be good friends some day." I look at the clock and see it's getting close to my visit time. My head is clear today. There's no anger or malice towards either of them. I know why they did what they did, and today, in this moment, I'm at peace with it. At least as much as one can be when they're separated from their 143. I go to the first room, lean against the door and lightly knock. "Hey, Ax. I hope today is one of your good days. I'm about to go see Sloane. I bet she misses you a lot. We got a newbie in today. Wait 'til you're out of there and meet this guy. I swear he's another version of Deck, it's wild." I push off the door and knock again. "Talk tomorrow, Ax."

I walk further down the hall until I reach my sweet clover's door. I put my back against the door and slide down to sit against it. I press my ear against the door in the hopes of hearing her, even if it's just her breathing. Movement catches my eye and I see one of the guards watching me. They learned pretty quickly that I would sneak in here whenever I can. They've been watching more often. At least during the day. Night shift doesn't give a fuck. I lean my head back against the door and remember the first night I snuck in here to see Sloane. To be close to her.

I walk through the empty halls and make my way to Sloane's room. I was given the all clear on my injury to come back to the psych floor. It's my first night back and the need to be next to her is all-consuming. At least while sedated, it didn't gnaw at me like it is now. I reach her room and the older guard who gave me a moment with Thumper stops, looks at me and then the door. He looks down at his watch and back up at me with a sigh. He slowly turns the other direction and says, "I really need a coffee."

I smile and then open the door. The moonlight shines over Sloane, little shadows cast across her body. Her eyes are open as she stares at the ceiling, tears falling down her face. "Clover?"

A small gasp falls from her lips and her head rolls towards me. Her voice barely above a whisper, "Slasher?" I walk over to her bed and crawl in beside her, cradling her in my arms. I kiss her temple and nuzzle in as close I can get. I bring my nose to her hair and breathe her in. She melts into my touch and sighs.

"I've missed you, sweets." I squeeze her hip. "Every inch of you. It all hit me like a freight train when the sedation cleared and I could think straight. I felt like I was drowning with how much I missed you and needed you. Seeing the beauty that is my clover. Touching you. Hearing you. I'm not supposed to be here, but there's no place I'd rather be. I don't know how long they'll let me stay, but I'll soak up every second I have."

She gasps and starts pushing my shirt up. "How bad is it? Let me see."

She shakes her head and frantically paws at my shirt. I help lift it. A choked sob falls from her lips when she sees the angry scar left behind. I push strands of hair behind her ear. "Hey, look at me." She doesn't listen at first so I make it a command. "Look. At. Me. Sweets." Her head shoots up and our eyes connect. "There's my good girl. I told you before. I'll gladly bear any mark you give me. I'm okay. I'm right here."

Her face crumples as the memory takes hold. "I-I'm s-so sorry. I'm so sorry, Slasher. I just didn't know what else to do. I-I needed to save you. I had to. Please, please forgive me." My eyes fall to the jagged scar across her cheek and I gently run my thumb down it. She squeezes her eyes shut and pulls away, placing her hand over it. "Don't look at it."

I pull at her hand until she stops fighting me. I place kisses along it, while whispering, "I'll never forgive myself for this, but scar or no scar, you're fucking beautiful, sweets."

I wrap my arms around her and cradle her to my chest, rubbing circles on her back. "You say that now, but you won't be saying that when you're mad at me."

"You know who I am, Clover. You know there will be times that I'll say fucked up things about that entire day. I'll be angry and hurt over everything that happened. That you dared find a way to hurt me and then leave me. I promise I'll do what you asked, but it's going to take time. I'm not going to be a changed man overnight. Even if it's what you deserve."

I start to roll us over when there's a jabbing feeling in my thigh. "Ow, fuck." I let go of her and pull back, remembering that I stole a pen to bring with me. I pull it out of my pocket and click it. She looks at it in confusion as I hold it up and wave it. "I know it's not the blue marker, but a blue pen was the closest thing I could get my hands on." She lies on her back with her hands over her stomach. I pull the left one from her and write, '143', on the side of her ring finger. I kiss over it and then toss the pen aside to hold her for as long as I can.

Sloane

I lay in my bed and look around the room. I run my finger along the fucked up scar running down my face. I know if I ever get to see Axel again, he'll be more upset about it than I am. I'm not mad at him about it at all, I just hate that I'm left with another reminder of that day. A reminder that everyone else can see and ponder on where it came from. I'm sure the stories are endless.

As much as I miss Karver, I know I did the right thing. I guess that's how you know that love is real. No matter how much I've struggled with feelings and emotions, I know what we have is real. You don't destroy your whole life and chance at happiness for just anyone. No matter how toxic we were at times, I was willing to fight every battle with him. I can hold him accountable for his words and actions, but not fault him for it. I know his demons scream in his head daily and it fucks things up, but I love him enough that I would stick it out until my final breath. I still stand by that. Even if I have to do it a bit differently now. Karver made me feel. He brought me back to life. What better way to return the favor than by taking the fall and allowing him a chance to live? I confessed to multiple murders for love. For Karver. Does that make me broken or a monster? Perhaps, I'm both. I bring my left hand up to my face and smile at the almost faded, '143', on my ring finger. I almost cried the first time he did it, but it's now become the first thing he does when he's able to sneak in here to lay down with me.

I look at the colorful calendar that he drew himself. July 1-22 is crossed out, and in big bold letters the 23rd says ***SLASHER'S BIRTHDAY***. I start humming 'Happy Birthday' when I hear a single knock on the door. Pause. Four knocks. Pause. Three knocks. I sniffle and then smile as I shed a tear. *Hi, Slasher.*

We may have survived Corbin, but at what cost? We still ended up with scars and bleeding hearts that day.

"You can not make everyone think and feel as deeply as you do. This is your tragedy, because you understand them but they don't understand you."

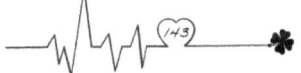

Resources

National Education Alliance for Borderline Personality Disorder
https://www.borderlinepersonalitydisorder.org/

https://www.borderlinepersonalitydisorder.org/list-of-recommended-bpd-resources/

https://dbtselfhelp.com/
Information about all aspects of dialectical behaviour therapy. Find handouts, worksheets, lessons, and research articles.

https://emotionsmatterbpd.org/
emotions matter, mental health, bpd, borderline personality disorder, borderline, treatments, dbt, cbt, border line personality, disorder, mental disorder

https://www.nimh.nih.gov/health/topics/borderline-personality-disorder
This excellent site thoroughly covers the subjects of What Is Borderline Personality Disorder, Signs and Symptoms of BPD, Treatment, Clinical Trials, Statistics, Finding Help, Suicide Prevention, and Publications. A link to Medline Plus gives a brief discussion in Spanish.

https://www.needymeds.org/
is a 501(c)(3) national non-profit information resource dedicated to helping people locate assistance programs to help them afford their medications and other healthcare costs. Great website for help finding low or no cost community programs and service (if available) within 20 miles of your zip code.

Resources

https://www.nami.org/

The Home page contains a link to useful information about BPD that describes symptoms, commonly asked questions, origins, treatment, suicide and self-harm, treatments, medications, plus additional resources and links. Individuals seeking recovery information will find this website quite useful and readable. This site provides a wealth of information on all mental illnesses and specifically on borderline personality disorder.

https://draonline.org/

This is the Dual Recovery Anonymous Resource Center for those looking for a 12-step or self-help group when one has a substance addiction issue as well as a mental health diagnosis.

https://nowmattersnow.org/

Skills and support for coping with suicidal thoughts.

https://bbrfoundation.org/research/borderline-personality-disorder

This organization is committed to alleviating the suffering caused by mental illness by awarding grants that will lead to advances and breakthroughs in scientific research.

https://borderlinesupport.org.uk/bpd-support/international-support/

Although our organization is based in the United Kingdom and primarily provides support to individuals affected by BPD within the UK, we do also receive requests for international support from people affected by BPD worldwide. In response to this, we have compiled a collection of valuable resources specifically tailored for those residing outside of the UK.

National Suicide Prevention Lifeline
1-800-273-TALK (8255)
suicidepreventionlifeline.org

Suicide & Crisis Lifeline
If you or someone you know need support,
call or text 988 or chat 988lifeline.org

Acknowledgments

There was an amazing quote I heard in a Tik Tok audio, from the 2007 movie, Stronger. The words and emotion behind it were so incredibly fitting for one of the scenes in this book. "I can'! I can't! I can't! I can't do it! Why do you even want me?! Why?! I'm such a fuck up!"

Rem!x - Thank you for being the Slasher to my Clover... welp that sounds dirty. But really, thank you for being my inspiration, for allowing me into your life and asking you the tough questions so I could properly portray Karver. There would be no Karver without you. Thank you for being so supportive, and listening to my rants, questions and breakdowns throughout this process. Thank you for gifting me a piece of you to put into this book. 143, Slasher.

Vanessa - To my ride or die bestie and editor. I've said it before and I'll say it again, these books would not exist without you. You, and you alone, gave me the push to pursue this when I was ready to give up before the journey even started. Nobody could ever possibly have a better editor than I do. So many chick flick moments happening. Yeesh.

The Horde - NO CHICK FLICK MOMENTS. But, seriously... thank you. You know that I know that you know what I'm trying to say.

SKDesigns - Thank you so much for the incredible artwork you did on the e-book cover. You went above and beyond for me. You do amazing work in every avenue that you pursue. Thank you for your guidance and for being my friend.

Hype Squads - Y'all know who you are. I am eternally grateful that I met every single one of you. From the very beginning, you have shown nothing but love and support along this journey. You've hyped me up every step of the way. Stay squirrely, my friends.

Also by K. iller

Astronomical Love Series

This Life and the Next (a VERY dark rom-com)

Next Life (a bodyguard/mafia princess forbidden romance)

Double Life (Release Date TBA)

Half Life (Release Date TBA)

Standalones

Bleeding Hearts (a toxic love dark romance)

… but wait, there's more